I0699805

CHICAGO RAILERS HOCKEY

HOLD ME TIGHT

USA Today Bestselling Author

JENNIFER SUCEVIC

Hold Me Tight

Copyright© 2025 by Jennifer Sucevic

Published by Tangled Hearts LLC

All rights reserved. No part of this book may be reproduced in any form or by any electronic or mechanical means, including information storage and retrieval systems, without written permission from the author, except for the use of brief quotations in a book review.

This is a work of fiction. Names, characters, businesses, palaces, events, locales, and incidents are either the products of the author's imagination or used in a fictitious manner. Any resemblance to actual persons, living or dead, or actual events is purely coincidental.

Model Cover Design by Mary Ruth Baloy at MR Creations

Special Edition & Illustrated Cover by Claudia Lymari at Tease Designs

Editing by Shauna Stevenson at Ink Machine Editing

Proofreading by Sisters Get Lit.erary Author Services

Interior Formatting by Silla Webb at Masque of the Red Pen

Cover photography by Michelle Lancaster www.michellelancaster.com

Model Lochie

Illustrated Artwork Efa

Join my Newsletter here!

1
CALLIE

It might have taken a few hours, but the bakery is finally quiet. The morning rush has come and gone, leaving behind a trail of empty coffee cups, a smear of frosting on the glass display case, and exhaustion after a sleepless night.

After wiping my hands on a towel, I lean against the counter.

Sloane exhales next to me, brushing away a streak of flour from her cheek. "I really thought that stroller mom was going to riot when we ran out of almond croissants," she says, grabbing her water bottle.

I manage a smile. "She's probably already drafting a Yelp review as we speak. And it won't be pretty."

We both laugh, and I let myself enjoy the moment. Just one blissful second of quiet. Until I spot the stack of mail on the back prep table. That's all it takes for my stomach to dip.

I gravitate toward the pile and then slowly flip through bills and junk mail. It's mostly routine stuff I'll dump in the trash, until a thin white envelope with an official logo from the bank catches my eye. My fingers tremble as I force myself to tear it open. Even before scanning the words, I already know what they'll say.

My loan payment is overdue.

We're now moving toward the sixty-day mark.

If I don't make a payment soon, I'll default. Which means I could lose the bakery.

My bakery.

The one I worked so damn hard for.

The room blurs slightly as I grip the edge of the table.

For the hundredth time, I rack my brain for a way out of this mess. I can't go to my parents. They'd help if they could, but there's nothing left for them to give.

And Zane, my ex?

The father of my daughter?

Ha!

He's a professional hockey player and makes millions a year, and yet, his child support is always late. How he manages to burn through so much money each month is almost unfathomable.

What I've learned over the years is that he's not someone who can be relied on.

Unfortunately, I was a little late to the realization.

From the time I was a kid, I've had to figure things out on my own, and this situation isn't any different.

There's no choice in the matter.

Failure isn't an option.

Not when Nora is counting on me to provide a stable home for her.

"What's that?" Sloane's question cuts through my mental spiral. I blink out of those thoughts and find her watching me with a furrowed brow.

I force a smile that feels like it might crack my face in half before shaking my head and setting the letter on the counter near the register. "Nothing. Just more junk mail."

Relief washes over me when the door opens. I don't want

Sloane asking more questions. Not only is she an employee, but she's a good friend. The last thing I want to do is lie.

I glance up, already shifting into business mode, as River Thompson strolls in.

He's tall, broad-shouldered, and far too good-looking for my peace of mind. It's the tousled blond hair and piercing blue eyes that seem to slice right through me. He makes me feel seen in a way that's not entirely comfortable. When he walks into a room, I feel it down to my bones. The man moves with the grace of an athlete. Of someone who's at ease with their space in the world.

It must be nice.

I don't think I've ever felt that a day in my life.

This morning he's wearing a simple Railers hoodie and jeans.

When he steps over the threshold, the temperature in the bakery rises.

Or maybe it's just me.

My pulse trips, and it takes effort to stomp out the attraction zipping through my veins.

I hate the way my body reacts to him.

He's Zane's friend.

Or was.

Quite frankly, it's not my business what their relationship is.

What I do know is that he stood by silently while Zane made a fool out of me.

I turn my attention back to the register, hoping he'll order quickly and leave.

If I'm lucky, Sloane will swoop in like usual and save me from having to make small talk. Those conversations are always awkward.

A woman with a small child walks in right after him. She gives me a smile before glancing in his direction and doing a double take as her eyes widen.

"Oh my God," she gasps. "You're River Thompson. My husband is obsessed with the Railers."

River gives her a friendly smile that's both easy and charming. "Good to know. Tell him I said 'hey.'"

The little boy at her side is probably around five or six. He peeks out from behind her leg while clutching a toy car.

Without missing a beat, River crouches down so they're nearly eye level. "Do you like hockey, buddy?"

The boy looks up at his mother before nodding.

River reaches into the back pocket of his jeans and pulls out a glossy puck. "If you have a marker, I'll sign it for you. Would you like that?"

The woman digs through her purse with frantic fingers before glancing at me in desperation. "You wouldn't happen to have a Sharpie, would you?"

"Umm," I glance around the counter before opening a drawer and pulling out a marker. "Here you go."

She squeals before plucking it from my fingers and passing it to River. "My husband is going to die when he sees this."

River scrawls his name across the smooth surface. "Here you go," he says, handing it to the boy. "That's for when you score your first goal."

I roll my eyes before I can stop myself. Of course he has a puck on hand to give out to fans.

Who doesn't?

And apparently, the man is also good with kids.

I hate the part of me that's touched by the small gesture.

It annoys the hell out of me.

I don't want to feel anything where this man is concerned.

The woman gushes for a few more minutes before pulling out her phone and asking to take a selfie, which he agrees to. After more than two dozen photos, she orders a donut for her son and then finally takes off, probably posting all the pics as she goes.

River's gaze resettles on mine as he steps up to the counter. "Hey, Callie."

His voice dips, turning low and intimate. The deep baritone of it wraps around me before squeezing tight. There's a gentleness to it. For some reason, I imagine this is the exact tone he'd use when attempting to calm a skittish animal.

"Hi." I go for cool. "What can I get for you?" When he continues to search my eyes, as if picking through all my thoughts, I blurt, "We're kind of busy here. So…"

He breaks eye contact long enough for his gaze to drift across the now-empty tables as he pops a brow. "Really? Kind of seems like I just missed the morning rush."

My face heats as I shift behind the counter. "I meant that we have prep to finish up."

The corners of his mouth tip upward, as if he's used to my iciness and doesn't mind the burn.

"Could I get a black coffee, medium roast?" He points to the second row in the display case. "And maybe one of those cinnamon things."

"Scones," I say flatly.

"Yeah, a scone," he echoes, like it's a foreign word.

I quickly bag the pastry and hand it over, hoping to put an end to this conversation.

Instead, he continues to linger.

"So, how've you been?" he asks.

My hands tighten on the counter as his eyes continue to probe mine for answers I refuse to give. "I'm fine."

What else am I supposed to say?

That I'm one bounced payment away from losing everything I've worked so hard for?

That I have no one to call?

No safety net to fall into?

He looks like he wants to say something else, but I turn away before he can get the words out.

A man is the last thing I need right now.

Especially one who stood on the sidelines while my life unraveled once before.

It's a relief when the door opens again and another customer walks in.

Dismissing River, I focus my attention on the woman.

2
RIVER

Newsflash: I don't need or want coffee.

I don't even like coffee.

And even though the pastries smell delicious, they're not something I usually eat. I'm more into protein, not empty carbs.

It took me a few years, but I finally worked up the courage to stop by Lakeshore Sweets. Now, I'm here every day after practice like clockwork. I couldn't keep myself away if I wanted to. I'm like a junkie in need of a fix. The five minutes I spend in here, or ten if I can find an excuse to linger, are the best part of my day.

I try to soak in every detail, knowing this encounter will have to sustain me until the next one.

The first time I caught sight of Callie Westbrook was years ago, when Zane started bringing her around like she was a shiny new toy he couldn't wait to show off. What I didn't expect was to fall for my teammate's pretty blonde girlfriend.

I wanted her from the second she smiled politely and looked me in the eye like she had no clue how beautiful she was. And I wanted her even more with the passing of each day.

Each month.

Each year.

And don't even get me started on when she was pregnant with another man's child, her stomach rounded, glowing in a way that had absolutely nothing to do with Zane and everything to do with the kind of mother she'd be.

And I hated every fucking second of it.

I hated watching her in the stands during games, wearing Zane's jersey. I hated knowing the guy couldn't keep his dick in his pants, even when she was carrying their daughter. I hated knowing she deserved the fucking world and got so little in return from him.

And now?

Now I hate that she watches me warily, like I'm no better than her ex.

She doesn't know I saw everything, and even though I detested the thought of them together, I still tried to make Zane see what he was risking. I hated knowing he was screwing around behind her back. What I hated most was seeing how much he hurt her.

The past fades away as I watch her gracefully move behind the counter, tying a box of cookies with a pink ribbon, smiling at a kid with chocolate smeared across his cheek.

That smile is like the sun peeking out from behind the clouds.

I shift closer, waiting for her to glance up and look in my direction, but she studiously avoids my gaze.

And there's only so long I can hang around before it becomes awkward.

Hell, I'm already way past that point.

Especially when she doesn't want me in her shop to begin with.

I take a reluctant step in retreat. Just as I'm about to leave, I spot a folded piece of paper on the floor near the end of the counter, half-tucked beneath it. I bend down and snag it from the tile. It never occurs to me not to scan the contents.

My gut twists as I glance at the first few lines.

Then I read them for a second time to make sure I haven't jumped to the wrong conclusion.

When I look up again, Callie is helping a new customer, completely unaware I've been given a glimpse into her financial situation.

Without thinking, I fold up the paper and slip it into the back pocket of my jeans. My brain whirls with possible ways to help her. The tricky part is that if I offer my assistance, she'll shut me down without so much as a second thought.

Callie has a lot of pride.

And then there's the fact that she hates my guts and doesn't trust me.

I need time to think.

Plan.

By the time she turns around, I've got my scone in one hand and coffee in the other. "Thanks."

Her gaze cautiously flicks to mine as the sunshine in her expression fades. "No problem."

And just like that, she slams the door shut again, locking me out.

How sad is it that I live for the rare moments when she looks at me?

It's the only time I feel like I can breathe.

I push into the crisp autumn air and nearly run into Evelyn Kingston, one of the owners of the Railers hockey team. She's dressed in a stylish faux-fur coat, her ebony-colored hair twisted into something elegant that only looks effortless. Her gaze dips to the bag and coffee in my hands, then back up to my face with a shrewd smile.

"Fan of the coffee and pastries, are we?" she asks, like she doesn't already know the answer.

"Among other things."

"Well, you aren't the only one. Callie's about to receive a lot more attention."

Everything inside me stills. "Oh? Why's that?"

Her smile turns sly. "Beau Masterson's going to reach out to Callie about featuring her desserts in his restaurants. Isn't that fantastic news?"

It is.

One hundred percent.

But it also isn't.

Now I'm imagining Callie in the spotlight, facing even more pressure. While she deserves a thriving business, part of me knows that kind of exposure comes with complications. Especially when you're a single parent without a support system to rely on.

And, if I'm being completely honest, I don't like the idea of Beau Masterson sniffing around Callie. The guy is a rich playboy, and Chicago is his hunting ground.

When I remain silent, Evelyn steps closer before pausing, her gaze pinned to mine. "If you're planning on making a move, River, I wouldn't wait too long."

The comment catches me off guard. Before I can come up with a response, she's gone, disappearing inside the bakery.

I stand there for a few seconds, watching Callie through the window.

Evelyn's right. I can't afford to wait any longer. I've already wasted too much time.

If I'm not careful, she'll slip right through my fingers.

And I'm not about to let that happen.

3
CALLIE

My nerves continue to riot beneath my skin. Even after the door swings shut behind River. His presence lingers, impossible to ignore. I don't understand why he affects me so much.

I press a palm to my chest and try to talk myself down from the ledge.

It's not that big of a deal. The man is a customer like everyone else who pops in for a coffee and pastry.

He just so happens to be a dangerously attractive, ridiculously tall customer with gorgeous blue eyes and a habit of making me feel things I've spent years trying to avoid.

It's no big deal.

None at all.

When the last of the mid-morning rush trickles out, I drop onto a stool behind the counter as Sloane finishes wiping a table before leaning over and shooting me a look that says she's dying to explode.

"For weeks now that man has been showing up every day." Her tone might be innocent, but her smirk is anything but. "Think he'll finally work up the nerve to ask you out?"

With a wince, I rub the back of my neck, as if it's possible to massage away the tension his presence stirs in me. "I really hope not."

"Girl… That man looks at you like you're a tasty cupcake."

I roll my eyes. "I'm not interested. In anyone. But especially not him."

The lie comes out a little too easily. A little too smoothly. For the first time in years, I feel a stab of disappointment behind the words.

The truth is, I'm tired of doing this all alone.

Even though I tell myself I don't have time for a man, that doesn't mean I don't want one.

So, yeah… Maybe I kind of want someone to ask me out.

Just not him.

River Thompson is a carbon copy of my ex.

This is the first time since Nora was born that I've even entertained the idea of going out on a date.

I mean, who has the time between late-night feedings, keeping the bakery operating in the black, and trying not to fall apart in the wake of the destruction Zane wrought? When he walked away, it was like a bomb detonated.

Romance died.

Along with hope.

And trust.

I loved Zane.

Really loved him.

I put my faith in that man and all the pretty promises he made. I gave him my whole heart along with my body and my future.

Instead of holding it carefully in his hands, he tossed it aside like it meant nothing at all.

Not only did he walk away from me, he walked away from our daughter without so much as a backward glance. I have no idea how he could have done that. All it took was one glimpse at her precious face seconds after giving birth, and I was a goner.

There's nothing I wouldn't do for that little girl. No number of hours I won't work to make sure we have a roof over our heads and food on the table. I'd gladly go without in order to give her the world.

It baffles me how he doesn't feel the same. Instead, he leaves us with crumbs of child support and explanations that make me feel stupid for ever believing he was my knight in shining armor.

How do you come back from something like that?

From learning the hard way that the only one who's going to give a damn and save you is yourself.

It was a painful lesson to wrap my head around.

But I did it.

And I'll be damned if I make the same mistake twice.

This is no longer about me.

It's about Nora.

"Are you sure about that?" Sloane asks gently.

The question snaps me out of my thoughts. She's been working at the bakery for a couple of years now, and it didn't take long for us to become fast friends. Sloane has the innate ability to read people. There's not much I can hide from her.

"One hundred percent." My tongue darts out to moisten my lips. "Plus, he's a hockey player."

Sloane doesn't blink. "So?"

"So..." I exhale. "Zane was a professional athlete too. I think we both know that lifestyle doesn't mix well with mine. Even if River's nothing like him, I refuse to do that again. I've already had my heart broken once."

Actually, broken is an understatement.

More like obliterated.

I push up from the stool, needing to move, to do something

to shake off all this pent-up energy. "I just want to focus on Nora and the bakery. That's it."

And it's more than enough.

Sloane opens her mouth to argue when the bell above the door chimes and Evelyn Kingston breezes in dressed like she's about to walk in a fashion show. I've never met anyone like her before.

It was a shock when she stopped by a few months ago, wanting to know if I'd be willing to supply a Railers event with desserts. As tempting as it was to pounce on the opportunity, I had to think long and hard about the fact that it would once again place me in Zane's orbit. In the end, it was an opportunity I couldn't pass up.

She gives us both a smile.

"I passed your number along to Beau," she says by way of greeting. "You can expect a call soon. He's very interested in working with a local bakery, and your lemon iced shortbread was all he could talk about."

Hope flickers in me like a candle catching flame.

"That's amazing. Thank you," I manage, trying to stay calm. Inside, I'm doing a little happy dance and praying this works out. I need this break more than she knows. It's one that will keep the lights on a little longer and buy me time to catch up on some of the bills.

Maybe even save this place for Nora's future.

The door swings open again, and I glance over as a tall man steps inside. He's broad in the shoulders and fills out the expensive suit he's wearing. His salt-and-pepper hair is perfectly in place, and confidence radiates off him in heavy waves.

It only takes a beat for recognition to slam into me.

Hugh Landry.

While Evelyn owns half of the Railers, Hugh owns the other part of the team.

Rina, one of our closest friends, also happens to be the Railers' PR manager. She always has the inside scoop on what's happening behind the scenes. Partly because it's her job to keep the team out of trouble and partly because she's nosy as hell. She's confided more than once that the man has been a thorn in Evelyn's side for over twenty years.

The older woman stiffens as her eyes narrow. Her easy disposition vanishes, replaced by razor-sharp tension. "Are you following me now?"

Hugh's smile is smooth as silk but edged in steel. "Follow you? Why would I need to do that?" He steps farther inside the shop before glancing around the interior. "I was simply out stretching my legs and thought I'd grab a coffee before our eleven o'clock meeting." Then, as if he can't resist poking at her, he adds slyly, "Besides, why would I follow you when you woke up in my bed this morning?"

My jaw drops.

Um... Excuse me?

My brain stutters, scrambling to process what just came out of his mouth.

From everything I know about Evelyn, she can't stand Hugh, and she doesn't bother to hide it.

I must be missing something here. The Evelyn I know would rather set herself on fire than warm his sheets.

Then again, don't they say the line between love and hate is a thin one?

Evelyn's spine snaps straight as murder fills her eyes. "That's not something we're going to discuss right now," she says through gritted teeth.

Holy shit.

Hugh's grin deepens, as if he's enjoying himself. "Oh, I don't see the harm, darling. Everyone loves a good romance."

Romance?

The word lands like a thunderclap in the middle of the bakery. Sloane's eyebrows practically hit her hairline as she glances at me with wide eyes. Her lips twitch, as if she's dying to fire off a million questions.

Can't say I don't feel the same.

I clear my throat, all the while trying not to stare. The tension that crackles between them is thick enough to choke on.

"Coffee?" I offer.

When Hugh turns that charming smile on me, my knees nearly weaken. He's that good looking. I never thought I was into silver foxes, but...

We'll just leave it at that.

"Please," he says. "Black. No sugar."

Evelyn releases a sound that's more of a hiss. As she crosses her arms against her chest, the diamond bracelet at her wrist glints in the sunshine that pours in through the picture windows. "Don't you have somewhere else to be? Our meeting isn't for another hour."

His fingers brush against mine as he takes the to-go cup, and a shiver shoots through me. It has nothing to do with the touch and everything to do with the way Evelyn looks ready to rip him to shreds with her bare teeth.

"Actually, no," Hugh muses, taking a slow sip of his coffee. "It's nice in here. Warm and cozy. Not to mention, it smells delicious." His gaze slides to me, then to the display case. "Callie, I didn't get a chance to talk to you the night of the event, but a few of our sponsors were impressed with Lakeshore Sweets. I wouldn't be surprised if it leads to several business ventures moving forward."

"Thank you, I really appreciate that."

He flashes another dazzling smile in my direction that nearly knocks me on my ass. "If you need anything, just let me know. Once you're part of the Railers family, you're always part of it."

From the corner of my eye, I watch Evelyn's expression

relax.

Marginally.

Or maybe it's a trick of the light, because when I look again, she's back to scowling.

Sloane sighs into her latte.

I have no idea how to respond. As much as I appreciate the sentiment, the Railers don't feel like family. More like something to be avoided.

Then again, that does sound like family.

Evelyn steps closer. "You've pushed your luck enough for one day. I think it's time for you to leave."

Hugh leans in and murmurs, "And yet, you continue letting me do it."

It feels like I'm watching a chess match where I don't understand the rules. What I do know is that this isn't romance.

Not really.

This is something far messier.

Darker.

Evelyn looks like she's fighting for air in a room Hugh controls.

Sloane nudges me and whispers from the side of her mouth, "You're seeing this, right? I'm not hallucinating?"

"No," I whisper back. "You're not."

As Hugh raises his cup in a mock toast to Evelyn, I can't shake the feeling that whatever's going on between them is on the verge of exploding.

We engage in stilted conversation for a few more minutes before the older woman leaves as gracefully as she entered. Hugh follows her out with a hint of a grin. It's like there's an invisible thread binding them to one another.

As soon as they're gone, my muscles loosen. "Well, that was certainly interesting."

Sloane cracks a smile. "I'm dying for the backstory."

The edges of my lips lift. "Same. We'll have to pump Lilah and see what she knows."

"Or Rina. They work closely together. Maybe Evelyn's mentioned something about her relationship with Mr. Tall, Dark, and Foxy."

With a snort, I glance toward the register.

Crap.

The bank notice.

I should probably tuck the letter back into the envelope and shove it in my purse before Sloane catches sight of it.

But it's not there.

With a furrowed brow, I check the floor, the shelf under the counter, and the stack of mail for a second time.

Panic flares in my stomach when my search turns up empty.

No one else was behind the counter this morning.

And I know it was there with the stack.

I swallow hard, hating the idea that one of my customers might have picked it up by accident and is now privy to my financial situation.

How mortifying.

If Sloane had found it, she would've asked out of concern. She's one of the most forthright people I've ever met.

I nibble my lip as the bell over the door chimes with the arrival of a new customer, and I paste a smile on my face and get back to work.

4
RIVER

ll right, I'll admit that I wasn't planning on making a detour after practice. If I were thinking clearly, I would've headed straight back to the penthouse to chill out for a while before tonight's team meeting. Maybe even watched some film.

The second Evelyn mentioned Beau reaching out to Callie, something in me snapped.

I know exactly who the guy is.

Chicago might be a big city, but it's also a small one in all the ways that matter.

After a while, you see all the same faces at parties or clubs.

From what I've heard about Beau, he enjoys having a beautiful woman on his arm to show off.

Callie isn't just a pretty face.

She's smart and hardworking. The last thing she needs is to get tangled up with a playboy who isn't interested in settling down or being a true partner in every sense of the word.

It's exactly how I end up at the downtown bistro, seated at a table near the window with an amazing view of the river, a glass of water in front of me as I wait for the owner to make an appearance.

"Are you sure there isn't anything else I can get for you?" the hostess asks, leaning closer, ample cleavage on display.

My guess is that she'd like me to ask for her number.

But there's no chance of that happening.

There's only one woman I'm interested in.

She owns a bakery and has the most adorable two-year-old I've ever seen.

My twin sister's kids excluded, of course. Autumn and Haven have some serious cute factor going for them. Especially when they flash their dimples.

"Nope, I'm good."

She takes a small step in retreat. "Okay. If you need anything, just let me know. Wave me down. I'll be watching from right over there." She points to the hostess stand near the entrance.

Umm, okay... That's not creepy at all.

I force a smile. "Thanks. Appreciate it."

She beams before reluctantly turning to a table who's been trying to get her attention for the past five minutes.

This kind of behavior isn't anything out of the ordinary. Women have been falling all over themselves to get to me since college. And when I turned pro, it was like the floodgates opened.

Did I take advantage of the fan adoration in the beginning?

Guilty as charged.

And for a while, the transient encounters filled a void.

Until I met my best friend and teammate's new girl.

Then, it was impossible to forget her face.

Even while fucking other women.

Since I could only keep that up for so long, I stopped hooking up altogether. I haven't had sex in three years.

Honestly?

I haven't even felt the urge.

Which is disconcerting to say the least.

I'm knocked from those thoughts when Beau Masterson slides into the chair across from me. He's all flash with an expensive Rolex wrapped around his left wrist and suit that's tailored to fit his large frame.

"To what do I owe the pleasure, Thompson?" he asks with a quick smile.

Like I said, it's a big city that feels small.

I lean back in the chair, aiming for cool and collected. "I heard you were interested in carrying some desserts from Lakeshore Sweets in your restaurants, so I thought I'd drop by for a quick conversation."

I have to fight the urge to groan when his eyes spark with equal parts humor and interest. "You don't say? Go on."

When I press my lips together, his smile widens.

Beau Masterson comes from money, and lots of it. He's used to getting what he wants. And if it's necessary to pay for the pleasure, he'll do that too.

"So tell me, do you have an interest in the little bakery?" There's a beat of silence. "Or the pretty blonde who runs it?"

"Callie's a good friend," I say casually, hoping he buys it. It would be pretty fucking embarrassing if he asks her about our nonexistent relationship. "I'm more interested in what your intentions are."

Beau laughs, clearly enjoying himself. "Look, I'll be honest. She's a beautiful woman. And obviously talented. She has that sweet, girl-next-door appeal working for her. I was thinking about taking her out and getting to know her."

Dammit. I knew it wasn't as simple as the desserts.

My fingers flex beneath the table. "Callie isn't like the women you usually date," I say, making a concerted effort to lower my tone.

He shrugs. "Maybe I'm looking for something a little different."

Even though I'm loath to give him more information, I admit, "She has a kid."

Beau tilts his head. "Little girl, right? So what's your angle here, Thompson?" He leans in slightly. "Are you this protective of all your friends? Or is there more going on behind the scenes?" There's a beat of silence. "From what I've heard, Zane Holloway's the baby daddy. Or do I have it wrong?"

A muscle in my jaw tics.

I'm holding on to my temper by a thread.

What a fucking douchebag.

I meet his gaze and hold it steadily. "She and Zane were together, and now they're not. Callie's not the type of woman you fuck around with. She's got Nora and the bakery. That's where her priorities lie. If you're only interested in carrying her desserts, that's great. Just know that anything else is off the table."

His smile sharpens. "You're the one who makes that call, huh? Is she aware of that?"

I don't bother with a response, since I don't have a good answer. At least, not one I'm willing to share with this asshole.

But Beau keeps going. "Who's to say she doesn't want a little fun in her life? Sounds to me like she deserves it."

It wouldn't take much to wrap my hands around his throat and squeeze the air from his body. Slowly. If he keeps talking shit, that's exactly what's going to happen.

"She deserves more than what guys like you are offering," I say flatly.

Beau raises both hands as mock innocence shines in his eyes. "Hey, if she tells me no, I'll back off. But if she says yes? I won't apologize for showing a woman a good time."

I drum my fingers on the table. "Steer clear, Masterson. Or you'll deal with me."

Beau stares at me for a long moment before releasing a

chuckle that's low and full of amusement. "Damn. You really have a thing for her, huh?"

When I remain silent, he relaxes against the chair. "Noted."

With nothing else to say, I rise to my feet and walk toward the entrance. Even though I came here with the intention of giving Beau a bit of friendly advice, I leave the restaurant with fire in my veins and one thought echoing in my head.

I can't afford to sit on the sidelines and bide my time anymore.

Not when it comes to Callie.

Or her daughter.

Not when some smug asshole thinks he can touch what I've been quietly guarding for years.

5

CALLIE

Nora's giggle echoes through the townhouse as I flip the pancake onto her plastic plate. It lands a little lopsided, but she cheers as if I'm one of those celebrity chefs we watch on TV.

Breakfast for dinner is one of Nora's favorites. And since it's budget friendly, it's one of mine as well.

"Mama!" She clutches her child-sized fork like it's a wand before pointing it at the bottle of maple syrup.

"You're gonna bounce off the walls if you have any more of that," I tease, drizzling the sugary syrup until she squeals.

For just a moment, everything feels uncharacteristically light and happy.

Nora babbles while eating. Her feet swing beneath the highchair, her blonde hair in messy pigtails that won't survive another hour. I can't help but watch her as a swell of emotion rises inside me. I don't know how I got so lucky with my sweet girl.

As much as I want to stay present in the moment, my financial issues keep shoving their way in at the edges until it's all I can think about. Trying to keep us afloat feels like it's becoming harder with the passing of each day.

"Mo', Mama," she says, polishing off the last bite of fluffy goodness.

I refocus my attention and flip the next pancake before buttering and cutting it up for her.

Once Nora's done eating, I clean up the kitchen and then we head to the bathroom for a little bubble time with her bath toys. She's like a little mermaid in the tub. Next summer, she'll be old enough for swim lessons. Hopefully, we'll be able to find some at the local rec department that won't cost an arm and leg.

When the time comes, I'll have to talk to Zane about it. The child support he gives me doesn't stretch as far as it used to. He's lucky my parents watch Nora for free when I'm at work. If I had to pay for daycare, buying groceries would be even more of a challenge. And I certainly wouldn't be able to afford this townhouse that's close to the bakery.

It's only after Nora's fingers turn pruney that I wrap a towel around her and dry her off. Once she's in her unicorn pajamas, we turn on a show, and she sits quietly next to me on the couch while flipping through a picture book with her pacifier. When she turned two, I told myself it was time to wean her off it. Now, a few months shy of three, I still haven't followed through.

It's not a fight I'm looking forward to.

Just as I'm about to put Nora to bed, there's a knock on the door. A sigh escapes me as I consider ignoring it.

I know exactly who I'll find on the other side.

Even though I've asked Zane not to, he has a habit of showing up without warning, usually right before Nora's bedtime. She'll get wound up and then settling her down for sleep becomes even more of a challenge.

Nora blinks the drowsiness from her eyes. "Dada?"

I force a smile and nod. "Yup, I think so."

It nearly breaks my heart when she claps her chubby hands together and races for the door. She's practically vibrating with excitement. She's so starved for his attention when she's nothing more than a passing thought to him. While Zane certainly isn't the worst father in the world, he'll never win any awards for going above and beyond.

All I want to do is give this little girl the world, and I can't even give her a father who's genuinely interested in her.

It's disheartening.

Nora dances at my feet in her footed pajamas as I open the door. Her face lights up as Zane waltzes in wearing designer sunglasses and a hoodie that probably cost more than my monthly grocery bill.

"Hey, kiddo." He reaches down and absently ruffles Nora's golden locks before beelining to the couch. As soon as he drops down, he reaches into his pocket and pulls out his phone.

"Nice of you to drop by," I say dryly.

With a grin, he puts the slim device away. "No problem. I've been sitting on some big news and I wanted you to be the first to know." Before I have a chance to steel myself, he announces, "Gigi and I are getting engaged and filming a wedding special. It's gonna be huge."

I blink as my mind cartwheels. I have no idea what to say as he stares at me expectantly. "Wow. That was, um, fast."

He laughs, not taking offense to the comment. "Fast is the new trend, babe. People eat that shit up. We've got the network behind us, a stylized beach shoot, two dress designers vying—"

His words blur as my gaze shifts to Nora, who has climbed onto the couch and is sitting beside him, staring up at him like a puppy who only wants a scrap of attention.

It's painful to realize that his gaze never drifts to her. Instead, it stays pinned to mine. I want to shake him for being so obsessed with chasing fame. He's got plenty of it with his hockey career.

But that's not enough. He wants more.

He has no idea how much it would mean to his daughter if

he just gave her twenty minutes of his undivided attention. A crumb of his affection. She doesn't need a camera crew or fake fairy tale weddings.

She just needs him to show up for her.

Unfortunately, Zane isn't capable of that.

After nearly three years of me gently pointing this out, he refuses to hear what I'm trying to say. He's missing out on so much. I'm sad for both him and her.

Zane continues talking, oblivious to the fact I no longer give a damn about his personal life. The only thing I care about is how it affects our daughter.

"It's gonna be a wild ride. Think ten-episode arc leading to the wedding. Gigi's working with a florist in Bali—"

"Zane," I interrupt before the entire conversation can spiral out of control. "I need to talk to you."

His brows rise as he glances at me. "What's up?"

As much as I hate asking him for anything, I'm out of options. So, if I have to swallow my pride to keep things afloat, that's exactly what I'll do. "I'm behind on the loan for the bakery. Business has been tough with the economy. I'm trying to make it work, but I could really use some help. Just this once."

He frowns. "Damn, girl. I wish I could, but everything's tied up in the show. We're putting money into production, styling, locations—"

I can only blink.

He's joking, right?

The man is wearing sunglasses that cost more than six months of rent.

"Zane," I say again, firmer this time. "I need help."

There's no way to say it plainer than that.

He shifts on the couch and then glances at Nora as she slips her smaller hand into his before grinning up at him. "Kind of funny timing, actually. I was going to talk to you about lowering the child support payments. Maybe taking a break for a while."

My mouth falls open as my brain short-circuits. "What?"

He shrugs. "Things are a little tight, and Gigi and I are looking at some investment properties. Maybe a fixer-upper we could add to the show. People eat that home improvement shit right up." He taps the side of his head. "You always gotta be three steps ahead at all times. Plus, I figured Nora's still young. How much does a two-year-old really need?"

His obliviousness slams into me, leaving me to reel.

"Do you think raising a child is cheap?" It's impossible to keep the waver from my tone. "You think rent, food, and clothes just magically appear? *Poof*. There they are."

"You're amazing, Cal," he says, untangling his hand from Nora's and popping to his feet before heading toward the door. "You'll figure it out. You always do."

He leaves without even saying goodbye to his daughter.

I can only stare at the now closed door.

"Bye-bye, Dada," Nora says, waving her chubby little hand even though her father is long gone.

As much as I'd like to fall to pieces, that's not an option. Instead, I scoop Nora up and force a smile. "How about we make popcorn and watch another show before bed?"

Her eyes brighten. "Pop-pop."

"Yup. Popcorn fixes everything," I mutter, carrying her into the kitchen.

Except rent.

And late loan payments.

Zane is right about one thing, though. Somehow, I always manage to figure it out.

And I'll continue to do it for as long as I need to.

This isn't just about me anymore. It's about making sure my daughter is taken care of.

6
RIVER

The hum of fluorescent lights and the faint trickle from the showers echo through the locker room as I pull off my jersey and run a towel over my sweat-drenched face. Steele, Knox, Oliver, Jax, and Laiken are mid-conversation about this weekend's game when Zane strolls into the locker room with a towel wrapped around his waist.

"Some of you really need to step it up out there," he announces. "This is supposed to be a team effort."

Steele glares before crossing his arms in front of him. "Is there anyone in particular you'd like to call out? Or is this more of a general statement?"

With a shrug, Zane whips off his towel. "Just saying. Unlike some of you clowns, I've got a lot riding on us winning a Stanley this year."

"Thanks for the pep talk, bud. Maybe after you hang up your skates, you can consider the motivational speaking circuit," Knox throws out with a shake of his head.

"How about you focus on yourself for a change instead of what the other guys are doing on the ice," Laiken adds.

"I think he's already a little too focused on himself," I mutter.

Jax snorts. "Ain't that the truth."

Zane catches sight of me and grins. "Yo, Riv. Any interest in coming out with Gigi and me tonight? We're gonna hit a few clubs."

"Nah." Spending any more time with Zane than I have to isn't even a consideration.

He rolls his eyes and whines. "Come on, man. When did you become so lame?"

When I realized what a dickhead he was. Admittedly, I was a little late on the uptake. I should have seen it sooner.

Undeterred by my silence, he claps me on the shoulder. "You probably already heard the big news." Before I can tell him that I don't give a damn about his announcement, he continues, "Gigi and I are getting hitched. The network's throwing some serious money our way. We're talking a wedding special, ten episodes, international honeymoon. And they're paying for everything. Shit's gonna be epic. And you need to be there for it, man."

My stomach twists as the full weight of his words sinks in. "Wait a minute, you're getting married?"

It takes effort to keep my voice even.

He grins like this is the greatest thing to ever happen to him. "Hell, yeah. Didn't you hear me, bro? They're paying for everything."

There's no *she's the love of my life.*

Or *I seriously can't wait to marry her.*

It's all about the dollar signs.

Does he even give a damn about this woman?

Or is she just part of the next big content drop?

The fact I even have to ask that question says it all.

The only thing I can think about is the woman he left behind.

The one who's still picking up the pieces of her life.

I shift on the bench, pulse ticking faster. "Does Callie know?"

He waves a hand like it's nothing before yanking on a pair of tighty-whities. "Yup, I stopped by her place last night. I thought it was the right thing to do, you know? She took it well. I think she's finally over it."

My jaw clenches.

How is he this much of a turd?

"And I figured I'd talk to her about cutting the child support too" he adds casually. "Things are tight. You wouldn't believe the cost of a wardrobe for the show. You'd think these companies would be vying for me to wear their brands on a national TV show. It's seriously insane."

That comment has me seeing red as I swing toward him and cock my head, praying I heard him incorrectly. "I'm sorry… You asked her to do what?"

Zane blinks, his stupid smirk still in place. "Relax, man. She's fine. That girl always lands on her feet. It's what I love about her. All these people around me want to take, take, take. But not Callie. She wants to stand on her own two feet. Gotta appreciate that."

I shove my pads into my stall with more force than necessary. "You realize that she's barely scraping by, right?" I snap. "And you're out here blowing six figures on a televised circus and your entourage?"

Zane straightens, the smugness falling from his expression as defensiveness flashes in his eyes. "What I spend is none of your damn business, Thompson."

"The hell it isn't." I step forward, fists clenched at my sides. "You don't show up for Nora or help Callie out at all. And now you want to take even more away from them?"

His eyes narrow. "Did Callie put you up to this?"

"No, but she damn well deserves someone who actually gives a shit about her. Both of them do."

Knox wedges himself between us before it can turn into a full-blown brawl. "Whoa. How about we cool things down," he says, holding me back. "This isn't the time or place."

"Callie and Nora are my business, not yours," Zane adds.

Adrenaline pounds through me as I shake off my teammate. I'm not even sure why I'm bothering with this guy.

He doesn't get it.

And it's doubtful he ever will.

He's too focused on himself.

"Maybe if you took care of your business, I wouldn't have to step in and do it for you." Instead of waiting for a response, I grab my bag and stalk out of the locker room.

If Zane won't step up for Callie, then I will.

There's no way I can continue to stand by and watch her struggle.

The question isn't *if* I'll help.

It's *how*.

7
CALLIE

The scent of vanilla, butter, and cinnamon from the batch of muffins cooling on the rack fills the bakery as sunlight spills across the counters.

Lilah leans her elbows on the table as one hand drifts to her barely-there baby bump. "Steele has been driving me insane. He keeps hovering like I'm made of glass."

Rina snorts. "And yet you sound suspiciously smug about it."

Lilah rolls her eyes as a smile lifts the corners of her lips. "That's not what I meant."

Sloane sips her coffee and teases, "But it's not *not* what you meant either."

The table bursts into laughter. These small moments with women who have become more like a family to me are part of what gets me through the tough times.

I can share anything with them.

Well, almost anything.

When the door opens, and a man walks in wearing a perfectly tailored navy suit with a wool coat draped over one arm like he just stepped off the pages of *GQ*, the conversation at our table grinds to a halt.

Rina's jaw drops as she mutters, "Holy hotness."

It takes a moment for recognition to slam into me.

The first thing I did after Evelyn mentioned that Beau Masterson might be interested in featuring my desserts at his restaurants was look him up online. Apparently, I'm one of the few people in the greater Chicago area who didn't already know who he was.

The man dabbles in everything.

He's a restaurateur.

An investor.

And from everything I found, a well-known playboy.

For some reason, he's considering adding my desserts to his menu.

He smiles at the group before his gaze zeros in on me. "Callie Westbrook?"

Looks like I'm not the only one who did their homework.

When I don't immediately respond, Rina elbows my side.

Hard.

I pop to my feet like a Jack-in-the-Box, and wipe my hands nervously on my apron before closing the distance between us. "Yes. Hello. That's me."

His gaze burns into mine. "Would you have a few minutes to talk?"

Rina grabs Lilah's hand. "She sure does. We were just about to leave." She winks behind his back as they slip out the front entrance of the bakery.

My attention lands on Lilah as she walks by the glass and mouths, "*Text us everything.*"

Sloane jerks her thumb toward the back. "I need to take care of something in the kitchen." Then she disappears around the counter and through the swinging door, leaving us alone. I swallow a groan and try not to fidget as he steps closer before extending his hand.

I take it automatically. His grip is warm and confident.

"I have to admit to being impressed at the Railers event a few weeks ago," he says smoothly. "Everything was amazing. I'd love to sit down and discuss the possibility of carrying some of your desserts in my restaurants."

When he continues holding on to my hand, I carefully tug it free and then take a small step in retreat. "I'd love that. Did you have a specific date in mind?"

Before he can respond, the door opens again, and a jolt of awareness shoots through me as River strides inside. His blond hair is still damp from the shower, the ends curling against his neck. His blue eyes are sharp and searching as they land on me. The pull between us is instantaneous.

More than that, it's infuriating.

The second River spots Beau, his eyes narrow before slicing to me again, as if assessing the situation. The intensity of his gaze makes my skin prickle. It's tempting to put more space between Beau and myself, but I refuse to do that.

River's jaw tightens as his shoulders turn rigid. A muscle tics in his cheek before he forces himself to relax, his expression settling into something that looks casual. But I know better.

"Hey," River says. He steps closer, hands loose at his sides. "Am I interrupting?"

"Actually," Beau replies easily, like he doesn't notice or care about the strange current that runs between us, "you were. Callie and I were just discussing getting together for dinner this Thursday evening." There's a beat of silence before Beau tacks on, "To discuss a potential partnership."

Dinner tomorrow?

"Oh. That's kind of short notice." My voice wavers even as I make a concerted effort to steady it. "I'll have to let you know. I need to find a sitter first. My parents usually watch my daughter during the day—"

"I'll do it," River cuts in.

My eyes widen as they slice to his. "I'm sorry?"

Even though he swallows up some of the distance between us, he doesn't crowd my personal space. That doesn't mean he's not close enough for the heat of his body to wrap around me like a second skin, cocooning me in comfort.

"I'll stay with Nora during your meeting."

Stunned by the offer, I shake my head. The thought of him babysitting my daughter sends my whole world into a tailspin. "I don't think that's—"

"You know you can trust me with her, right? I would never let anything happen to Nora," he says quietly, as if it's meant for my ears alone.

The seriousness in his eyes has my throat tightening. Somehow, I do know that.

"Yes."

It should be Beau who flusters me. By every logical standard, he checks all the boxes. The man is handsome, successful, and if I can trust my instincts, interested in more than a business partnership.

Instead, it's River who makes my pulse race and tangles me up inside.

Beau grins, mischief flickering in his whiskey-colored eyes. "Looks like we're all set. I'll pick you up tomorrow at six."

My lips part to say... I'm not even sure what, when River leans in, his warm breath ghosting over the shell of my ear. "Wouldn't an afternoon meeting be more appropriate for a business discussion?"

"Nope." Beau's grin grows. "We're planning on mixing business with pleasure."

A low growl rumbles up from River. The deep reverberation of it sends a shiver through me even as heat curls low in my belly.

When neither man speaks, I say, "I'll see you tomorrow."

Beau heads to the exit, tossing one last parting shot over his shoulder. "I look forward to spending more time with you, Callie. It'll be fun."

The door clicks shut behind Beau, leaving me with River. The air shifts, thickening with tension that sparks hotter now that it's just the two of us.

My hands twist in front of me, a feeble attempt to ground myself before I swing toward him and blurt, "I don't understand why you did that."

8
RIVER

The good news is that Callie doesn't sound mad by my unexpected offer. More like thrown off.

As if she can't quite figure me out.

And that's okay.

For the time being.

"I think we can both agree that it's a great opportunity," I say honestly. "Even if I don't like the idea of you spending time alone with Beau Masterson."

She blinks, clearly not expecting that response.

"I'm thinking about what's best for you," I add. "Not me."

Confusion flickers in her expression for half of a second before it's masked again. "I can check with my parents. I'm sure they'll watch Nora."

"That's not necessary," I insist. "I've got you covered."

She swallows before glancing toward the front of the bakery, as if needing a moment to collect herself, before her narrowed gaze slices back to mine.

"And you're really okay watching her?"

"Of course. Believe it or not, I've spent time around kids."

Her expression turns even more skeptical. "You've actually held a toddler?"

A grin tugs at the corners of my mouth. "Yup. My twin, Willow, has two. A three-year-old and a one-year-old who screams like he's auditioning for Broadway."

Her eyebrows lift. "You have a twin?"

"Yup." Unable to help myself, I swallow up the little bit of distance that separates us. "There's a lot you don't know about me, Callie."

Even though she stands her ground, I catch the flash in her eyes and the pulse that flutters faster against the delicate flesh of her throat as she realizes just how close we are. Heat flares to life between us as the scent of her floral shampoo mixes with my cologne.

She has no idea how much I want to get my hands on her.

With one blink, she pulls herself back together again as her tongue darts out to moisten her lips. "Are you sure about this?"

"Absolutely. I wouldn't have offered if I wasn't."

I lean in close enough that she has to tilt her chin upward to hold my gaze.

"Besides," I say, "I'll be there afterward to make sure you get home safe and sound. And Beau knows it."

It would be impossible not to notice the way she stills as I slip my fingers beneath her chin. "If he touches one hair on your head, it'll be the last thing he ever does."

Her eyes flare as her lips part, but not a single sound comes out. For a second, all her quiet defenses falter as she stares up at me like she's never heard words like that before.

Which kills me.

She deserves them.

This woman deserves to be worshipped like a queen.

It takes a moment for her to recover. "I don't need a knight in shining armor."

No, she doesn't.

She's more than capable of taking care of herself.

She's had to.

"I never said you did. Looks to me like you've got it all under control. You're a single mom and a business owner. No one needs to ride in and save you, Callie. But that doesn't mean we don't all need a helping hand every once in a while. And I want to be that for you."

"Why?" she asks, brow furrowing.

"I think the answer is pretty obvious."

I see the exact moment she swallows hard and decides not to push for more answers.

When she remains silent, I attempt to lighten the mood. "Do you really think I can't handle Nora?"

"It's not about you handling her. It's about me not trusting just anyone with my daughter."

"That's fair," I admit. "But you can trust me."

Unable to help myself, my gaze dips to her mouth.

Just for a beat.

Long enough for her to see it.

Long enough for her to feel it too.

She turns away, grabbing a rag to wipe the counter. "If you're sure—"

"I am."

"Okay then. I guess I'll see you tomorrow night. Do you need my address?"

"Nope, I already have it." Mission accomplished, I waltz out of the bakery with a smile on my face.

It might not be a ton of progress.

But it's more than enough.

For now.

9

CALLIE

I t's just a business meeting, I remind myself.

Nothing more than that.

I repeat the words like a prayer as my hands flutter over a dress I haven't worn in three years. It's a little snug at the hips and a lot more low-cut than I remember, but it's one of the few things in my closet that screams *I'm still put together,* even if I feel anything but.

And it shouldn't matter because this isn't a date.

Just as I swipe on lip gloss, there's a gentle tug on my leg.

"Me!" Nora demands, pointing to my lips with the commanding tone only a toddler can pull off.

With a grin, I bend down and give her a gentle kiss, smacking my lips together for effect. "There. Now we both sparkle."

She giggles with delight before running off with her stuffed giraffe clutched in her arms. My heart aches as I watch her. She's growing up so fast, and I'm doing everything I can to give her the life she deserves.

When the doorbell rings, my stomach flips.

I tell myself it's nerves about the meeting.

That it has more to do with what's at stake and absolutely

nothing to do with the man who volunteered to watch my daughter for a few hours.

My hands smooth over the fabric of my dress one last time before opening the door and finding River on the other side with a crooked smile and wind-tousled hair.

He's wearing a blue crewneck sweater that is the exact hue of his eyes and hugs his chest like it was tailored specifically for him. He shrugs out of his jacket, and the way his muscles shift beneath the fabric makes me forget how to draw oxygen into my lungs for half a second.

Maybe more.

His gaze slowly sweeps over me. "You look beautiful."

My cheeks heat, and I find myself trapped within his stare. "Thanks." My voice comes out sounding unsteady, and it only makes my face flame more.

Pull it together, Callie.

I spot the tote in his hand, and latch on to it like a lifeline. "What's in the bag?"

He hands it over. "Why don't you open it and see."

I peek inside and find coloring books, oversized crayons, and a few toddler-safe toys that have clearly been picked out with care. This isn't just random junk thrown together. Nor is it expensive or flashy.

It's surprisingly thoughtful.

Everything inside me constricts. "You didn't have to—"

"I wanted to," he says, cutting me off before stepping inside the townhouse. "I figured something new would keep her occupied for a while."

The man isn't wrong. "It will. Smart thinking."

"Me?" Nora peeks around my legs to stare at River with interest. This isn't the first time they've met, but she doesn't spend a lot of time with men. Just my father. So I'm not sure how this will go. I'm bracing myself for her to get upset when she realizes I'm leaving.

"Hey, sweetheart," River says, squatting down to her level. "That's a pretty cool giraffe you got there. Mind if I check him out?"

My fingers tunnel through her curls. "Do you remember River?"

It's almost a shock when Nora takes a hesitant step from behind me before carefully setting her beloved stuffy in his hands. It would be difficult not to notice how much bigger and masculine they are than hers.

He handles the toy with care, turning it one way and then the other, as if he's inspecting it.

"Does he or she have a name?"

"Gaffy," Nora whispers.

River nods, his expression turning thoughtful. "I like it. Does Gaffy like to color?"

Nora takes another step closer.

"Do you want to check out some of the things I brought for you to play with?"

When she glances up at me, I nod and give her an encouraging smile. "You're going to have so much fun while I'm gone."

River holds out the bag, and Nora peeks at the contents before dipping her hand inside and pulling out the oversized crayons.

She stares at the colors before glancing at him. "Me?"

"Yup. All for you."

As much as I try to keep the walls in place where River Thompson is concerned, they're already starting to crumble. Watching him interact with my daughter is all it takes to melt my normally icy reserve where this man is concerned. He's paid more attention to her in five minutes than Zane has in the past year.

That realization is enough to bring tears to my eyes.

I blink them away when Nora grabs River's hand and tugs him into the living room. He pops easily to his feet and follows her. His gaze locks on mine as he settles on the couch. It doesn't take Nora long to plop onto his lap as she digs through the bag, pulling out toys and playing with them.

I don't think she's ever taken to someone with such ease. For a long moment, I stare, silently watching them interact.

He's not just babysitting.

He's engaging with her.

With a smile, River listens as Nora talks, even though he can't possibly understand everything she's saying. The ache that blooms within me is too big to name.

I cough lightly to break the silence. "I'm going to run to the bathroom before I leave."

"No problem," River says. "We're all good here."

Yes, it seems like they are. And I couldn't be more surprised.

Once I'm done, I pick up my purse from the table and glance through the contents, making sure I have everything I need.

Hmmm. My phone.

I look around, spotting it on the coffee table near the couch. What's strange is that I don't remember leaving it there. Although, it's not uncommon for Nora to play around with it. River watches me as I scoop up the slim device and shove it in my bag. The heat of his gaze is enough to singe me alive.

Tension crackles in the air between us, ratcheting up until it's enough to choke on. It's almost a relief when there's a knock at the front door. I open it and find Beau in a stylish gray suit, his hair combed away from his face. He offers a charming smile that should make my pulse race but does absolutely nothing.

"Evening, Callie." His gaze slides past me toward the living room. "And this must be Nora."

My daughter glances at him from where she sits perched on River's lap before thrusting a toy in his face.

Beau gives a slight chuckle before dismissing her as his attention returns to me. "Cute kid."

For a brief moment, I'm disappointed he doesn't make more of an effort with Nora. The second that thought slips in, reality crashes over me.

Right.

This isn't a date.

He doesn't have to make friends with Nora.

Still, a tiny part of me wishes he'd tried.

Beau extends his arm, clearly in a hurry to get out of here, and in all honesty, so am I. When I turn to River, I find his attention already pinned to me.

"My number and Nora's schedule for the evening are on the kitchen table. She just needs a bedtime story before she goes down at eight."

River nods. "Got it."

This is so much harder than I anticipated. "Call if you need anything."

Instead of brushing off my concern, he offers a supportive smile, as if he understands exactly how hard this is for me. "I will. We'll play for a bit and then read some stories. We'll be fine. I promise."

With a nod, I turn to leave, but something makes me glance back at them. River is smiling at Nora as she chatters excitedly on his lap.

When I remain frozen in place, captivated by the sight, Beau slips an arm around my waist before steering me out the door. "Shall we?"

I nod. "Yes, thank you."

With one last look at the pair, I close the door behind us as we step into the chilly night air. Beau leads me to a sleek black car with tinted windows that idles near the curb. A man wearing a black suit jumps out of the driver's side as soon as he sees us before rushing around the vehicle and opening the door.

I hesitate a beat too long before sliding into the back seat.

Beau follows me inside the luxurious sedan. For just a split second, I can't help but wish I were staying home.

Or maybe I wish it were River taking me out instead.

I shove that thought deep down and lock it inside a vault where it'll never see the light of day, then I force myself to smile.

This is business.

Something that can save the bakery and get us back on even footing again.

What I need is for this to work out.

10
RIVER

"**R**ivvy!"

Nora plops into my lap like she's been doing it her whole life, her little fingers clutching a green crayon like it's a sword. She's been calling me Rivvy all night, and I swear to God, every time she says it, it hits me right in the chest and knocks the air from me.

Even though I've only been here for an hour, it already feels like she's got me wrapped around her little finger.

How isn't Zane totally obsessed with his daughter?

It doesn't make a damn bit of sense.

And then there's her mother...

Nora pulls my attention back to her when she holds up a lopsided drawing. It could be a unicorn or a dinosaur. Possibly both. Or maybe it's just a bunch of scribbles. She beams, as if she just painted the *Mona Lisa*.

How can I not smile back?

"Should we hang it on the fridge, ladybug?" I ask. "Your mama is going to love it."

She scampers into the kitchen and stares at the refrigerator. I grab a couple magnets and place them strategically on the drawing. As soon as that's done, she grins at it before racing back to the living room and climbing onto the couch. With a small sound, she pats the cushion next to her.

How is this kid so damn cute?

No, seriously.

It's mind-boggling.

When Nora points to the television, I grab the remote and turn it on, flipping through a few channels until it lands on a cartoon that looks age appropriate. Nora plucks the pacifier off the coffee table as she snuggles Gaffy in her arms.

My thoughts wander to Callie as I sneak a peek at my phone. Beau better be talking about pastry orders and not trying to flirt with her.

With an exhale, I drag a hand through my hair. The idea of Callie out on a date with another man eats away at my insides.

I glance down at Nora. "Think we should check on your mama? Make sure everything's good?"

If it's not...

She plucks the pacifier from her mouth. "Mama!"

I nod. "Exactly what I was thinking, ladybug."

With my phone in hand, I type out a message.

Me: *Just wanted you to know that Nora has tied me up and is running wild through the townhouse. JK. We're fine. She colored a masterpiece for you, and we hung it on the fridge. Now she's watching a show. Then we'll read a few books, and it's lights out for this girl.*

I hit send and then wait for a response. When one doesn't pop up right away, I grow impatient and hit her name until a map appears on the next screen.

Did I happen to turn on her share location when she went to the bathroom before walking out the door with another man?

Damn right I did.

Looks like she's at one of his restaurants. It's only a couple of miles from here. Nora and I could be there in less than ten minutes if we needed to.

Me: *If I don't hear from you in two minutes, I'm coming to get you. FYI-I know where you are.*

It takes less than ten seconds for her response to come through.

Callie: *Okay, I'm calling your bluff. Where am I?*

I fire off the answer.

Me: *Sweet Surrender.*

There's a longer pause this time before she responds.

Callie: *Did you turn on my location?*

Me: *Consider it a safety measure.*

Callie: *That's a little stalkerish.*

Me: *Agree to disagree.*

Callie: *Is everything okay?*

I snap a pic of Nora sitting contentedly next to me watching TV, totally engrossed in the show.

Me: *She's perfect. I just wanted to check on her mom.*

Callie: *I'm fine. I won't be out much longer.*

Me: *Good.*

Callie: *Thank you again.*

Me: *Enjoy the rest of your evening out.*

As soon as I hit send, I tack on—

Me: *Not too much, though.*

Callie: *I'll try not to.*

I stare at her last message, my thumb hovering over the screen.

Does she have to try hard?

Are she and Beau hitting it off?

It might have started out as a business thing, but has it turned into more?

With a yawn, Nora leans against me, her head settling on

my arm. I reach for the blanket and tuck it around her small body so she's cozy.

And I let myself imagine what it would be like if this were more of a permanent situation.

If she were mine.

If they both were.

11

CALLIE

The second I step inside Beau's restaurant, my suspicions grow that this is more than a business meeting. The space is dimly lit, with muted music playing and pretty votives that flicker on every table.

The atmosphere is intimate.

More romantic in nature.

It's the kind of place where a man proposes and future plans are talked about.

This is supposed to be a business meeting about potential contracts and wholesale orders for desserts. But when Beau pulls out my chair and gives me a slow, confident smile, I realize he's not thinking about dessert trays.

He's staring at me like I'm a tasty treat on the menu.

And I don't know what to do with that.

I'm totally out of my element.

Beau orders a bottle of wine along with our dinners before I even have a chance to look over the menu. He charms our waitress with a smile the entire time.

I was with a man like that. Someone who was quick to cajole you into bed, all the while thinking about his next conquest.

That's not a mistake I plan to make again.

Once the wine arrives, I take a sip out of politeness and then set the glass down.

Beau is handsome. Smart. Put-together. Women literally turn their heads to stare when he walks by.

I should be into him.

Instead, all I can think about is whether River figured out that Nora insists on reading *Goodnight Moon* twice. Or if she made him do the voices. Or if she talked him into letting her eat chocolate chips straight from the bag by batting her big brown eyes at him. Will that affect him the same way it does me?

I blink and realize Beau asked me a question.

"So, you and River... What's the story there?"

My fingers tighten on the base of my wine glass as our steaks are set down in front of us. "River?"

Beau tilts his head, smirking like he already knows the answer. "You two seem close."

"We're not," I say a little too quickly, cutting into the steak and then smearing butter on the potato.

His smile widens. "Good. Although, it wouldn't matter if you were. I've never been afraid of a little competition."

My stomach twists at that pronouncement.

The rest of our meal is filled with talk. And what I mean by that is Beau does most of it. He tells me about his restaurants, his investments, and plans for future expansion. I nod, murmuring at appropriate intervals, all the while waiting for him to ask a few questions about me or even the bakery. Maybe the kinds of desserts I specialize in.

He doesn't.

Not even once.

I carefully check my phone under the table for any missed messages, but there aren't any. Which is a good thing. It means Nora isn't giving River any problems.

I refocus my attention on Beau's face. On the words coming out of his mouth. On the candle that flickers between us.

It's no use.

In my head, all I see is River crouching down to talk with my little girl. And the bag of toys he brought for her. The way she handed over her stuffy, as if she'd known him forever. Then there's the sound of River's quiet, steady voice when he said I could trust him with Nora.

We're midway through dinner when my phone buzzes, and I pounce on it as if it's a lifeline.

River: *Just wanted you to know that Nora has tied me up and is running wild through the townhouse. JK. We're fine. She colored a masterpiece for you, and we hung it on the fridge. Now she's watching a show. Then we'll read a few books, and it's lights out for this girl.*

A sharp pang cuts through me.

Not at the part where he says he's been tied up, but that he's so good with her.

"Callie?"

My head jerks up, and I reluctantly set the phone on the white-clothed table. "Sorry."

He takes a sip of his wine. "Is there an issue?"

I force a smile as our plates are cleared away. "Not at all."

"Good. So, I was telling you about my restaurants."

"Yes. It's really interesting."

He launches into how his parents owned a few and then he built upon their empire. And that's certainly impressive. I'm sure it takes a lot of work to oversee so many different ventures. But he didn't start from nothing or build his business from the ground up. It's a lot harder when sweat equity is the only thing you have to invest.

Beau continues to drone on, and it takes a moment to realize I've tuned him out again.

"Wow," I say, hoping he didn't notice my lapse.

"You have no idea."

I hum in agreement as a man in his late forties stops by the table. With a grin, Beau rises to his feet before they shake hands and talk about their golf game.

When my phone buzzes with another incoming text, I slip it into my palm and scan the message.

River: *If I don't hear from you in two minutes, I'm coming to get you. FYI-I know where you are.*

My pulse kicks up as I peek at the screen.

Does he?

I glance at Beau, relieved that he's still talking and laughing with his friend.

Me: *Okay, I'm calling your bluff. Where am I?*

The response is immediate.

River: *Sweet Surrender.*

My belly dips, and I slowly type out the question uppermost in my mind.

Me: *Did you turn my location on?*

River: *Consider it a safety measure.*

Me: *That's a little stalkerish.*

River: *Agree to disagree.*

I should be angry that he thought it was perfectly normal to invade my privacy. But how can I be when a pic of Nora sitting contentedly next to him while watching TV rolls in?

Honestly, it's the strangest thing.

Who knew River Thompson, superstar hockey player, was actually a toddler whisperer in his spare time?

Maybe he's right and I don't know as much about him as I assumed.

Me: *Is everything okay?*

River: *She's perfect. I just wanted to check on her mom.*

Ugh. This man. I'm not sure what he's playing at, but I don't like it one bit.

Me: *I'm fine. I won't be out much longer.*

I hope.

River: *Good.*

I'm not touching that comment with a ten-foot pole. For all I know, he's eager to get on with his evening now that he's done his good deed for the year. I'm sure he has women on standby for booty calls. That thought sits at the bottom of my gut like a heavy stone. Instead of dwelling on it, I shove it aside, but it continues to nag at me no matter how much I pretend it doesn't.

Me: *Thank you again.*

River: *Enjoy the rest of your evening out.*

Another message immediately pops up after that.

River: *Not too much, though.*

Me: *I'll try not to.*

I stare at the screen a little too long as a strange warmth blooms within me.

"Is everything all right?" Beau asks.

I quickly flip my phone over. "Yup. Just checking in with River. I should probably get home soon."

Beau frowns. "Really? I was hoping we could check out one of my clubs afterward."

A laugh tumbles from my lips.

When I realize he's not joking, my chuckle fades into awkward silence. "Sorry, I'm not really into the club scene anymore."

Surprise flashes across his face before he shrugs and waves our waitress over. "I hope you enjoyed dinner."

"I did," I assure him. "Everything was fantastic."

That said, tonight hasn't gone the way I expected. I still have no idea what he thinks about the bakery or my desserts.

Just like he has all evening long, Beau talks the entire ride home. One thing's for sure, the man certainly has a lot to say. I force a polite smile and nod, all the while counting down the minutes until I can escape the confines of the sedan.

What's become apparent is that tonight has been a total bust.

Even though I didn't want to get my hopes up, I was counting on this partnership to pan out. It would have made life just a bit easier and given us a little wiggle room. It's been so long, I almost don't remember what simple feels like.

Thankfully, it doesn't take long to reach the townhouse. As the vehicle rolls to a stop, Beau swivels toward me, and our knees bump.

When he leans closer, panic sparks in me, and I blurt, "Well, thanks again for dinner." I flatten myself against the door and yank the handle. "Let me know if you have any questions about the desserts."

"I was thinking we could start with a few hundred a week," he says with a chuckle. "Gabby, my assistant, will be in touch with exact numbers on Monday."

My mouth falls open. "Really? That's amazing."

His grin softens as his gaze drops to my lips. "I'd also like to take you out again."

Well, hell.

"Oh. I'm, ah, flattered. I just... I'm not sure I'm in a place to start dating."

He shrugs. "Is it really necessary to slap a label on whatever this turns out to be?"

Um...

It takes effort to keep the smile pasted in place. "As much as I appreciate the offer, I'd prefer to keep our relationship strictly business."

He arches a brow. "Perhaps I can change your mind about that."

Unlikely.

I shake my head. "Thank you again for the opportunity. I look forward to hearing from your assistant."

Before he can attempt to change my mind or rescind the

offer, I'm tumbling out of the car and onto the curb. It only takes a moment to straighten and dust myself off before I'm halfway up the steps to the townhouse. Once there, I turn and lift a hand to wave. Using the key, I slip inside the safety of my home. Only then does the tension I've been carrying around all night ease from my shoulders.

No matter what River texted earlier, I'm fully expecting to walk into pandemonium. Nora's probably running wild, refusing to go to bed, and every toy she owns will be strewn around the place.

Instead, I find the lights dimmed and the TV volume on low. My footsteps stall when I spot River in the armchair and Nora curled up against his chest, fast asleep with her cheek mashed against his sweater and her hand clutching the fabric.

I freeze as everything inside me constricts.

They look so cute together.

Kind of like they belong.

What hurts even more is that Zane never cuddled her like this. He never held our daughter like she was his whole world or acted like she was the best part of his day.

But River?

He does it as if it's the most natural thing in the world.

His lips curve in a slow smile as our eyes stay locked. I slip off my jacket and then my shoes. Every step I take feels deliberate. Magnetic. Like some kind of invisible force is drawing me to him. It's one I don't have the strength or the will to resist.

I've never felt this way before.

Not with anyone.

Including Zane.

Back then, I mistook his attention for affection. I was swept up in the whirlwind of being wanted by a pro athlete who said all the right things... until the shine wore off and the truth came into sharp focus. He didn't love me. He enjoyed the chase.

By the time I figured it out, I was already pregnant and in too deep to turn back.

But with River...

This isn't a storm.

It's something I don't recognize.

And I'm not sure if I should step closer... or run.

12
RIVER

ora's completely sacked out on my chest, one arm flung across my ribs like I'm her personal stuffed animal. Her lips are parted slightly, and her fingers twist in the fabric of my sweater.

I should probably get her to bed before Callie walks through the door. I want to make things as easy as possible for her.

But I don't move a muscle.

Instead, I remain in the armchair, content to have this little girl snoring in my arms. There's something comforting about the warmth of her body. The trust that had filled her face when she stared at me with eyes the exact shade as her mother's. She could have asked me for a pony, and I would've wanted to know what color she had in mind.

I'm knocked from those thoughts when the front door clicks open and Callie walks in.

For just a second, I eat her up with my eyes.

All right, let's be real.

It's for way more than a second.

Anytime this woman is near, I find myself forgetting about everything else going on.

It's a relief that she looks the same as when she left earlier. Gorgeous, calm, and pulled together. She shrugs out of her jacket and hangs it on the hook before bending to unfasten her shoes one at a time.

That shouldn't be so sexy.

Our gazes cling as she closes the space that separates us until she's no more than a foot away.

"I take it the meeting went well?" I ask, refusing to call it a date.

"It did. He agreed to carry my desserts."

"That's great," I say, meaning it. "I'm happy for you."

I brace myself as she leans in to pick up Nora. Her scent hits me first. It's something light and floral. It's unfair just how quickly it goes straight to my head. I inhale a lungful of her before I can stop myself.

Her eyes widen as they dart to mine, and we freeze for a beat.

Maybe less.

But it's enough to leave me reeling.

Nora stirs, and Callie pulls back, as if she touched a live wire, before easily adjusting her daughter in her arms. It's almost like Nora is an extension of her own body. Watching them together makes something inside me ache.

Without a word, she disappears down the hall. I give it a couple of minutes before trailing after her. I find Callie standing over Nora's crib, arms folded, watching her daughter sleep, as if she's trying to take in the moment.

She startles when I step beside her.

"Just in case you were wondering, she was really good for me," I whisper, not wanting to wake the little girl.

A smile lifts the corners of Callie's lips. It's not an expression I'm used to seeing. Especially aimed in my direction. "I'm glad. I was kind of worried. She's always with me or my parents. I thought she might cry the whole time I was gone."

I shake my head, only wanting to give her reassurance. "Nope. She was great." My brow furrows as I stare at the toddler. "She looks like she's outgrown her crib."

Callie huffs out a tired laugh. "Yeah, I know. I need to move her into something bigger."

The words are simple, but they land heavy.

I wonder if it's the money.

Or the time.

Or maybe everything that's weighing on her all at once.

"We could do it this weekend," I suggest.

Her head jerks toward me. "What?"

"I've got some time. And a truck. We could go and pick something out, then I can put it together for her."

"You don't have to do that."

It would be impossible to miss the confusion that flares to life in her brown eyes.

"I want to," I say, stepping a little closer.

When she remains silent, I add, "Remember when we had a conversation the other day about how it's okay to accept help every once in a while? This would be one of those times."

Her shoulders fall just a bit as she glances away. "There hasn't been anyone to help in a long time."

I lift my hand, gently slipping my fingers beneath her chin. Her skin is so damn smooth, and warmer than I expected. It's almost a surprise when she doesn't fight me as I tilt her face toward mine.

"I know," I murmur. "And I'm sorry about that. If you'll let me, I'd like to help."

She studies me in silence for a handful of moments. Even with the dim lighting, I see all the emotions that jockey for position in her eyes. Both her pride and fear. The never-ending exhaustion of being a single parent and running a business without anyone to support her. And maybe the flicker of something she doesn't want to admit.

To herself or me.

"Fine," she whispers.

I don't move.

Or speak.

I just stand beside her, close enough to catch the rise and fall of her chest.

And in the quiet that follows, something delicate settles between us.

Something that feels dangerously close to a softening I didn't think was possible.

13

CALLIE

By the time I finally make it to the bakery the next morning, I'm running on caffeine and nerves. Nora woke up with a low-grade fever. Even though it wasn't anything serious, I couldn't shake the anxiety that clawed at my insides. She seemed fine by the time I dropped her at my parents' house, but I'm still bracing for a phone call.

So when I walk in and see a glittery purple banner that reads *Congratulations*, I stop short. There's a cake on the counter with bright pink frosting. Before I can jumpstart my brain, I'm swallowed up in a group hug.

Rina squeezes me hard enough to crack a rib. "We're so proud of you!"

Sloane grins. "I knew you had him in the palm of your hand. By this time next year, you'll be opening a second location in the suburbs."

Lilah offers me a mug of my favorite mint tea. "You've earned this, Cal."

It's almost a shock when tears fill my eyes and a lump rises in my throat. All I can do is press a hand to my chest and try to contain all the emotion attempting to break loose.

"Thank you. Seriously. I really appreciate this."

The four of us squeeze into the back table by the window and dig into the cake while Rina waggles her brows.

"So... Beau. Talk about one hot man."

"He's definitely handsome," I agree.

Sloane leans forward. "Tell us everything. Was this a business dinner..." She waggles her brows. "Or a *business dinner*?"

I laugh. "It was just a business dinner. Although, the restaurant felt more romantic than I expected, and he ordered wine. Then, at the end... it kind of seemed like he might try to kiss me."

"And?" Rina demands, sitting up straighter. "And then what happened?"

It's almost embarrassing to admit the truth. "I might have told him that I didn't think it was a good idea to mix business with anything personal before fumbling with the door handle and launching myself out of the car."

Lilah giggles. "Oh no."

Rina throws her hands in the air. "Girl. I would've been all over that man like glaze on a donut."

"Yeah, well..." I shrug. "It didn't feel right. Not that he did anything wrong. I just wasn't feeling it."

Sloane tilts her head. "Hmmm... Is that because you were too busy thinking about a certain blond hockey player with muscles for miles?"

I roll my eyes. "Of course not. He watched Nora for me and nothing more."

"That was so sweet of him," Lilah says.

It was.

It's impossible to fight the smile that lifts my lips. "Okay, I'll admit it. He was really great with her. I thought she'd be upset when I left, but she barely noticed I was gone. They colored, played with toys, and watched a show. When I came home, I found Nora passed out on him." A beat of silence follows that admission. "Seeing how good he was, how kind and patient he was with her, meant more than I expected."

Sloane arches a brow. "Go on. I'm totally loving this."

Rina smirks. "You mean it melted your icy, independent heart just a little?"

Before I can respond, the door chimes behind me, and just like that, he's standing in the entrance, as if I conjured him straight out of my thoughts.

He's tall, golden, and infuriatingly hot in a worn hoodie and pair of jeans. His gaze settles on me, as if I'm all he sees. I feel the spark of electricity we always seem to generate down to my toes.

Rina mutters, "Speak of the devil."

Sloane grins. "Just like clockwork."

River heads straight toward us, giving the other women quick glances of acknowledgement.

"Heard you babysat last night," Rina calls out. "Giving up hockey for a nanny position?"

He doesn't even blink as his attention stays locked on me. "Depends on who I get to watch."

That comment has warmth creeping up my neck.

Unsure how to respond, I rise to my feet. "I'll grab your usual."

It would be hard not to feel his masculine presence as he follows me to the counter.

My mind blanks as sweat springs to my palms. It's the most ridiculous thing ever. I rack my brain for something to say before blurting, "Thanks again for watching Nora last night."

"It was my pleasure."

Shivers erupt across my flesh.

"Are we still on for Sunday afternoon?"

If I were smart, I'd back out of this shopping excursion ASAP. He's giving me the perfect opportunity. I just need to take it.

Instead, I nod. "Yes."

I bag the bagel and pour a cup of coffee before handing it over to him. He swipes his credit card before glancing back at the girls and nodding a quick goodbye. The second the glass door shuts behind him, the bakery explodes in a barrage of rapid-fire comments.

"Oh. My. God," Rina says. "My panties almost self-combusted. Can't say any of my Tinder matches have had that much chemistry lately. Or maybe ever."

"Talk about the difference twenty-four short hours makes," Sloane adds with a shake of her head.

Lilah gives me a wistful smile. "I'm on the verge of swooning. Honestly, if you don't kiss him soon, I might."

"Pretty sure Steele would have something to say about that," Rina says with a snort.

I sink back into my seat with a belly full of butterflies. "No, it's not like—"

"Don't even say it," Sloane cuts in.

With my palms pressed to the table, I will myself to cool down as the truth sinks in with a crushing weight.

I'm no longer sure if I want River to stop pushing his way into my life. But I'm scared to death of what will happen if he actually succeeds in doing it.

14
RIVER

By the time I pull up outside Callie's townhouse, I've triple-checked the bed straps in the back of my truck and adjusted the brand-new car seat I installed last night. I don't want her to worry about a damn thing today.

She must have been waiting by the window. The moment I throw the truck into park, she steps outside, carrying Nora on her hip and a diaper bag slung over one shoulder. Her hair is up in a knot, and she's wearing something simple like leggings and an oversized sweater. There doesn't appear to be a speck of makeup on her face.

And I swear, she's never looked hotter.

"Hey." I hop out, slamming the door.

"Hi." She adjusts Nora's weight as I round the front of the truck to the sidewalk.

As soon as I'm standing next to them, I reach out and stroke my finger along Nora's downy cheek. "Hey, ladybug. It's an exciting day! Are you ready for a big girl bed?"

She grins, showing off her pearly white teeth. "Rivvy!"

Callie blinks, staring first at her daughter and then at me. "Rivvy?"

"Seems easier than saying River. So, we're just rolling with it." When Callie's brows pull together, I let out a low cough and change the subject. "Ready to go?"

"Yeah." She points to a small SUV parked up the street that has seen better days. "I'll take my own car and meet you there since I've got the car seat."

I pop open the door to the passenger side of the truck and show her the brand-new seat I bought. "No need to do that."

She stutters to a stop. "Wait a minute… You have one?"

I nod. "Yup."

"Why?" Her voice comes out sounding uneven, like the question has too many layers and she's afraid of the answer.

I shrug, trying to keep it casual. "I didn't want you to have to unbuckle yours and then deal with reinstalling it. Those bases are a real pain in the ass."

For the second time in a matter of minutes, she stares at me, lips parted slightly, as a storm of emotions crosses her face. Surprise, confusion, and something that looks suspiciously like gratitude.

"You didn't have to do that," she says, quieter now.

"I know. But I wanted to. It makes things easier."

Without saying anything more, she gently straps Nora in before sliding onto the passenger seat up front. When she doesn't immediately do the same for herself, I step close enough for the faint scent of her shampoo to wrap around me. My fingers brush her side as I reach for the seat belt, taking my time before drawing it across her chest.

She stills on a sudden intake of air as my knuckles graze the side of her breast before I click the latch. Instead of moving away, my hand remains in place, fingers resting lightly on the buckle.

When I finally look up, her wide eyes are locked on mine. Her pupils are dilated and her lips are parted ever so slightly. The air between us turns charged, as if the smallest movement might tip us over the edge.

"Thank you," she whispers.

My gaze drops to her mouth and lingers there before lifting to meet her eyes again. "Anytime."

I close the door gently, then hustle around the hood and slide in beside her. There's something about having her so close that hits deeper than I expect. Honestly, it's not a moment I ever thought I'd get to enjoy.

With a press of the button, I start the engine and pull away from the curb. Nora kicks and babbles the entire drive to the baby superstore. Callie remains quiet, fidgeting next to me. I rack my brain for something that will break the tension, but it remains stubbornly silent. As soon as we pull into the parking lot, Callie unlatches her seat belt and jumps out of the truck. By the time she opens the back door, I'm already there, nudging her out of the way and unhooking Nora from the seat.

"I can take her," Callie says, reaching for her daughter.

I shake my head, already shifting Nora in my arms. "Nah, the two of us are tight now. We bonded the other night." I glance at her. "Didn't we, ladybug?"

Nora giggles and clutches a handful of my jacket, as if in total agreement.

Callie mutters, "I really don't understand this at all. She doesn't go to just anyone."

A slow smile spreads across my face. "Guess it's clear I'm not just anyone, then."

Inside, the store smells like lavender wipes and baby powder. I carry Nora as we stroll the aisles, Callie beside me, her gaze flicking between the toddler beds and me like she's trying to process both at the same time.

A sales associate sidles up to us. She's all enthusiasm and big energy. "Oh my gosh, your daughter is adorable! And she looks just like you!"

When Callie opens her mouth, more than likely to clarify

our relationship, I say before she can get the words out, "Thank you."

Callie goes quiet beside me, but I feel her gaze as Nora flashes me a grin and rests her head on my shoulder.

We tell the associate what we're looking for and she leads us to a fancy selection of toddler beds. We find one that's all sleek lines, high safety ratings, and costs as much as a playoff ticket.

Callie takes one look at the price tag and shakes her head. "No, that's too much—"

"Do you like it?" I ask, cutting in. "Do you think Nora would enjoy sleeping in it? Is it something she can grow into?"

Callie studiously avoids my gaze as she nibbles her lower lip. "Yeah."

"Then there's nothing more for us to discuss." I pull out my card before she can argue, and hand it over to the saleswoman. "We'll take it."

The woman practically squeals. "What about the mattress?"

"We'll take one of those as well."

She raises a brow. "And an extended warranty?"

"Yup."

With my credit card in hand, she scurries off to ring up the purchase.

As soon as she disappears around the corner of the aisle, Callie swings toward me. "River, I love the bed, and I think Nora would too, but..." A flush creeps into her pale cheeks. "It's way too much. I can't afford it."

I hold her gaze. "It's a gift. There's no need to pay for anything."

"I don't expect you to buy us the bed. Nora's my responsibility. And I'm more than capable of taking care of us." She lifts her chin as her bottom lip trembles. "I've been doing this on my own for nearly three years."

That admission makes my heart ache. It's tempting to lift

my hand and massage the pain away. "I know. You're one of the strongest women I've ever met, Callie. I really admire that about you."

She blinks, and her jaw stays locked tight, as if she doesn't know how to respond to the compliment.

As tempting as it is to tug her close and wrap her up in my arms, to soothe some of the hurt within her, I remain still. "Nora deserves a bed that'll grow with her. You do too. So let me do this."

Just when I think she'll continue arguing or flat out refuse the gift, she jerks her head in a tight nod. "Fine. But just this once."

Her surrender feels like a small victory.

Like I'm one step closer to her letting me into her life.

After signing the sales receipt, we load the oversized boxes into the bed of the truck and strap them down tight. Callie watches me the whole time with a slightly furrowed brow, like she sees something she doesn't quite know how to handle.

Nora chatters all the way home as she stares out the window and smudges it with her fingers. I can't help but smile. Even though Callie remains silent, her thoughts are loud.

I glance at her before returning my attention to the road stretched out in front of us. "Are you all right?"

She nods a little too quickly. "Yeah. Just tired."

"I'm sorry you've had to do all this alone. Zane should have been a better partner." I look at Nora in the rearview mirror, and everything inside me turns to mush. "A better father, at the very least."

She swallows hard as her gaze finds mine. "Believe it or not, I don't regret getting involved with him. If I hadn't, I wouldn't have Nora. And she's my entire world. She's the reason I get out of bed every morning and work as hard as I do. I wish Zane were more involved, but maybe it's better he isn't. The last thing I need is for Nora to get attached, only for him to flake when she's old enough to understand and be hurt by his indifference."

I don't think about reaching out and wrapping my hand around hers.

I just do it.

From the way her eyes widen and she stills in her seat, she's just as shocked by the unexpected offer of comfort as I am. It's not a total surprise when she slips her fingers free before twisting them nervously in her lap.

Neither of us say a word for the rest of the ride. The silence isn't uncomfortable, but it's heavy. Thick with things we're both avoiding. My grip stays steady on the wheel, my focus on the road ahead, even as every part of me is attuned to her. The way she shifts in her seat. The slow rhythm of her inhalations. The faint scent of her perfume as it weaves through the air.

I tell myself I need to be content with whatever she's willing to give me.

But the truth is, I'm already past that point.

I want more.

More than she's ready for.

More than she might ever be ready for.

And no matter how much I try to reel it in, I know there's no going back.

15
CALLIE

I'm still thinking about the way River's warm fingers were wrapped around mine as we pull up to the curb outside the townhouse. The moment he cuts the engine, I slip from the truck and open the door to get Nora. It's only then I realize she's fallen asleep.

River stops by my side, his gaze settling on her.

His expression turns tender. "How is it possible that she's even more adorable when she's asleep?"

I snort as a smile tugs at my lips. "No clue. But I do know she's a total tornado when she's awake, and she's starting to outgrow her naps. I was hoping for at least another six months."

He shifts slightly. "Should we wait until she wakes up, or do I try to lift her out now?"

"Let's give it a shot. I'm sure you want to get the bed inside and set up. You've probably got plans for this evening."

"Nope. None." His eyes meet mine. "I'm all yours for as long as you want."

I falter on a sharp inhale, searching my brain for a response.

But there's nothing. I'm totally blank.

I force out a cough to steady myself. "You should probably get her."

He gives me a lopsided smile before unlatching the harness and lifting it over Nora's shoulders, trying to make room to maneuver. Nora shifts but doesn't wake. At least, not yet. He carefully slips his hands under her arms and eases her from the seat. As soon as her limp body is free, he pulls her against his chest and holds her close so that her head is tucked beneath his chin.

Seeing my daughter nestled against this man does funny things to my insides. Other than the help my parents provide by babysitting, this is the first time in years I haven't felt like I had to do something alone.

As we head up the walkway to the townhouse, River says, "Looks like there's something taped to the door."

I blink out of my thoughts. "Huh?"

He nods toward it, and that's when I see the envelope. Bright white with my name and address typed out on the front. It looks official. A vise grips my insides.

Is it from the bank about the late loan payments?

They wouldn't actually come to my home on a weekend, would they?

My footsteps falter as dread pools within me. I'm scared to find out what's waiting inside. I already know that whatever it is won't be good.

With River looking on, I force myself to reach out and carefully rip it from the door. My fingers tremble as I open and scan the contents. I frown and reread it for a second time, trying to make sense of the paragraphs. Without warning, it feels like my world has been upended.

"Is everything okay?" River asks from behind me with Nora still sleeping in his arms.

Notice of Rent Increase: $500.00 effective next month.

The words blur on the paper.

Five hundred dollars.

I'm silently reeling at that number.

Even with the dessert order for Beau's restaurants, it's not going to be enough to cover all my expenses. No matter how hard I work, something always comes along and eats away at my savings.

It's exhausting.

How much longer can I continue to do this?

I'm like a hamster on a constantly spinning wheel.

What's frightening is the realization that I'm only one disaster away from losing everything.

A sound that's caught between a laugh and a sob tears from me. "My rent is being increased by five hundred dollars," I whisper as the paper flutters in my hand. "The landlord isn't even giving me a thirty-day notice."

I don't realize tears are rolling down my cheeks until River's hand is at the small of my back. "I'm sure there's a way to fight it. At least for a full thirty or sixty days. What he's doing has to be illegal."

I shake my head. "I've heard from a few of the neighbors that he wants to sell the place to a developer. And jacking up the rent is one way to force me out."

He takes a step closer. "What if I could offer you a solution?"

I glance at him as my brain somersaults. "A solution?"

There's a beat of silence as his blue eyes sear into mine. "Move in with me."

My brow furrows.

There's no way I heard him correctly.

"You and Nora can stay with me," he repeats. "There wouldn't be any rent. No stress. I can help out with her. You won't have to do this all on your own."

He can't possibly mean it.

I shake my head and search his face. "Why would you offer that?"

His expression never wavers. "Do you want the truth? Or a version that's easier to swallow?"

My pulse stutters. "The truth."

His steady gaze stays locked on mine. "I've wanted you for years, Callie. Not just in passing or as a fantasy. I've wanted *you*. The real you. The you who bakes when she's stressed and bites her lip when she's overthinking. The you who built a life for her daughter with no one's help. You walked into my world and blew apart every plan I had. And it feels like I've been waiting for my shot ever since."

The force of his words slams into me, stealing every thought, every defense I thought I had.

When I remain silent, unsure how to respond, he reaches out until his hand cups my cheek. His thumb brushes just beneath my eye.

"I've felt this way since the first time Zane introduced us," he says quietly. "It was after a game. Some club downtown. You walked in wearing this black dress and strappy heels, and I swear, the whole damn room disappeared. I couldn't stop looking at you." His tone turns rough. "At the time, I considered Zane my friend. But seeing you at his side? Watching the way you stared at him? I don't think I've ever hated anyone more. And I've been secretly coveting what he never appreciated ever since."

I can't catch my breath.

Every word leaves me spinning.

"You have?"

He nods once. "The entire time."

I shift, my eyes searching his for any sign of hesitation, any crack in his sincerity. I've been wrong before, and I don't want to take a chance on being wrong again.

One question rises to the surface. One that's too heavy to ignore. "What do you want in return?"

He doesn't flinch or look away. "I want you in my bed. And when you're ready to give yourself to me, I want that too. But what I want goes so much deeper." There's a pause. "I want all of you, Callie. Every messy, complicated, brilliant part."

Just like that, the air vanishes from my lungs.

I have no idea how to respond.

My brain is screaming at me to run away, but what choice do I have?

I need a safe place for Nora.

If it were just me, I could figure something else out.

My gaze flicks from his face to my daughter, who is still slumbering in his arms. I'd be lying if I didn't admit that part of me wants to tell him to go to hell. I've spent years fighting on my own, and I can continue to do it.

But my heart...

It's so damn tired of standing alone.

Of continually swimming upstream.

My shoulders collapse as that last thought rings in my head. "Do I even have a choice?"

He leans in, his hand sliding to curve gently around the back of my neck, anchoring me in place. "There's always a choice, Callie. One is to keep doing it all on your own." His gaze drops to my mouth before returning to my eyes. "The other is to let me help you."

"For a price," I murmur, needing to speak the truth aloud.

He lowers his head, lips brushing the shell of my ear. "I promise it won't be one you'll mind paying."

His voice is low.

Confident.

Intimate.

And just like that, a shiver sizzles through me, setting every nerve ending on fire.

I search his face, every shadow and line, but can't find a single reason to say no. If I'm being honest with myself, part of me doesn't want to. There's no way this respite will last long. River watched Nora once for a few hours before bedtime. He has no idea what living with a toddler 24/7 is like. After a week or two, day in and day out, his tune will change. If I'm lucky, it'll last a month. Just enough time for me to figure out a permanent living situation.

"Okay," I whisper.

Relief flashes across his face along with something else.

Something I wasn't prepared for.

Possessiveness.

Almost as if now that I've said yes, he has no intention of ever letting me go.

I have to remind myself that I've seen that look before.

Zane wore it in the beginning too.

This time around, I'm older.

Wiser.

I won't be fooled by pretty words wrapped up in nothing more than empty promises.

"When does this arrangement begin?" I ask.

"Right now. Go inside and pack what you and Nora need for the next few days. I'll hire a moving company to get the rest on Monday."

A jolt runs through me at how fast this is happening, and I hesitate. "Are you sure about this, River?"

"I've never been more certain about anything in my life."

I force out the next question. "What about Zane? He's your friend and teammate. Won't this cause problems?"

He swallows up the remaining distance between us until he's close enough for me to feel the gentle press of Nora against my chest.

"Zane and I haven't been friends for a long time," he says in a low tone. "I've spent years waiting patiently for you. And now I'm done waiting."

His words send an undeniable thrill shooting through me.

In this moment, I can't tell if I've just made the best decision of my life...

Or one that will shatter me completely.

16
RIVER

The bed is assembled, and Nora's sleeping soundly in her new room.

Callie stands beside me with her arms folded tightly, as if she's bracing for impact.

I don't blame her for being cautious. After blurting out how much I've always wanted her, you could have knocked the woman over with a feather.

And she's still reeling.

"Are you hungry?" I ask, wanting to turn her attention to something else.

I picked her up this morning and couldn't help but notice that she hasn't eaten a single bite all day. Not even when we made a pitstop to grab Nora some nuggets and fries on the way to my place.

I shoot her a sideways glance.

That ends now.

Callie needs to take better care of herself. The woman should be eating well and getting enough sleep. She can't keep running on fumes.

What she deserves is a man who will put her first.

Every damn time.

Every damn day.

Little does she know that she's found one.

She might not think there's a difference between me and her ex, but I'm going to show her exactly how wrong she is about that assumption. Zane and I are nothing alike.

Maybe early in my career, I let the fame and money go to my head. I hung around with players who made headlines every time they stepped onto the ice or walked into a club. It didn't take long for me to straighten myself out.

All right, fine... if you want to get technical, my twin sister, Willow, might've had a hand in knocking some sense into my head. Getting to be a good role model for my niece and nephew were just the icing on the cake.

She shrugs. "Maybe a little."

"Come on," I say. "We can talk more over dinner."

She glances toward Nora one last time, as if reluctant to leave her alone, before following me into the kitchen. Her gaze roams over the interior. It's all open space, clean lines, and windows that spill light across the hardwood floors. There are gray marble counters, chrome fixtures, and glass cabinets.

As much as I want to know what she thinks of my home, I keep the question buried inside. She's already a nervous ball of energy. I don't need to freak her out by telling her that we could find a new place, one she likes better.

"Wine?" I ask, congratulating myself on keeping the convo light as I grab a glass from the cabinet.

"That would probably be a good idea. I need something to take the edge off."

Once the wine is poured, I pass her a half-filled glass before leaning against the island and letting my gaze linger on her just long enough for color to bloom in her cheeks.

She can't be totally ambivalent toward me if I can make her blush so easily.

And that, I can definitely work with.

"I promise, it won't be that bad."

With her gaze pinned to mine, she lifts the glass and takes a long sip.

"Do you like spaghetti?" I ask, changing the subject to safer terrain.

"Yeah. Where are you going to order from?"

I smirk. "Nowhere. I'm going to make it myself."

She takes another sip of wine. "Well, color me surprised."

My gaze flicks to her again as she settles at the marble island. I can't say I don't like the sight of Callie making herself at home in my kitchen, drinking a glass of wine while I cook us dinner.

It's one I could definitely get used to.

She remains silent as I prep our meal. A big pot of water is filled and set on a burner to boil. From the fridge, I pull out a container filled with sauce I made a few days ago, and add it to a pan. Then I grab half a loaf of Italian bread, cut it lengthwise, and slather on a mixture of butter, garlic, and parmesan cheese. It doesn't take long for the sauce to simmer and the water to boil. I add the fresh noodles I picked up at an Italian specialty market. Three minutes tops and they'll be al dente.

Everything should come together around the same time. Spaghetti is an easy and comforting meal. The entire time I work, Callie sits on the stool across the island and watches me. It makes me wonder how often she finds herself being waited on instead of the one who does all the serving.

Way too often from the expression on her face.

"Do you cook a lot?" she asks.

"More than you'd think," I say, stirring the sauce. "It was something I picked up after college. Believe it or not, takeout gets old. And it turns out that I actually like cooking. The rhythm of it is relaxing. It's a great way to unwind at the end of the day."

She hums into her wine. "I never would've guessed that."

I glance over my shoulder and meet her inquisitive gaze. "I'm not sure why it should surprise you. It's not like you know very much about me."

With a frown, she sets her glass down with a clink. "There's plenty I know. You were Zane's friend, and that was more than enough."

Once the pasta is ready, I serve our meal and set a plate in front of her before settling on a stool at the island.

I remind myself that changing Callie's perception is going to take time and patience.

Luckily, I have enough of both.

"You're right," I admit. "I was his friend. But we haven't been close for a while."

She jerks her shoulders but doesn't respond.

Instead of pushing the topic, I let it drop. We eat in silence for a few minutes. It's the kind that simmers rather than settles.

She finishes about half of her dinner before setting her utensils down and saying quietly, "I really don't understand why you're doing this."

I don't answer right away. Instead, I study her, taking in the way she's sitting ramrod straight, her muscles full of tension. It would be impossible not to notice the guarded edge that's crept into her tone.

"You deserve better, Callie. You deserve more. And I want to be the one who gives it to you."

Her fingers tighten around the delicate stem of her glass.

"Even when you were with him…" My voice drops as I swivel toward her. "I saw you. And I saw how he treated you."

She blinks at me like she's trying to process a foreign language.

"But there was nothing I could do," I add. "You were with him, and I respected that. Even though I hated every fucking second of it."

This time she lifts the glass with a shaking hand and takes a larger gulp of wine. It's so damn tempting to reach out and wrap my fingers around hers to steady them.

But I've waited this long for the right time.

I can wait just a bit longer.

When I'm done with this woman, there's nowhere else she'll want to be and no one else she'll want touching her.

I'll make damn sure of it.

She stares down at her nearly empty glass and says quietly, "Would you just... do me a favor?"

"Anything."

When she tries to avoid my gaze, I slip my fingers beneath her chin, angling her face up until her eyes meet mine.

I need her to see me.

Really see me.

If we're going to do this, if I'm going to give her every damn thing she deserves, she needs to understand I mean it.

Her lips part, and when her tongue flicks out to wet them, my self-control wavers. It would be so easy to lean in, close that last inch, and taste her.

Instead, her words slice through the haze.

"I know you think this is what you want, but trust me, it isn't. Give it a couple of weeks and you'll be over it. You'll get bored, change your mind, and want us gone. Just... give me a little notice so I have time to find another place to live."

I shake my head, my gaze dropping to those plush lips I haven't stopped thinking about since the day we met. "That's not going to happen, Callie. Not in a few weeks. Not in a few months. Or years. Not ever."

Her brows snap together. "How can you say that? You live alone and are free to do whatever you want. You don't know what it's like to take care of a little kid. Just like takeout, it'll get old. Trust me, it didn't take long for Zane to get bored. And just like him, you'll want us out."

The thin, bitter waver in her tone nearly guts me.

In that moment, I want to find Zane Holloway and wring his damn neck with my bare hands for making her doubt her worth, for turning love into something that left scars she still feels. He didn't just break her heart. He ripped away her sense of security. Her belief someone could choose her and stay.

With my fingers beneath her chin, my thumb glides across her lower lip. It's such a small touch, but the tenderness I find there has everything inside me stilling.

"I'm not him," I say. "I don't make promises I don't intend to keep. And I don't walk away when things get hard."

Her eyes flash, something fragile sparking in them, but she reins it in. She wants to believe me.

She just can't.

Not yet.

"You weren't with a man before," I continue. "You were with a selfish little boy who didn't know how to value what he had. You gave him your heart, your loyalty, a family, and he threw it away. But I see you, Callie. I see everything you are. Everything you've built. Everything you carry. And I want it. All of it."

She goes motionless, the silence between us thick with things that have been left unsaid.

"I'm not going anywhere," I add. "So don't ever confuse me with the kind of guy who would."

Her lips part on a shaky exhale. "What is this to you, River?"

I don't hesitate.

"This," I say, pressing my forehead to hers, "is everything I've ever wanted. You. Nora. This life."

She swallows hard. "I don't believe you."

Even though I'm disappointed by the response, I'm not surprised.

A slow nod follows as I continue to hold her face. "That's okay. You don't have to. Not yet. Zane did a number on you, and

I get that. Just know I'm going to prove it every single day until the only thing you believe is me."

Her eyes shine with unshed tears, but she doesn't pull away.

It's a small thing, her staying still and letting me in even just this tiny bit.

But right now, it feels like everything.

17

CALLIE

"*I see you, Callie. I see everything you are. Everything you've built. Everything you carry. And I want it. All of it.*"

As much as I want to believe him, I just... don't.

Can't.

The thought of opening myself up to the same kind of pain as before is too scary. I'm not even sure this living arrangement will survive a week.

Two, tops.

This man has no idea what he's gotten himself into.

From the corner of my eye, I watch as River strips down to his boxer briefs like it's routine and we've been doing this for years. All the fangirling on Railers Rumors about River Thompson being one of the sexiest hockey players in the league is one hundred percent accurate. The guy has more in common with a Greek statue than a flesh and blood man.

As much as I don't want to be totally entranced by the sight of him, I am.

At this very moment, I'm having a difficult time ripping my attention away. My gaze drags across the broad line of his shoulders, the sculpted muscles of his chest before sliding over the deep ridges of his washboard abs. And then there are the tattoos. But it's the sharp cut of muscle just above the waist-band of his boxer briefs that melts my brain.

I have no business looking that low, and yet... here we are.

It's official.

I'm way in over my head.

When I'm finally able to shake myself out of my River Thompson induced trance, I snatch my duffel bag off the floor and flee to the en suite bathroom to clear my thoughts.

It's the best option.

The only one available to me.

The second I step inside the massive bathroom, I come to an abrupt stop, momentarily stunned by the sheer luxury of it all. Like the kitchen, the walls are a rich charcoal gray that somehow feels both sleek and soothing. The color perfectly complements the gleaming white marble floors laced with subtle gray veining. Chrome fixtures catch the muted ambient lighting, casting a quiet elegance over the entire space.

A freestanding soaking tub sits beside a floor-to-ceiling window that frames a spectacular panoramic view of the city skyline. It's the kind you only see in luxury hotel ads or dream real estate listings. Across from it, a deep mahogany vanity stretches along one wall, topped with a matching marble counter, and outfitted with double sinks. The open shelving beneath holds neatly folded towels that practically beg to be wrapped around bare skin.

I trail my fingers along the polished stone, taking it all in with wide eyes before they land on the glass-enclosed shower at the far end of the room. The bathroom is easily bigger than my entire living room.

Probably twice the size.

And just like that, I'm already imagining the feel of warm water pouring over me, the steam curling around my body as I let myself unwind, even if only for a few minutes. I'd be crazy not to take full advantage of the spa-like features while I can. In a week or two, this won't be my reality.

But right now?

It's calling my name.

Shoulders squared and chin lifted, I head back to the bedroom. River is sprawled across the king-sized mattress with his hands folded behind his head like he doesn't have a care in the world. The position draws my eyes to the curve of his biceps, flexed just enough to make my mouth turn cottony. He glances over, his gaze tracking me as I pause at the doorway, suddenly more aware of myself than I want to be.

"Is it all right if I take a shower?" I ask, trying to sound casual.

His brows lift just a fraction. "Callie, you don't have to ask permission to do anything. This is your home now. Nora's too."

The way he says it tugs a string loose inside me. A string I've kept wrapped tight for too long. The ache that blooms within me at the sound of my daughter's name on his lips catches me off guard. Like he already sees her as part of his life.

It takes effort to swallow the lump of emotion rising within me. "Thank you."

His lips lift. "No problem."

With a nod, I turn and slip back inside the bathroom. The moment the door clicks shut behind me, I reach for the lock and twist it.

Not because I don't trust him.

I do.

It's probably what unsettles me the most.

I lean against the solid wood and try to gather my composure. There's something dangerously comforting about this space. About him. About the quiet, steady way he keeps showing up.

It's unfamiliar territory.

And yet, it doesn't feel wrong.

It feels like the start of something I have no idea if I'm ready for but can't bring myself to walk away from.

More than anything, I need a sliver of control in a situation that feels like it's slipping further from my grasp with each passing second.

I twist the shower handles and watch as water cascades from the rainfall head mounted in the ceiling. For a long beat, I stand and stare at it, letting the sound calm my frayed nerves. Then I move on autopilot, peeling off my clothes and dropping each piece into a neat pile on the cool tile. I dig through my duffel for a ponytail holder and then twist my hair into a messy bun before stepping into the enclosure.

The second the warm spray hits my skin, I exhale.

Not just a sigh, but something that sounds a little too close to a sob.

I close my eyes and tilt my face toward the heat, letting it wash over me, melt into my muscles, and sink deep beneath the stress that's been living in my bones for months. It feels so good I could cry. Instead, I press my palms to the wall, let my forehead rest against the tile, and try to regain my bearings.

It feels like it's been years since I've been able to do that.

There's no rushing.

No multitasking.

Nora's not screaming from the other room.

There isn't a clock ticking down until the next crisis.

There's just stillness.

It's blissful.

As dangerous as the thought is, I can see how easy it would be to get used to this.

To River.

To how patient he is and how he anticipates needs I have yet to verbalize. Everything about him, from his quiet protectiveness to the thoughtful way he speaks, feels like a balm on raw, exposed skin. It's the kind of comfort I've stopped letting myself long for.

I shove the thought from my mind before it can take root.

No one sticks around forever.

Especially when it gets hard.

Even though I want to stand under the water until my skin prunes, I force myself to turn the dial off. I grab one of the plush towels from the open shelf and wrap it around my body. After drying off, I pull on the only clean clothes I brought in here with me. Sleep shorts and a comfy ribbed tank top.

They're not meant to be sexy.

But when I glance in the mirror, my stomach flips. The fabric clings to every curve, the chilled air in the bathroom highlighting just how thin the top is. My nipples are clearly visible through the cotton. I tug at the material, but it's hopeless.

There's nothing else in the bag to wear.

Perfect.

My pulse stutters as I crack the bathroom door open, just enough to peek into the bedroom. River's head turns immediately, his eyes locking on mine with laser focus. His gaze drops as I step into the room, raking over my bare legs, pausing at my hips, lingering at the hem of my tank before climbing slowly back up to my face.

Heat crawls up my neck as I tug at the edge of the shirt, even though it does absolutely nothing to hide what's already on display.

He remains silent.

There's no smirking or teasing.

But the intensity of his stare says everything.

I practically scurry to the bed and climb in, pulling the sheet and blanket up to my chin like some sort of protective shield. My heart finally begins to slow once I'm cocooned beneath the covers.

The mattress is more like a cloud, and the sheets are cool and silky against my skin.

And yet, nothing about this moment feels harmless.

The real danger isn't the man next to me.

It's how easily I'm starting to want him.

He doesn't say a word as he remains stretched out beside me. He's all lean muscle and quiet strength, the kind of man who seems comfortable, confident, and unshakable.

Like having a woman in his bed is nothing new.

I stare at the ceiling as my mind spins with doubts and questions. Instead of staying buried, they rise to the surface like bubbles in boiling water.

Before I can stop myself, the one that's been uppermost in my mind slips out. "What is it exactly that you expect from me?"

He shifts, turning toward me. His elbow sinks into the mattress, bringing him even closer. My nerves snap to full attention.

He watches me for a beat before his gaze drops to my mouth and then lifts back to my eyes. "Nothing."

The word lands softly, but it feels like a seismic shift.

His hand moves slowly, like he's giving me time to pull away. When his fingers brush my cheek, I flinch out of reflex, not fear. But he doesn't withdraw. Instead, he lets the touch settle.

"I don't expect anything from you, Callie," he says gently. "I'm not here to take anything you're not ready to give. I'm not going to sleep with you just because we're in the same bed. Not until you want it too."

It's the kind of thing a man says in a movie. Something scripted to melt a woman on the spot.

My eyes go wide.

And then, to my own surprise, laughter spills out. It's more of a sharp release from all the pressure that's been building. I clap a hand over my mouth, trying to muffle the sound, but it's too late. The tension shatters.

"That is never going to happen," I say once I'm able to steady my nerves.

River's mouth curves into a lazy smirk. "We'll see about that."

Without another word, he rolls onto his back and reaches for the bedside light before clicking it off.

Even though darkness settles around us, my thoughts refuse to be silenced, and my pulse doesn't show any signs of slowing. I lie there for a long time and stare into the shadows above. The steady sound of River breathing next to me is both oddly comforting and completely unsettling.

After everything that happened today, from the way he ignited a fire inside me to the tenderness he showed Nora, to the words he said that reach straight into the parts of me I didn't know were aching, one thing is painfully clear.

I don't have River Thompson figured out.

Not by a long shot.

And that might be the most terrifying realization of all.

18
RIVER

A quiet, broken sound slices through the dark, and I jolt upright, adrenaline rushing through my veins. For a second, I'm disoriented, still caught between sleep and waking.

That's when I remember I'm not alone.

Callie's curled up next to me, her faint inhalations brushing against the pillow. The floral scent of her shampoo wraps around me before slipping slyly around my heart until it's impossible to untangle.

Before I can shift closer and take it all in, another sound cuts through the silence.

A hiccupping sob.

And just like that, everything inside me freezes.

Nora.

My body moves before my mind can fully catch up. I glance at Callie. She's out cold with one hand tucked beneath her cheek. Her features have relaxed and are finally at ease. She needs this sleep. I've seen how hard she pushes herself, the exhaustion she carries like an extra weight she's gotten used to.

I slide quietly from the bed, careful not to jostle the mattress. The floor is cool beneath my feet as I pad into the hallway. The door across from ours is cracked open, the glow of a tiny nightlight casting a warm pool of amber against the dark.

I nudge the door open wider and step inside.

Nora's sitting up in bed, her tiny body trembling. Her hair is mussed and her cheeks are damp with tears. She blinks up at me with wide, watery eyes, and the second she sees me, her bottom lip wobbles as her arms reach up.

"Rivvy…"

Her voice is barely more than a whisper, but it hits me like a freight train. An ache fills me as I cross the room in three strides and scoop her into my arms. She clings without hesitation, as if she already understands I'm someone she can trust. Her arms wind around my neck as I press a kiss to the top of her head.

"Hey, ladybug," I murmur, rocking her gently. "Did you have a bad dream?"

She doesn't answer, just lets out a tired whimper and rests her head on my shoulder.

As I settle into the chair in the corner, I grab the fleece blanket draped over the back and wrap it around her. Nora lets out a sleepy sigh, her thumb slipping into her mouth as she nuzzles closer.

I shift her slightly, cradling her small body against mine, and start rubbing slow circles along her back. It's meant to soothe her, but it ends up calming me too.

The tension I didn't realize I was holding bleeds out of my muscles.

She settles deeper into me, all warm limbs and trusting. That's all it takes for something within me to pull tight. It's the kind of tightness that makes it hard to breathe, but in the best possible way.

I glance around the room, my gaze landing on the bare corner where a cozy armchair rocker would fit perfectly. The first thing I'm doing tomorrow is ordering the one we saw at the store.

Minutes pass.

Maybe more.

The room is dim and still, lit only by the nightlight and the faint glow from the hallway. The hush of the city hums through the windows, but it feels a world away from where I am right now with this little girl curled up against me, her heartbeat syncing with mine.

Nora hasn't even been here a full twenty-four hours, and already she's got me wrapped around her little finger.

I don't know what that says about me.

Or maybe I do.

I rest my head back against the chair and let my eyes fall closed for just a moment. My arms stay wrapped tight around her, like I'm anchoring us both in place.

I tell myself I'm just resting.

Giving her a minute or two to fall into a deeper sleep.

But the truth is, I don't want to move.

Or be anywhere else.

Not on the ice.

Or at the Rail Yard.

Or even in my king-sized bed.

With this little girl sleeping soundly in my arms and her mom just across the hall, it feels like everything I've ever wanted. Like I'm exactly where I was always meant to be.

Now I just have to convince Callie she belongs here too.

19
CALLIE

Pale morning light filters through the curtains, casting a golden glow across the room. I don't wake to the sound of Nora crying or the familiar rush of panic clawing at my chest, reminding me of everything I forgot to do the day before. There's no alarm, and all hell isn't breaking loose.

It's just silent.

Somehow, that quiet is more disorienting than the storm I've grown used to over the years.

I lie still, letting the softness of the mattress cradle me as the lingering warmth of the sheets cocoons my limbs. They feel heavy in the best way. I can't remember the last time I felt like this.

Not just rested but refreshed.

With a yawn, I glance around the room and realize that nothing looks familiar. For a split second, panic shoots through me. That's all it takes for recent events to come crashing back in a jumbled wave.

The bakery's late loan payment.

Shopping with River.

The eviction notice taped to my door.

River's offer to let us stay with him.

Falling asleep in his bed.

My pulse flutters as I roll onto my side, inching toward the other edge of the mattress. It's been a long time since I've slept in a man's bed. And even longer since one touched me with something that didn't feel like an expectation or obligation.

Just care.

I brace myself before finally peeking at the spot beside me only to find it empty. The sheets are cool to the touch and his pillow is undisturbed.

He's already gone.

I tell myself I shouldn't care even as a sharp pinch settles beneath my ribs.

This isn't about River.

I'm not here for a man or some whirlwind romance. I'm here because there weren't any good choices. I needed help and, for once, someone offered it.

This is about survival.

Mine.

And more importantly, Nora's.

Still, the disappointment of waking up alone continues to linger.

It's a quiet ache I refuse to acknowledge.

Like a bruise I pretend not to feel until something brushes against it, reminding me it's still there.

With a quiet sigh, I push back the covers and swing my legs over the edge of the bed. The chill in the air makes me shiver as my bare feet hit the hardwood. I rake my fingers through my hair, trying to shake off the weight of sleep as I pad into the hallway.

It's time to get moving.

I need to get Nora dressed, drop her off at my parents' house, and hustle to the bakery. I've got custom orders stacked a mile high, and my inbox is already overflowing. There isn't time to delay.

There's no space for anything except work, deadlines, and responsibilities.

As usual, my brain kicks into overdrive. I'm already itemizing tasks and prioritizing what needs to get done first. I need to order more flour and eggs. Reprint the catering invoice. Call the supplier about the vanilla extract. Prep for tomorrow's delivery. Text Sloane to check the display case. The list builds with every step I take until I'm standing outside Nora's door.

One glance inside stops me in my tracks.

River is sprawled in the oversized chair in the corner, head tilted back, jaw slack with sleep. His chest rises and falls rhythmically as my daughter lies curled on top of him.

Nora's tiny hand is fisted in the light smattering of hair on his chest, her cheek resting against his skin. Her legs are tucked beneath her, one foot poking out from the blanket wrapped around them both. His arm is looped around her protectively, as if even in sleep, he's trying to keep her safe.

Something about the sight cuts straight to my core.

This quietly tender moment is what I used to dream about back when I was pregnant and still foolish enough to believe Zane would be the kind of father who got up in the middle of the night without being asked. The kind of man who'd hold his daughter with both arms and his whole heart. Who'd love her the way she deserved. The way every child should be loved.

That dream died long before Nora ever opened her eyes. So I buried it and told myself it didn't matter. That I'd love her enough for both of us. That I'd be everything she needed. But now River's here, and he's holding her like it's the most natural thing in the world.

Like she's his.

Like she belongs with him.

To him.

Maybe the cruelest part of all this is knowing he's not mine.

Not really.

Not officially.

Not in any way that counts.

And yet, here he is. Doing what the man who should have never questioned it, wouldn't, without hesitation or complaints.

Unable to help myself, I watch them in silence, the ache growing heavier with every heartbeat. For a moment, all I can do is press a hand to my sternum and wonder how I'm supposed to keep him out when he's already found a way in.

My gaze drifts over him.

In sleep, he looks softer.

Younger.

More vulnerable.

And still so devastatingly handsome it's almost unfair. It's not just his face or the sharp cut of his jaw, or the annoyingly long lashes most women would kill for.

I don't realize I've crossed the room until I'm standing in front of him, close enough to feel the heat of his skin. My fingers twitch with the urge to touch his face, to trace the curve of his cheekbone or the sleepy smile tugging at his mouth.

But I stop myself just in time, and curl my hand into a fist at my side.

Letting River in any further would be all too easy.

And much too dangerous.

Somehow, I already know that if I let myself fall for him, there won't be a cushion to catch me. There'll be a crash I won't be able to walk away from.

His lashes flutter and his eyes open before finding mine. A drowsy smile curves his lips. Almost as if seeing me here, first thing in the morning, is the best part of his day.

A rush of warmth floods through me.

It's like I'm sixteen all over again and hopelessly out of my depth.

I force myself to move, gently scooping Nora into my arms.

She stirs only slightly, giving a sleepy sigh before tucking herself against me.

"You should've woken me," I whisper, focusing my attention on my daughter even as I feel his gaze burning into me. "She's my responsibility. I should be the one to take care of her."

River stretches, the movement slow and lazy as his arms lift above his head. "You were out cold and she was upset," he says, words still husky with sleep. "I figured I could handle it." His steady gaze returns to mine. "And I told you that while you're here, she can be our responsibility."

Our.

That one small word punches right through my ribs.

It doesn't hurt because I'm offended.

It hurts because I want it.

More than I want to admit.

Even to myself.

I clutch Nora tighter, like maybe if I hold her close enough, she won't hear that word and get the wrong idea.

As if I haven't already gotten it myself.

He's making this feel too easy.

Too safe.

Too right.

And that's the real danger, isn't it?

There'll come a point when River decides he's done playing house and walks away after worming his way into both of our hearts.

It won't just break me.

It'll break Nora too.

And I don't know if either of us could survive it.

20
RIVER

"As soon as the season is over, we're gonna start filming. You can't believe how much money the network is dumping into this. It's like we're gonna be printing cash."

Zane slides one palm against the other, like he's handing out Benjamins at a strip club.

I stare at him for what feels like the hundredth time, and wonder how the hell we were ever friends in the first place.

Was it him who changed?

Or me?

Maybe it was both of us.

We came in together as rookies. We were green, hungry, and ready to take the league by storm. We clicked right away. Same line. Same grind. Same goals.

But now?

Every damn word out of his mouth is laced with bullshit.

It's tiring.

He's sprawled across the bench in front of his locker, towel barely hanging around his hips, yapping loud enough for the entire room to hear. I pull my sweatshirt over my head, jamming my arms through the sleeves like the motion will keep me from losing it.

Even though no one is asking questions, he keeps yammering about his reality star dreams.

"The producers want to feature Nora in a few of the episodes. You know, give it a wholesome, family vibe. Viewers eat that shit up."

My head snaps toward him as I scowl. "Your daughter isn't a prop."

He barks out a laugh and claps a hand on my shoulder like we're still bros. "Relax, man. It'll be good exposure. I'm sure Callie will be fine with it. And who knows? Maybe this little setup can be lucrative for all of us. Callie can play the part of jealous ex who just wants her man back."

The muscles in my jaw go tight and my hand curls into a fist at my side. For a second, I can actually picture my knuckles crashing into his face.

Just once.

Hard enough to knock some goddamn sense into him.

Like he hasn't hurt Callie enough?

Now he wants her publicly humiliated on national TV?

And to bring Nora into it?

Neither of them should be used as pawns in Zane's next publicity stunt.

They deserve better.

Every time Zane opens his mouth, it becomes more obvious that he's not worthy of either one of them.

He never was.

I close the distance between us before dropping my voice as he yanks on a pair of joggers. "Did you know the bakery's struggling? If Callie's the one supporting your kid, maybe you should do the right thing and help her out instead of being a selfish tool and only thinking about yourself."

He scoffs like I'm being overly dramatic, and that pisses me off even more. "You think I've got extra cash lying around?" He grabs his cologne and sprays it twice. "I need to head out. We've got a photoshoot tonight, and Gigi's hair takes, like, an hour."

He winks at himself in the mirror before strutting out of the locker room. The door swings shut behind him as the silence settles like dust in his wake.

Oliver shakes his head. "That guy is on such an ego trip. If Gigi dumps him, he'd probably marry himself."

Laiken lets out a low whistle. "That guy needs a reality check that's not on TV."

Jax's brows furrow. "Did he really say he wants to put Nora on camera? On a reality show?"

"Yup," Steele says, crossing his arms as he leans against his locker. "That's exactly what he said. There's no way Callie will let that fly."

"There's no way *I'm* going to let it happen," I grit out. Just saying it makes my blood pressure spike.

Steele lifts a brow. "Is that so? You get a say in the matter?"

I meet his gaze without flinching. "Yeah. I do."

Respect flickers in his expression before one side of his mouth hitches with amusement. "Does Callie know you're making decisions for her now?"

"Nope," I admit, "but she will."

I'm done watching her carry the weight of everything while Zane coasts through life without consequence. And I'm done watching Nora grow up without the kind of steady, safe presence she deserves.

Zane might be her biological father, but let's be honest, that's where his contribution ends. I'm not going to sit back and let either of them pay the price for his failures.

Steele nods. "Good for you, man. She deserves someone who's willing to step up."

"Thanks." I sling my bag over my shoulder, offer a quick goodbye, and push through the locker room door.

The second it clicks shut behind me, my phone buzzes in my pocket.

I don't have to look at the screen to know who it is.

Twin intuition is a legit freaky thing.

I swipe to answer. "Hey, Willow. What's up?"

"Is everything okay?" She sounds like she's on full alert.

"Yeah, everything's fine. Why?"

"I don't know," she mutters. "I just had this feeling you needed me."

I huff out a quiet laugh. "Have I ever told you how unsettling that sixth sense of yours is?"

That comment makes her chuckle. "Welcome to being a twin. There's something in your voice. You sound like you're about to punch someone or profess your undying love. Which is it?"

"The situation is complicated," I say with a groan.

"So," she muses, "not hockey."

I scrub a hand down my face as I step into the corridor. "Her name's Callie, and she has a daughter. Along with an ex who doesn't deserve either of them." There's a pause before I admit, "He also happens to be one of my teammates. Zane."

The beat of silence from her end says it all.

"Damn," she whispers. "You're already in deep, huh?"

"I've been in deep for a while now. And there's no way I can continue to sit back and do nothing. Not when she's carrying the weight of the world. She and her daughter deserve better. They deserve someone who'll show up for them every damn day. Not just when it's convenient and fits into his schedule."

Willow doesn't joke or tease. "Whatever you need to do, I'm one hundred percent behind you. Always have been. Always will be."

Just like that, the last of the tension leaks from my shoulders as I push through the exit and head toward the parking garage. "Thanks, sis. That means more than you know."

"This woman must be really special to have you tangled up like this."

"She's so much more than that," I admit. "You're going to love her. And Nora? She's incredible. Smart as hell, sweet as can be, and funny in that way that sneaks up on you. She's got this little dimple when she smiles..."

I stop myself as a slow grin spreads across my face.

"I can't wait to meet her. Hopefully soon. Like the next time you guys play Mav's team. Hint, hint."

"We'll see about that. It might be a little too soon." I click the button to unlock the truck as I step into the cold air of the garage before admitting, "I want them so damn much, but I don't know if Callie will ever believe I'm not like her ex."

"Then show her. Every day. Not with big promises, but with small things. Real things. Until she understands the difference."

I jerk the door open, climb into the driver's seat, and start up the engine.

Zane had his chance and he blew it.

Now it's my turn.

And I'll be damned if I let Callie or Nora slip through my fingers the way he did.

21
CALLIE

From beneath my lashes, I steal a glance at River.

He's smiling at Nora like she hung the moon in the sky, completely captivated by the way she insists on feeding herself. Her fist is wrapped around the handle of her fork as she stabs noodles and tender bites of beef with toddler-like determination. There's sauce on her chin, cheek, even eyelashes, but he doesn't seem to mind. If anything, he looks enchanted. As if she can do no wrong.

Why can't I stop staring?

Even when I force myself to refocus on the plate in front of me, my gaze unconsciously drifts back to him. It's easier to watch River when he's so wrapped up in Nora and doesn't notice me looking.

It's just another thing that makes this situation feel dangerous.

The way he so effortlessly rearranged his life and opened his home to us. The quiet rhythm we've slipped into. The shared dinners and laughter, along with the warmth that's sprung up between us. The way he moves through his space like it was always meant to include us in it.

It shouldn't feel this easy.

Nothing in my life has felt this simple in years.

I twirl my fork through the noodles, trying to shake off the heaviness pressing down on me.

When I can't take another moment, I glance across the table at him again and am shocked by the words that tumble out. "You're going to spoil me."

They sound more like an accusation.

He doesn't miss a beat. "That's the plan."

I reach for my glass of water, needing something to keep me from totally unraveling. The coolness grounds me, but only for a moment. I take a sip and try to swallow the feelings that are starting to take root inside me like stubborn weeds.

Nora babbles to herself between bites, already seeming completely comfortable in this new place.

In this new life.

With River.

I never expected her to adjust so quickly or with such ease.

After dinner, I busy myself in the kitchen, clearing plates and loading the dishwasher. Every few minutes, I peek into the living room out of habit. I've grown so used to multitasking. Working, cleaning, and parenting. There's never a time when I'm fully off-duty. It's strange and a little unsettling to know that my daughter is being cared for by someone who isn't me.

Or my parents.

I catch sight of them at the window. River's holding Nora in his arms and pointing out the glittering skyline. Her hand is pressed against the glass, no doubt leaving behind smudges and tiny fingerprints. Instead of flinching or correcting her, he just lets her be.

And that affects me in a way I don't have words for.

This impossibly steady, gentle, quietly protective man is unlike anyone I've ever known. The more I let myself feel it, the more I realize how desperately I want to believe it's real.

Even if I'm not sure if I should.

All right, that's not totally true. Steele Sanderson is like that. The man is hopelessly devoted and utterly obsessed. He's been in love with Lilah for a decade. That much has always been obvious to anyone with eyes. It was only a matter of time before he stopped pretending otherwise and made his feelings known.

And honestly?

I love that for her.

My friend deserves someone who looks at her like she hung the stars. A man who shows up without question and stands by her side no matter what.

Steele is going to be an incredible father. You can see it in the way he's already taking care of Lilah and planning their future. He has quiet strength and unwavering loyalty to those he loves.

It's a rare find these days.

I would be lying if I didn't admit to being a teeny bit jealous.

Not in a bitter way, just wistful. Like I'm watching someone live out the dream I once had for myself, only to see it crumble before it could come true.

By the time I finish cleaning up the kitchen, Nora and River are curled up on the couch. The TV plays a movie at low volume, casting a muted glow over the room. Nora's nestled against him, her head resting on his thigh like it's the most natural thing in the world.

I settle beside her on the other side of the couch, careful not to disturb the moment. The three of us, side by side, in a home that's not really mine. And yet, the scene unfolding around me feels domestic in a way that's foreign.

This is exactly what I used to picture back when I was pregnant and still foolishly believed Zane would rise to the occasion. That he'd love our unborn baby the way I already did. That we'd build a life together, a family, a home.

But he never showed up.

Not in the ways that mattered.

River, though?

He didn't just show up. He opened his door without hesitation. He's been kind, patient, and steady.

And now my daughter is snuggled against him like she's known this man her entire life.

About thirty minutes in, Nora's eyes start to close. I stroke a hand down her back. "Okay, baby. Time for bed."

She lifts her sleepy gaze to mine before shifting her attention to River and reaching for him with her arms stretched wide. "Rivvy."

The softness and trust threaded through her words slice right through me.

River doesn't even blink. He lifts her carefully into his arms and kisses the crown of her head. "You stay here," he says to me. "I've got her."

Then he disappears down the hallway with Nora. Her arms are looped tight around his neck like she was made to fit there.

I count to sixty.

Sixty full seconds before tiptoeing after them and pausing outside the doorway. I peek around the corner and find them sitting in the armchair. Nora is wrapped in a blanket and tucked into his lap. River's voice is low and soothing as he reads *Goodnight Moon,* turning each page with care. Every so often, my daughter gazes up at him with eyes that are full of wonder, as if he's her whole world.

And maybe he is.

It's getting harder to keep telling myself he's not.

I step back and swallow down the lump of emotion welling within me. My hand presses to the center of my chest, as if that'll be enough to physically hold my unsettled feelings in place.

Unsure what to do with myself, I wander into River's bedroom and pause just inside. My gaze drifts around the space, taking in the details, looking for clues as to who he really is.

I'm not sure if I know anymore.

He's not the man I originally pegged him to be.

He's deeper.

Gentler.

Kind in a way that feels effortless.

And when it comes to my daughter, he's so patient and attentive, it brings tears to my eyes. If there's a way past my defenses, it's through her.

Whether he realizes it or not, every day he's chipping away at the walls I've spent years building around myself. Not with big, dramatic gestures. But with quiet, consistent moments that sneak in when I'm not paying attention.

A silver-framed photo on the nightstand catches my eye, and I gravitate in that direction before picking it up and studying it. River's with a beautiful blonde, both mid-laugh with their arms looped around each other. There's no mistaking the resemblance. This must be his twin sister. She's a delicate, more feminine version of him, with the same strong features and warm blue eyes.

Does she know he invited a woman and her toddler to shack up in his home?

Would she judge me for not being able to keep a roof over my daughter's head?

Or think I'm a clout-chasing gold digger looking for a meal ticket?

I cringe at the thought, and gently set the photo back in its place before backing cautiously away.

In all likelihood, I won't be here long enough for it to matter.

Still, the thought remains as I move toward the bathroom and close the door behind me. My gaze lands on the massive soaking tub in front of the floor-to-ceiling window. I can't remember the last time I took a real bath.

Who has time for that with a small child, a business, and a never-ending mountain of responsibilities waiting for them?

Not this girl.

I tilt my head and listen for signs of Nora's distress. Anything that'll tell me I'm needed. That he's not as capable of handling her as he'd assumed. A handful of seconds slip by, and still, the penthouse remains silent.

Peaceful.

I chew my lower lip as a silent war rages inside my head.

Duty versus exhaustion.

Just fifteen minutes.

That's all I'll allow myself.

If River needs me, he'll figure out where I am.

Decision made, I turn the tap and begin filling the tub. The water steams as I strip off my clothes and slide into the heat, letting it cradle me. Once I relax against the smooth curve of the porcelain, it doesn't take long for my eyelids to flutter shut and the tension in my shoulders to melt away.

For the first time in forever, I exhale.

It should feel like a release.

Instead, it feels like a trap.

I know better than to believe this break from reality will last. It's just an interlude. A moment of quiet before everything changes again.

A knock at the door is what pulls me from the tangle of my thoughts. I sit up slightly as the water sloshes against the rim of the tub. "Yeah?"

The door creaks open and River steps inside with a glass of wine in his hand.

"Nora's asleep," he says quietly. "She didn't even make it to the second book."

His eyes find mine and stay locked there. As tempting as it

is to cross my arms over my breasts, I don't. Instead, I hold his steady gaze, letting him see me.

When I don't ask him to leave, he closes the distance between us before setting the glass on the edge of the tub. "I thought you could use this. Do you need anything else?"

"No," I murmur. "I'm good."

The air between us grows heavy with something I can't quite name.

River lingers. "Should I leave?"

It's a fair question.

The kind that demands honesty.

It's almost a shock to realize I don't want him to go.

I shake my head once.

That's all it takes for his eyes to darken. Now that I've given him permission, his gaze dips over my naked body. There's nothing rushed or lewd about his silent appraisal. It's the look of a man who is savoring something rare. Something he waited a long time to have and wasn't sure he'd ever get.

His tone drops, becoming low and rough. It scrapes against a part of me that's been dormant for years.

"Would you like me to wash you?"

A response sticks in my throat.

A tight nod is all I can manage.

River pushes up the sleeves of his Henley, revealing strong forearms that are dusted with dark hair, before kneeling beside the tub.

That shouldn't be so sexy.

"Lean forward."

I do as he says, my body shifting through the water with a ripple. The heat wraps around me, but it's nothing compared to the fire spreading beneath my skin.

His hands, slick with soap, find my back. He moves slowly, working in gentle circles. My shoulders loosen as my jaw unclenches. The stress I wear like armor begins to slip from my bones.

He's so careful. As if I'm something breakable.

Something that matters.

His fingers rise, gliding over my shoulders, then down my arms. They drift across my ribs, the curve of my waist, teasing a shiver out of me. When he reaches around to my front, his palms flatten against my stomach, and everything in me goes still.

He pauses, as if waiting for me to say no.

To stop him.

But I don't.

Can't.

His hands rise before cupping my breasts. His palms are warm and steady, but it's the way his thumbs sweep in unhurried circles over the sensitive peaks that has me going motionless. The feather-soft pass of his touch sends a wave of heat down my spine, a ripple that blooms through me until I feel it in places I didn't know could ache.

A gasp slips free before I can stop it, and my back arches instinctively, offering myself to him before my mind has even made the choice. His movements are slow and purposeful. Measured in a way that feels like more than seduction.

It's worshipful.

His hands trail lower, mapping every curve like a man memorizing a language he never wants to forget. The lush swell of my hips. The inviting curve of my thighs. Each stroke is maddening in its restraint. It's not meant to tease but to savor.

My body hums with want, hips lifting from the porcelain in a silent plea for more, but he doesn't rush.

Even as I tremble beneath him, I force myself to stay still and let him explore, to simply *feel*. Somewhere deep inside, I realize this is going to leave a mark. Not on my skin, but on the parts of me no one's ever touched.

When his fingers finally graze the heat between my thighs, the pleasure that surges through me isn't just sharp and electric, it's surrender. It's about being handled like something precious instead of something broken. It's about being seen, scars and all, and still being wanted.

River touches me like he already knows every fragile piece I've tried to hide and he wants every single one of them.

"Should I keep going?" he asks, his tone rough and frayed, as if the words are scraping against the very edge of his control.

The warmth of his breath ghosts over the shell of my ear, and the low rasp of his question sets every nerve ending ablaze.

I nod, unable to stop myself, too overwhelmed to form words.

Instead of moving, he goes still, his hand resting just shy of where I need him most. Not pressing or teasing. Simply waiting for more than a silent yes.

"I need to hear you say it," he says. "Use your words, sweetheart."

A shaky sound slips from me. "Yes," I whisper, barely louder than the ripple of water. "I want you to touch me."

The effect is immediate.

I turn just enough to see his eyes darken, the blue turning stormy as something primal flashes in them. His jaw tightens as his hand flexes on my thigh like he's holding himself back by sheer willpower alone.

"How long's it been since you came?"

Heat floods my cheeks as shame slips in at the edges. "Before Nora."

River curses. For a beat, he tips his forehead to mine. His fingers tighten at my hip, anchoring me in place.

"Jesus, Callie." The way he says my name makes something deep inside me clench. "What about toys?" he asks quietly, eyes searching mine. "Nothing to take the edge off when you need it?"

A nervous, self-deprecating laugh catches in my throat. "No."

His brow furrows as he leans back just enough to study me. "Why the hell not?"

I shrug in embarrassment. "There was never time. And it never felt important."

His expression softens, the desire in his eyes not fading but transforming into something that feels like possession wrapped in devotion, fierce enough to protect me from the world, and gentle enough to make me want to hand over everything.

"You're important," he says. "And your pleasure is important too. Do you understand me?"

His mouth skims the corner of mine. It's barely a kiss and more of a promise. "Now, I want you to ask for what you need."

I swallow, the words coming easier this time. "I want you to touch me."

"Good girl," he says.

The praise lights through me like a spark catching tinder. His hand finally moves, slow and sure, exactly where I need it.

He shakes his head as something fierce and unyielding flickers in his eyes. "You're wrong about that," he says, his tone carrying the kind of conviction that brooks no argument. "Orgasming isn't a luxury you have to earn. It's not a reward for being good enough or working hard enough. It's basic self-care. Every woman deserves that kind of release. To remember what her body can feel and is capable of."

His hand slides higher, grazing skin already tender and alive from his earlier touch. "You should know that. You should feel it often. And if no one else has reminded you lately..." His gaze locks on mine. "Then let me."

The tenderness in those words slices straight through me, splitting me open in places I didn't realize were still locked tight.

His fingertips move with quiet purpose. Every stroke is

patient, as if he's determined to commit each reaction to memory.

The water rocks gently around us, ripples lapping against the porcelain. My breath hitches as my hips lift, chasing more without meaning to. There's a plea coiled in my throat, but the words refuse to form.

His mouth finds the side of my neck, the warmth of his lips brushing that sensitive spot just below my ear. The contact is electric, but it's what he says next that ties me in knots.

"As long as you're here," he tells me, each word sinking in deeper than the last, "I'll take care of you. Whatever you need."

The promise in his voice doesn't just touch me. It surrounds me, settling over my skin like something warm and immovable. A shield I didn't know I'd been craving.

My head tips back, lips parting, his name spilling out on a ragged cry as the ecstasy builds to something wild and unstoppable. It crests and breaks, scattering my thoughts until I'm nothing but sensation. My body shakes beneath his hand, every shudder pulling me further under, every beat a reminder that he's the one holding me there.

When my lashes flutter open, he's still watching me. Not with arrogance, but with quiet awe.

Droplets cling to his forearms where I've splashed him, running in slow, silvery trails down his skin. I expect him to strip off his clothes and climb in with me, to close the last bit of space left between us.

Instead, he leans in and gently brushes a damp curl from my forehead, his touch so careful it threatens to break me open all over again. His thumb rests against my temple, his eyes locked on mine, as if memorizing this exact second.

"You deserve to be touched like that every damn day," he says. "To be cared for until you can't remember what it felt like to go without."

His words strike deep, unlocking a part of me that's been sealed up and silent for years.

And then he straightens, walks out of the room, and closes the door behind him with a click.

The quiet rushes in like a tide as I sink deeper into the water, my limbs loose and my skin still buzzing from his touch.

But my mind is anything but calm.

The warmth wraps around me like a blanket, but it doesn't soothe the storm he's left in his wake. My body betrays me, chasing a truth I'm not ready to admit.

I know this wasn't just about pleasure.

It was about him and what this meant.

How everything just changed between us.

I stare at the ceiling, hoping for a little bit of clarity.

For answers.

For something to tell me how the hell I'm supposed to make sense of this thing that shouldn't matter but suddenly feels like everything.

It should've just been a release.

A simple favor.

A fluke.

But it doesn't feel like any of those things.

Not even close.

What River gave me wasn't just pleasure. It was much deeper. Something real.

And that's terrifying.

The last thing I want to do is fall for River Thompson.

But... What if it's already too late and that's exactly what's happening?

22

RIVER

Touching Callie in the tub was supposed to take the edge off. It should have settled the wildfire burning in my blood since the second I caught sight of her.

If anything, it made the desire rampaging through my veins a hundred times worse. Now I know exactly how smooth her skin feels beneath my fingertips and the way she arches her spine and gasps when she's dancing on the edge. How she says my name, not like it's a curse or a challenge, but like a promise.

Like it meant something.

Here's what I know: I want so much more than her body.

I want every guarded glance, every quiet breath, all the pieces she keeps locked away because the world taught her not to trust. I want her laughter, the easy kind she's forgotten how to let loose.

I want her mornings, her nights, her forever.

I pause outside Nora's room before easing the door open, careful not to make a sound. The nightlight casts a pale glow across the space, painting shadows on the walls. My gaze finds her small form right away. Her cheeks are flushed with the warmth of sleep as one small hand clutches the edge of her blanket while the other is wrapped tight around Gaffy.

She looks peaceful. Like nothing in the world can touch her. A knot pulls tight inside me at the sight.

At the weight of what I want to give them both.

I glance at the bare walls with their neutral tones, the rug that's more practical than playful. It's functional and serves a purpose. But it doesn't belong to a child.

Nora deserves better than this.

They both do.

I make a mental note, already planning. Tomorrow, I'll call a decorator. Someone who knows how to bring color and light into the space. Someone who can give this room life. Pink walls if she wants them. A canopy bed draped in gauzy fabric. Maybe some twinkle lights. Or a cozy reading nook filled with pillows and stuffed animals. We could add a mural. Bunnies and stars, or even a rainbow.

Whatever Nora dreams of, I'll find a way to make it happen.

Maybe it's too much, too fast, but I don't give a damn.

I want to build something for them.

No, I want to build something *with* them.

A home.

A future.

A life that feels like more than going through the motions.

With one last glance at Nora's peaceful form, I close the door. I'll figure out a way to keep both Callie and her daughter, no matter what it takes.

When I step back into the bedroom, the bedside lamp casts everything in honeyed light. Callie is already curled beneath the covers, her silhouette outlined in shadows. Her blonde hair spills across the pillow like silk, and the sight of her in my bed, tangled in my sheets, looking like she belongs there, makes every instinct within me roar with need.

She glances up as I enter, her gaze meeting mine in the quiet hush of the room. For a beat, everything goes still. The heavy weight of what I feel for her presses in, coiling around my ribs like a vise.

Without a word, I tug my shirt over my head. The cotton catches slightly on my shoulder. Her gaze never leaves me. I feel the heat of it like a brand on my skin. The rustle of denim fills the silence as I unbutton my jeans and let them fall to the floor.

Still, she doesn't look away. Her breathing changes, becoming shallow and slower as she grips the edge of the blanket like it has the power to steady her.

Even more surprising is she doesn't try to hide her interest.

It's a small thing, maybe. But it means everything. It's a tiny crack in the walls she's built around herself. A glimpse of the curious and brave woman hiding behind the facade.

God, I want her to stop fighting this.

I want her to lean into whatever's building between us.

I want to be the soft place she finally lets herself rest.

Her comment breaks the quiet. "You have tattoos."

I pause, catching her eyes as I let her see all of me. "A few."

Her gaze dips, tracing the ink on the left side of my ribcage, her curiosity fighting to break free. "What's that one for?"

Each step is careful, like I'm approaching a skittish animal that will bolt if I move too quickly. "That one's for Willow."

Her gaze roves over me. "You two must be close."

I nod, settling on the edge of the mattress, close enough for us to touch.

"Yeah," I murmur. "She was diagnosed with leukemia when we were in high school. And for a while, it was bad. Really bad." When the words get stuck in my throat, I swallow them down and keep going. "There were times when I thought we'd lose her."

Callie's features relax, and for a moment, all the guarded distance she keeps between us dissolves.

"I'm sorry," she says gently. "That must've been terrifying. I can't imagine."

"It was." I glance down at my hands, at the ink on my skin, before looking back at her. "But she's okay now. Married, actually. To Maverick McKinnon."

Her eyebrows shoot up, and the tension in the room lightens as she smirks. "Wait... are we talking about *that* Maverick McKinnon?"

I grin. "Let me guess. You think he's good-looking."

Her eyes sparkle with amusement as she shrugs. "I mean, who doesn't?"

The smile tugs wider at my mouth as heat pools low in my stomach. "Is that so?"

I pounce in one fluid motion, bracing my weight and pinning her wrists to the mattress as I hover inches above her. Our bodies don't quite touch, but the space between us crackles like a live wire. It's electric and volatile, pulsing with all the things we haven't said.

Her lips part on a shaky exhale as her chest rises. The desire she's trying so damn hard to bury, flares in her eyes, breaking through the surface like a spark catching flame.

Her pulse flutters beneath my fingertips where I hold her wrists as her gaze stays locked on mine. It's wide, filled with something raw and unspoken.

It's so damn tempting to kiss her.

Hell, I'd like nothing more than to devour her in one tasty bite.

Instead of giving in to temptation, I hold still and inhale her sweet scent, letting her feel the power in this moment and know that it belongs to her.

I'm not here to take.

I'm here to give her the choice.

The permission to decide.

When she doesn't pull away, I dip my head close enough to taste the air between us and feel the hunger clawing at my ribs.

"You better be careful, sweetheart." My voice is low and rough as it frays the edges of my restraint. "Keep talking like that, and I won't be able to control myself."

She swallows hard as a shiver courses through her and her legs shift restlessly beneath me. There's a war being waged in her eyes. She's unsure if she wants to surrender or escape.

Should she give in to the want or cling to self-preservation?

God, I want this woman.

Not just tonight.

Or for now.

I want her forever.

My gaze dips to her mouth. The slight tremble of her lower lip and the subtle invitation written across her expression calls to something primal deep inside me.

Even when her lips part and her eyes darken with desire, I don't move.

Callie isn't a distraction, a temporary fix, or a one-night escape from reality. She's the future I didn't know I was missing until the moment she walked into my life.

The sad truth is that she's not ready yet.

Not in the way I need her to be.

Not for what I'm offering.

I want more than just her body pressed beneath mine.

I want her trust.

Her truth.

Her heart.

Every scar.

Every shadow.

All the pieces she never lets anyone see.

Already, I realize that if I push now and take more than she's ready to give, I could lose it all.

So, I do the only thing I can, and force myself to retreat.

My fingers loosen from around her wrists, the contact slipping away even though every part of me protests. I sit back slowly, putting space between us, even when it feels like I'm ripping out a piece of myself to do it.

The silence stretches as I watch her closely. It would be impossible not to notice the way her expression shifts. How she processes what *didn't* happen.

Even though it's only been a few days, I'm getting better at reading her.

Disappointment flashes in her eyes before she can hide it. And that nearly undoes me on the spot. I could have kissed her and given her what we both wanted. Confusion settles in next. She doesn't understand why I stopped or what it means.

And finally, the one that confirms I made the right call.

A burst of relief that's small and fleeting, like it was caught inside for too long.

When I reach up and gently brush the backs of my knuckles along her cheek, she leans into my touch before she can think better of it.

It's instinct.

The beginning of trust.

And it's everything.

"Get some sleep, Callie." My voice is rough with everything I'm fighting to keep locked up.

Like how I'd burn the world down to make her feel safe.

How I'd wait a lifetime if that's what she needed from me.

How she already owns my heart and doesn't even realize it yet.

Before she can respond or I can change my mind and give in to the gravitational pull between us, I rise to my feet. Every muscle screams in protest as I circle to the other side of the bed. The mattress dips beneath my weight as I lie beside her, careful to leave a sliver of space between us.

Not because I want the distance.

But because she needs it.

Getting impatient and rushing her now would be the quickest way to lose her.

The room falls into silence. It's the kind that buzzes with everything that hasn't been said.

It's the kind that holds its breath and waits.

I stare up at the ceiling, all the while steadying the storm inside me and trying to forget the way her skin felt against my hands. The way she looked at me like I could be something more than the man she thought I was.

Like maybe I could be the one she lets in.

Beside me, the sheets rustle.

A small shift, then another, and I know she's turned to face me.

I don't move.

I wait as a long moment stretches between us and then her chest begins to rise and fall in a slower rhythm, the tension in the room easing with each passing second.

Inhale.

Exhale.

Steady and trusting.

As if whatever battle she was waging inside herself has finally quieted enough to sleep.

Even though our bodies aren't touching, I've never felt closer to her. Never felt something more intimate than her turning toward me in the dark and letting herself rest.

She doesn't have to say it. Not out loud.

Because I *feel* it.

She's letting me in.

Inch by inch.

And I'll earn each and every one of them.

This thing between us isn't about lust.

It's not about the high of the moment.

It's about her.

It's about showing up and being the kind of man she and Nora can count on.

Every damn day.

So I stay exactly where I am as the silence wraps around us. And in the dark, I make a promise I don't need to speak out loud to mean.

I'm not going anywhere, sweetheart. When you're ready for more —when you're ready for me—I'll be here waiting.

23
CALLIE

I wake gradually from the kind of deep, consuming sleep that seeps into your bones and lingers in your muscles long after your eyes have fluttered open. The room is quiet, the light subdued, and my body feels boneless, wrapped in warmth and something even rarer.

Security.

It takes a second to register it. A beat longer to realize how foreign this complete sense of safety is. Like I've finally stopped bracing for the next hit. It's been so long since I've let myself relax. Since I've allowed myself to sink into the comfort of it.

The reason for that hits me.

River.

The thought spreads through me like a ripple across still water. Gentle but impossible to ignore.

I'm curled into him, my cheek pressed against his hard chest, where the steady thump of his heart drums against my ear. One of my legs is tangled with his, my knee slung over his thigh. His skin is warm and firm beneath mine. His body is all strength and quiet steadiness.

How did I not notice the effortless way he makes me feel small and protected all at once?

As if nothing outside this bed could harm me.

And, God, the man smells delicious. Like soap and something I can't name but instantly recognize as him. I should move before he wakes up and realizes I've practically crawled on top of him.

Before I forget that this isn't real.

Instead, I remain motionless. The heat radiating off him feels way too good.

He feels way too good.

And even more than that, I don't want to.

After years of keeping my guard up, I'm not seconds away from falling apart. I feel safe.

The kind of safe I didn't even know I'd been craving. The kind that makes me ache because I'd forgotten it was even possible.

Zane never made me feel like this.

Not even when things were good.

Or when I tried to convince myself he loved me.

And now River is doing it without even trying. He calms the storm that rages inside me just by being himself. There haven't been any grand gestures or sweeping declarations. There's just been this quiet, unshakable presence that makes everything in me loosen.

I shift slightly, attempting to untangle the mess of thoughts crowding my head, all the while trying to convince myself I'm not already too far gone. That's the moment I feel his thick erection beneath the covers, straining against the thin cotton of his boxer briefs.

My breath catches and my eyes fly open.

Oh.

Heat floods through me like lava.

I don't move.

Or even think too hard.

If I do, I might not be able to stop myself from wondering

what it would feel like if I reached out and touched him. That's all it takes for temptation to build low in my belly, until it's impossible to ignore, simmering just beneath the surface and spreading warmth through every inch of me. My fingers twitch as the need to touch him pulses through me with a force that's impossible to shut down.

I really need to stop.

Or roll away and take some much-needed space, all the while reminding myself why this is a terrible idea. Before I can list every reason I shouldn't do this, my hand slowly moves. A knot pulls tight within me. I haven't even laid a hand on him yet and already I feel like I'm on the verge of exploding.

"You can touch me, Callie. I promise, I won't mind one bit."

His comment cuts through the silence, and my head jerks up so fast, I nearly give myself whiplash.

His eyes are open, and there's nothing casual about the way he watches me. There's no trace of uncertainty or doubt. Just steady, unflinching hunger.

I should stop before the situation spirals further out of control.

Instead, I throw back the covers. My hand trembles as I reach for him, pressing my palm against the front of his briefs and wrapping my fingers around his hard length. His hips twitch as a sharp inhale hisses through his teeth. His muscles tighten beneath my touch, as if he's holding himself together by a thread.

Need rolls off him in heavy, suffocating waves.

It's almost shocking just how much I want this.

Not just the physical part, but the way he looks at me like I'm something he never thought he could have.

Something worth waiting for.

It doesn't take long before the cotton beneath my hand dampens with moisture. A low groan rumbles from him, and I swear it's the sexiest sound I've ever heard. His restraint, the tension in his jaw, the way his hands stay clenched at his sides, it all makes my pulse skitter. He's allowing me to set the pace and giving me the space to choose. And that choice is its own kind of power.

The words are out of my mouth before I can stop them. "How long has it been for you?"

Almost immediately, I regret the question.

If he says something careless, something that breaks the fragile connection forming between us, I don't know if I'll be able to stop myself from pulling back and rebuilding every wall I've allowed him to pull down.

I brace for his answer.

He doesn't look away or even blink. "Three years."

My eyebrows pull together. "Seriously?"

He nods.

I search his face for a tell, any hint he's lying. "I don't believe you."

One side of his mouth lifts into something that's not quite a smile. "It's true. I got tired of hookups that didn't mean anything." His voice dips, turning rough around the edges. "Plus, it didn't help that the woman I wanted was with someone else."

I don't ask who he's talking about because I already know.

That's all it takes for the sexual tension between us to ratchet higher, the silence growing so heavy it presses in until the rest of the world slips away into nothingness.

There's just River.

And me.

Along with the attraction that pulls us together with a force I don't fully understand.

"No matter how many times I tried to pretend with other women," he says quietly, "they just weren't her. Not even close."

My fingers still as the words hit hard.

They're too much.

Too honest.

Too real.

And some stubborn instinct tells me to turn away, to shield myself before I get pulled in any deeper.

No matter how much I try to deny it, a piece of me still aches to believe him. To trust that this is different. That what's happening between us isn't another mistake I'll regret down the road.

The hardest thing is how real it feels. Like a truth that burrows deep and settles into my bones.

Still, I know better than to fall for pretty promises that never come to fruition.

Instead of pulling away, I move slowly, watching the way his body reacts to my touch. The tension in his jaw. The way his chest rises faster, breath quickening, hips twitching beneath my hand, as if he's fighting every instinct not to lose control.

His head falls back against the pillow as his eyes squeeze shut. "Callie..." My name comes out sounding more like a rough warning. "I won't last long if you keep that up."

There's no way I can stop.

Not when I'm the one in control and making him come undone.

The significance of what's about to happen pools low in my stomach. This isn't just about giving back what he gave me last night. It's about the knowledge that I can affect him so easily. That I can be the one to pull him apart when he's always so composed. The realization is intoxicating. It makes me feel powerful, wanted, and achingly alive in a way I've never experienced.

His fist tightens in the sheets, knuckles turning bone-white, while his other hand wraps around my wrist. The hold isn't rough or meant to stop me. It's steady. Like he needs that point of contact to keep himself tethered to the earth.

"I mean it," he grits out. "I'm gonna come. And that's not something I was planning on."

The warning sends my pulse racing as my thighs press together in sharp anticipation. My steady grip tightens around him. "Good. I want to watch you fall apart."

The low sound he makes is like a groan of surrender, and it rips straight through me. His hips jerk once, twice, before finding a desperate rhythm, thrusting into my hand like he can't help himself anymore. The muscles in his stomach flex under my gaze, each hard line shifting.

He's completely at my mercy now.

Every rough, erratic thrust pushes him closer, the tension winding tight through his body until it finally snaps. With his head tipped back, a hoarse curse rips from his mouth as heat spills, hot and thick, into my palm, soaking through the thin cotton of his briefs.

Even when the waves of his release ebb, his chest continues to rise and fall in jagged pulls as sweat beads his temples. My fingers stay wrapped around him, easing the pressure as my strokes turn slow and coaxing. My thumb traces lazy, feather-light sweeps over the damp fabric, feeling every twitch and aftershock. His lashes flutter and his mouth relaxes as I continue touching him.

In the quiet that follows, with his body loose under my hand and his control stripped away, I realize this moment isn't just about his surrender.

It's about mine too.

When his eyes finally open, they're darker than before, and yet, somehow softer. "Holy shit. That was intense."

The air between us shifts. Not just from what we did but how it felt. Something deeper settles in, something I'm not sure I'm ready for.

He catches my wrist before I can pull away, his fingers wrapping gently around it. Then he slowly lifts my hand and presses a kiss to the inside, right over my pulse. It's unbearably tender. And, somehow, it unravels me more than anything else.

"I hope you realize that wasn't just about getting off," he says, gaze fastened to mine. "It meant something."

The crazy part is that I feel it too.

But the words refuse to come.

They sit in the back of my throat, too tangled in fear to push forward. I don't know how to say them without risking everything.

Instead, I force a small smile. It's weak and doesn't quite reach my eyes.

"You should probably clean up." I'm already pulling back the covers, needing to put some space between us. My feet hit the floor, and I cross the room on shaky legs, heart thudding so loud it drowns out everything but the sound of my own fear.

Because he's right.

It did mean something.

24
RIVER

An hour later, Callie's halfway through zipping Nora into her jacket when her phone rings. Her expression shifts as she answers. Neutral at first before tightening with concern. Whatever is being said on the other end isn't what she wants to hear, and her posture tenses. Her free hand rises to her temple, pressing lightly, as if it'll be enough to hold the stress at bay.

"No, it's totally fine," she murmurs. "Get some rest, okay? I hope you feel better."

With a sigh, she ends the call. It's the kind of sigh that sounds like the weight of the world just landed on her shoulders.

"What's going on?" I ask, already bracing for what she's about to say.

Her brow furrows as she meets my eyes. "My mom's sick. The flu, apparently. And my dad's not feeling great either. So, no babysitting today."

I nod slowly, already thinking through our options. "Sounds like what we need is a plan B."

"Yeah." Her hand sweeps down Nora's arm before squeezing her smaller fingers. "I have a neighbor who's watched her before, but she also babysits a couple of other kids. Nora always ends up sick after spending time there."

The way her voice dips at the end tells me everything I need to know about the situation. She's dreading the idea and already talking herself out of it.

"How about I watch her?" I offer.

Callie blinks before refocusing her attention on me. "What?"

"She can stay with me," I repeat. "The team has the day off. The two of us can hang here while you're at the bakery."

She stares at me like I've lost my mind. "For the whole day? That's like, eight hours."

I shrug. "Sure. We'll build a pillow fort, watch a few shows, maybe make a mess. Right, ladybug?"

Nora perks up like she understood every word. "Rivvy!"

I grin and scoop her into my arms. "See? She's in. Problem solved."

Callie hesitates as an internal debate plays out in real time across her face. "Are you sure?"

"Positive."

"If something comes up, or she gets fussy, or it's more than you can handle—"

"That's not going to happen."

Her eyes plead with mine. "Just promise you'll call me. Please?"

I step closer, adjusting Nora in my arms until I can meet Callie's eyes. "I promise. If anything comes up, you'll be the first one I call."

She wavers for another beat, brushing a kiss against Nora's curls. "You probably don't realize it, but she can be a handful."

I catch her fingers before she pulls away, giving them a quick squeeze. "Nora will be fine. And so will you. Go to work. I've got this."

Callie studies me like she's trying to decide whether she can trust me. Just when I think she'll balk, she gives a small nod before heading toward the elevator.

The moment she disappears around the corner, I turn to Nora, who's still snuggled against my chest. "All right, ladybug. What should we do first?"

Ten minutes later, she's settled in her highchair, and it's a total shitshow. She's eating strawberry yogurt like it's a competitive sport. There's more on her cheeks, hands, and on the tray than in her mouth. I'm pretty sure some made it into her hair, and I'm starting to rethink my breakfast choice. Unless I plan on giving her a full-on bath, I'm not sure how I'm going to clean her up.

My phone buzzes just as I'm wiping a blob of yogurt off Nora's forehead. I glance at the screen and see that it's my sister before swiping to answer.

"Hey, what's up?"

"Nothing," she says casually. "Just checking in about the situation."

With a frown, I rack my brain. "What situation are we talking about?"

"Come on, River. Keep up. The single mom you've got your eye on."

"Ah. That situation." I glance at Nora, who's trying to feed me a spoonful, her hand wobbling as she holds it out. "I really wish you would have called fifteen minutes earlier. You probably would have told me that letting a two-year-old feed herself yogurt was not going to work out in my favor."

"Rookie mistake," Willow says with a laugh. "Although, if you don't mind, I'd love some photographic evidence."

"So you and Mav can laugh your asses off at my expense? Hard pass."

"Aww, come on. We're an old married couple. Don't take away all our fun."

I snap a quick selfie of me and Nora. The yogurt definitely made it into her hair and onto her nose.

Willow sighs, "Oh my God, she's adorable."

"Yup, that she is."

"Speaking of which." Willow none too subtly changes the topic of conversation. "Have you taken Callie out on a date yet? Wined and dined her a little bit? Busted out that famous Thompson charm? What's your game plan here? I want all the details."

I lean back in my chair, still holding the spoon Nora handed me. "Didn't I mention she's living here?"

There's a moment of stunned silence before Willow practically shouts, "I'm sorry, what?"

I wince. "Yeah. It's a temporary situation. It just kind of happened."

"How was that not the lead of your last ten texts?"

I rub a hand over my face. "She and Nora were in a tough spot, and I offered to let her stay here until she figures things out."

"And how's that going?"

I glance at the toddler, who's smearing the pink dairy product all over the tray with both hands like she's finger painting. "Honestly? Better than I expected."

"You sound different, Riv. Like you're really into this woman."

"I am," I admit. "I like her a lot." Even saying that feels weak. Like it's not nearly enough.

"I love that for you. Truly. I want you to be happy."

"I know." I pause, swallowing hard. "She doesn't know it yet, but I don't want her to leave. I want this to turn into something real."

"So... she has no idea this is more of a permanent situation?"

A crooked grin tugs at my lips. "Not yet."

Willow laughs. "I can't wait to see how this unfolds."

"Yeah, well, I'm terrified that I'm going to mess it up or scare her away."

"You won't," she says with certainty. "Just keep showing up for her. Every day. That's what matters."

A lump forms in my throat. One I have to clear away before I'm able to speak again. "She's been hurt before. And I can see how scared she is. Every time I get close, she pulls away, as if expecting it all to fall apart."

Willow hums. "Then be the one who doesn't leave."

I nod, even though she can't see it. "That's the plan."

"Oh, by the way, Autumn and Haven say hi. They miss their uncle like crazy."

"I miss them too. Bet they've shot up another couple inches since I last saw them."

"Feels like I'm buying new clothes every month. It's crazy."

"Maybe when you're in town for the game, you can stop by and meet Callie and Nora" I say before hesitating. "You'll like them."

There's a pause on her end, like she understands everything I'm not saying. "That's a big step."

"It is. One I'm ready to take." The acknowledgment sends a heavy thrum through my veins. "Although, let's keep that between us for now. Do me a favor and don't mention anything to Mom. You know how she gets. She'll have a venue and flower arrangements picked out before Callie even meets her."

There's a beat of silence.

"Oh, about that…"

"Willow," I say with a groan.

"Hey! She was bugging me about when we're having a third kid. I panicked."

"Well, that certainly explains the five voicemails she left me before seven this morning."

"Sorry." She doesn't sound remotely apologetic for throwing me under the bus. "You have fun with that, okay?"

Before my sister and I can say goodbye, the ding of the elevator cuts through the air. I glance toward the entryway, half-expecting it to be Callie. As much as I'd love to see her, the last thing I want is for her to come back because she doesn't trust me with Nora.

Instead, I find Knox, Laiken, Steele, Oliver, and Jax.

Laiken's holding his daughter's hand. Her smaller fingers are swallowed up in his larger ones, and she's wearing a pink tutu over her leggings. The second the guys step into the kitchen and catch sight of Nora, who's currently channeling her inner Picasso as she gleefully smears yogurt across the tray of her highchair, they all freeze.

A beat of stunned silence hangs in the air as they collectively take in the sight.

"Um, I'm no expert on kids," Knox says, lifting a brow as he studies the mess, "but I'm pretty sure she's supposed to eat that, not wear it."

Steele chuckles and claps me on the shoulder. "Jumping straight into the deep end, are we? I like it. Shows initiative."

Jax lowers his voice like he's narrating a nature documentary. "Observe the domesticated male in his natural habitat. Notice the unshaven jaw, the weary eyes, and yogurt-splattered clothes. What's become clear is that he has accepted his fate."

Laiken doesn't miss a beat. He strides forward, rips off a few sheets of paper towel, and crouches in front of Nora like he's been through this exact scenario a dozen times.

"You're letting her win, man. Rule number one: stay ahead of the mess. Once they gain control, it's all over."

Nora giggles and kicks her legs, clearly delighted by all the attention.

Elody tugs gently on Laiken's sleeve. "Daddy, can I help?"

He smiles down at her before ruffling her hair. "Of course,

baby. Once we clean Nora up, maybe you can show her your sticker book."

Knox nudges Steele with his elbow and nods toward the scene. "Take notes, Cap. This is your future."

Steele smirks. "Bring it on. I'm ready."

When Oliver's phone buzzes, he pulls it out of his pocket and glances at the screen, immediately typing out a reply, his thumbs moving at lightning speed.

Jax leans over, trying to sneak a peek. "Who's blowing up your phone this early in the morning? Wait, wait. Lemme guess... Is it some poor girl you ghosted before she could figure out whether round one even happened?"

Oliver doesn't bother looking up. "It's none of your damn business."

Knox's eyes gleam. "Which means Jax nailed it."

Oliver slips his phone back into his pocket, flipping him off behind Elody's back without missing a beat. "Nah, that's your signature move."

"It feels like you're hiding something," Jax says with a grin. "I thought we were all friends here."

Oliver quirks a brow. "Define the term 'friends.'"

"That's fine." Jax rubs his hands together like he's hatching a plan. "I'll just put my elite detective skills to work."

"Hate to break it to you, man," Steele says with a laugh. "You've barely got skills on the ice. If I were you, I'd focus on keeping my day job."

"Ouch. Shots fired," Knox adds with a laugh.

Before Jax can respond, Oliver tips his chin toward me. "Hey, Thompson, didn't you mention that the girl who works with Callie was just asking about our boy over here?"

Jax whips around so fast he nearly trips over his own feet. "Wait, Sloane was asking about me? And you didn't tell me?" His voice hits a pitch only dogs can hear. "Seriously, man, what the fuck?"

Laiken groans before smacking the back of Jax's head. It's just hard enough to get his point across. "Language. We've got little ears in the room, genius."

He angles his head toward Elody, who's now watching Jax with wide eyes and the kind of intense focus that means every word is being stored for later use.

"Laiken's right," Steele adds with a chuckle. "You wanna be the reason she starts swearing at school?"

"I said A-S-S once," Laiken mutters, "and I had to hear about it every day for a week."

"You spelled 'ass,' Daddy!" Elody pipes up. "You said it was a bad word!"

Laiken drops his head into his hand. "I was telling them *about* the word, not *saying* it. There's a difference."

"But I *like* saying it," she announces proudly. "It's funny."

Knox chokes on a laugh as his shoulders shake. "She's not wrong about that. It is pretty funny."

Laiken shoots him a glare. "Yeah, well, you're not the one getting the side-eye from her grandparents when she starts showing off her new vocabulary."

The room quiets after that, amusement fading as something heavier slips in.

"Any word on the custody situation?" Knox asks in a hushed tone so the girls won't hear.

Laiken watches Elody and Nora as they run toward the living room, Elody leading the way. His gaze softens, but the tension in his jaw doesn't ease. "They hired a new lawyer. Looks like they're not backing down anytime soon. They must think if they keep pushing long enough, I'll cave. And that's never going to happen."

"What about Sarah?" Oliver asks quietly.

Laiken runs a hand through his hair as a muscle in his jaw tics. "No one's heard from her in months. But her parents? They've suddenly decided they want a second chance with

Elody. Like maybe they can rewrite history and do it 'right' this time."

My stomach turns. "That's total bullshit. You're a damn good dad, Laiken."

My teammate jerks his shoulders, but the weight behind his eyes doesn't budge. "I'd like to think so."

"Seems like they're trying to take something that doesn't belong to them," Knox mutters.

Before the mood can sink any lower, Elody bounds back into the kitchen, face flushed as she beams. "Daddy! Nora likes my stickers!"

Laiken's expression relaxes in an instant. "That's great, sweetheart. Keep showing her, okay?"

The little girl nods before spinning on her heel and skipping back to the living room.

We all watch her go, and I realize there's nothing I wouldn't do for this group of guys. What I've learned is that blood isn't the only thing that makes you family.

It's showing up.

And all of us?

We're just trying to figure it out as we go.

One messy, yogurt-covered day at a time.

25

CALLIE

When I step into Lakeshore Sweets, Sloane is already behind the counter with her sleeves rolled up and her hair twisted into a messy knot, restocking the pastry case with practiced ease. She looks up when the bell above the door chimes, shooting me a smile.

It's the voices coming from the back of the shop that have me pausing.

I glance over and spot Lilah and Rina huddled at the corner table, a half-eaten cinnamon roll sitting between them. Rina's laughing while Lilah gestures animatedly with her teacup like she's mid-story.

I lift a hand and wave. "Hey. I didn't know you two were stopping by this morning."

Rina doesn't answer right away. Instead, she gives me a slow once-over, eyes narrowing in a way that immediately makes me self-conscious.

"Hmmm. There's something different about you," she says, pointing her coffee stirrer at me.

"Is there?"

Sloane leans an elbow on the counter and raises an eyebrow. "Actually, Rina's right. You've got that look."

I blink. "What look?"

"The   I-just-got-laid-and-I'm-still-enjoying-the-afterglow look," Sloane says.

Lilah chokes on her tea, coughing into her sleeve as Rina smirks. "That's exactly what I was thinking."

The laugh that slips free is a little too quick and a little too loud. "Oh, come on. Give me a break."

"Hold up." Rina rises to her feet. "That was in no way a denial. It was more of a deflection. We're onto you, girl."

"You're kind of scary, you know that?" I grumble as she saunters closer.

A wide grin spreads across her face. "Thank you. I always strive for intimidating with just a hint of menace sprinkled in."

"Someday she might actually decide to use her powers for good instead of evil," Lilah calls out.

"I wouldn't count on it," Sloane says, already pouring a fresh pot of coffee. She grabs a honey lavender cruller from the case and sets it on a small plate. "But in the meantime, this definitely feels like a pastry-and-interrogation kind of morning."

A few minutes later, we're all gathered at the back table, our coffee cups steaming and a spread of sugary goodness set out between us. The cinnamon rolls are joined by a couple of croissants, the cruller, and something Sloane swears is the best lemon scone she's ever made.

After a bite, I have to agree.

Delicious.

There's a warm hum in my chest I didn't expect. A feeling of comfort. Of being seen and understood.

Growing up, I didn't have a lot of girlfriends. Not the kind who showed up for you without being asked, or teased you like this but would also go to war for you if needed. Somehow, without me even realizing it, these three have become exactly that for me.

They're my people.

As I sit here, laughing with them, a little embarrassed and a lot grateful, I know I wouldn't trade this for anything.

I wrap my hands around my mug as the warmth steadies me. "Okay, fine." I meet their eyes one by one. "I'm staying with River."

Three jaws drop in perfect sync. Sloane's cruller falls back onto her plate. Lilah jerks forward so fast her elbow nearly knocks over her mug. And Rina just blinks at me, stunned, like her brain is buffering.

Sloane's the first to recover. "*Staying* with him... or *staying with him*?"

I lift a brow. "Is there a difference?"

"Uh, yeah," Lilah says. "The first one means you're sleeping under the same roof. The second means you're sleeping under *him*."

Rina lets out a bark of laughter. "You did *not* just say that."

Sloane leans in. "We're gonna need you to start from the very beginning, and don't you dare leave anything out. And if you skip the spicy parts, I'm quitting on the spot."

A gurgle of laughter bursts out before I can rein it back in. When my chuckles fade, what's left feels lighter.

Freer.

Like the weight I've been carrying isn't quite so crushing with these three sitting beside me.

And yeah, maybe nothing about River and me is easy. Maybe it's messy and complicated and full of things I don't know how to say out loud. But right now, with their expectant faces and warm drinks and easy camaraderie, I realize that I don't have to necessarily figure it out alone.

Rina blinks again. Then once more. I'm not sure I've ever seen her rendered speechless. "I'm sorry, did I just black out? I'm almost positive you just said you're staying with River Thompson. As in your ex's best friend. The same guy you refused to make eye contact with a few weeks ago."

"Although…" Lilah lifts her tea with a knowing smile. "He did watch Nora last weekend."

"That's still a pretty big leap," Sloane says, arching a brow. "From babysitting duty to living under the same roof."

With a shrug, I try playing it cool as the corners of my mouth twitch. "You didn't black out. And if you did, blame Oliver. Not me."

Rina groans as her head falls back. "The only O word I want to talk about is *orgasm*. Not *Oliver*."

Sloane perks up like she's been waiting for this exact moment. "Any chance we'll get to hear those two words used in the same sentence?"

Rina flings a napkin at her, but the flush climbing her cheeks gives her away.

Lilah grins and shifts in her seat, one hand resting lightly on her growing baby bump. "Now that's definitely a situation we need to circle back to. But right now, I want to hear all about how this whole surprise-roommate thing happened with River."

I let out a sigh as my brain tumbles back to the weekend. "My landlord taped a notice to my door that the rent would be going up five hundred dollars."

Lilah's eyes widen. "*Five hundred*? That's—"

"Insanity," I finish for her. "With everything else going on, there's no way I can swing it."

"And River just offered up his home?" Surprise crosses Sloane's face "Like, here's a spare bedroom and built-in support system, no strings attached?"

I nod slowly, omitting the part about sharing his bed. "Yeah. He said he had space. That it wasn't an issue for Nora and me to stay with him until I figured out my next move."

There's a pause and then Lilah lets out a quiet laugh. "Yeah, if you remember correctly, I got the same speech." She rubs her stomach with a smile so tender it tugs at something deep in my chest. "Now look at me."

Rina nudges her with a grin. "You've never looked more content or happy. So we all know that man is doing something right."

"I *am* happy," Lilah says dreamily. "Settled in a way I didn't think was possible. It didn't all happen overnight, but moving in with Steele was the beginning. That's when everything started to shift between us."

"You deserve it, babe," Rina says, giving her hand a squeeze. "Steele adores you. Relationship goals right there."

I take a long sip of coffee, hoping they'll stay focused on Lilah's fairytale romance for just a little longer.

No such luck.

I feel the moment the attention boomerangs back to me.

Three sets of eyes. Zero escape routes. Each one of them is looking at me like they've got follow-up questions locked and loaded.

Sloane points her cruller at me. "Okay, explain why you walked in here glowing. Not pregnancy glowing," she adds. "But something *definitely* happened. And I, for one, need the details. I think we all know that my love life's been DOA since... honestly, I don't even want to slap a date on it. So, make me happy and just spill."

Even though we're the only ones here, I glance around the bakery before leaning in. "He gave me an orgasm last night."

For the second time this morning, three jaws drop in perfect unison.

Sloane nearly drops her cruller.

Again.

"Wait, *what*? You *slept* with him?" Sloane nearly shouts.

"No!" I say quickly, hands flying up. "But he"–I widen my eyes and nod my head—

"you know."

Lilah stares at me wide-eyed. "I was *not* expecting that. But just to be clear, I love that for you."

With a grin, Rina leans forward. "It's about time someone worthy of you stepped up to the plate."

Sloane exhales dramatically. "God, I'm totally jealous. I mean, the only thing I've been doing in bed lately is cuddling up with my heated blanket and binge-watching murder podcasts. If anyone needs help disposing of a body, I'm your girl."

That gets a round of giggles, but then Lilah's expression grows serious, and I know what's coming next. "So, how do you feel about everything?"

The laughter fades, and the truth slips out. "I'm not sure."

I pick at the edge of my napkin, trying to find the right words. "River is turning out to be different than I expected. And he's amazing with Nora." The fear that's been simmering beneath the surface rises, and before I can stop it, I blurt, "I can't afford to get hurt again."

Silence stretches across the table. It's not awkward, just real. Like they all get it. Like they've all stood in the same place, waiting for the other shoe to drop.

"It's not just the sex, or I guess I should say, the non-sex," I murmur. "It's the way he looks at me. Almost like he sees me, along with all my baggage, and it doesn't make him want to run for his life."

Rina reaches across the table and lays her hand over mine. "That's how it's supposed to feel, babe. That's exactly what it looks like when a real man shows up."

Before I can respond, my phone buzzes. I slip it from my pocket before glancing at the screen.

River: *Just wanted to show you that we're doing fine.*

There's a photo attached.

Nora has two slightly crooked pigtails that look way too good for a rookie attempt. Her cheeks are sticky with strawberry yogurt, and she's grinning, as if having an absolute ball. River's beside her, face pressed close, blue eyes crinkled from smiling. He looks like he's having just as much fun as she is.

Squeals erupt from around me.

"Oh my God," Sloane gasps. "He *did* her hair. And it's actually good. Like, shockingly good."

"Are we sure this man is real?" Rina asks. "This feels more like a Hallmark movie, and I mean that in the best way."

Lilah lifts a brow, her smile knowing. "Are you sure you're not in deeper than you thought?"

That question makes my pulse skip and stumble in protest.

There's no way to hide the smile that spreads across my face. "I think it's a definite possibility."

I type out a reply while they all watch on.

Me: *Looks like you've got it all under control. Thanks again.*

The second I hit send, Rina narrows her eyes and points at me. "That look right there. That dreamy, slightly turned-on look? That's not casual. It's endgame energy."

Before I can respond, the door opens and Beau steps inside the bakery. He flashes a confident smile that makes Sloane straighten in her seat before he beelines for our table.

His gaze stays locked on mine. "Hello, Callie. Do you have a minute to talk?"

"Sure." I rise to my feet, acutely aware of the whispering that explodes behind me the second I turn around.

We stop near the register, and Beau lowers his voice. "I spoke with Gabby yesterday. Everything's set. We'll start featuring your desserts at two of the restaurants next month. If the feedback's strong, we'll look at gradually expanding the menu."

"That's amazing." A genuine smile forms. "Thank you again for the opportunity."

He takes a small step closer. There's a pause, and when he speaks again, his tone gentles. "I really enjoyed the other night.

I know you said you wanted to keep things professional, but I was hoping you might reconsider."

I hesitate.

Beau's handsome. Polite. Charming in a way that feels harmless. But there's no pull or spark between us. There isn't a rush of heat in my chest like there is when River walks into a room.

"I don't think that's a good idea," I say gently. "But I really did have a nice time."

His smile falters just a bit, and I get the feeling this man isn't told no very often. "Is there anything I can say to change your mind?"

I shake my head. "No, I'm sorry. There isn't."

He studies me for a moment, reading between the lines. "Is there someone else?"

I pause before admitting, not just to him but myself as well, "I think there might be."

There's a flash of disappointment in his eyes before he recovers quickly. "If anything changes, I hope you'll let me know."

"I will."

With a nod, he offers a polite smile to the table, then turns and walks out, leaving behind a strange mix of relief and guilt swirling within me.

Once he's gone, I make my way back to the table.

"Well," Sloane says, breaking off a piece of her cruller, "that was a little hot and a lot awkward."

Rina's phone buzzes, and her face lights up the second she looks at the screen.

Lilah leans in, already grinning. "Hmmm. I wonder who's got you smiling like that."

"Excuse me?" Rina asks, a little too casually.

Lilah arches a brow. "What do we have here? A new Tinder match?"

Rina grabs her purse before rising to her feet and making her way to the door. "Just a guy with good banter. Trust me, it's nothing serious."

"Wait a minute, that's all we get after I just bared my soul?" I call after her.

She glances over her shoulder with a devilish smile lifting her lips. "And don't you feel better for it?" Then she winks. "If it turns into anything more, I'll be sure to bring it to the circle of trust."

With that, the door closes behind her.

Lilah sips her tea and lets out a content sigh. "Never a dull moment around here, is there?"

"Nope," I murmur, watching the door a beat longer before turning back to the table, to the people who now feel more like family. "Not even close."

26
RIVER

ora's sticky fingers tap the glass display case, leaving behind faint smudges from the half-eaten cookie I gave her ten minutes ago. We're in a sports shop at the mall, and the jersey I'm holding is already wrinkled from her enthusiastic attempts to help me pick it out.

She's wearing a sparkly pompom hat that covers her ears and makes her look like a walking snowball.

The teenager working the register leans over the counter, practically swooning. "Your daughter is such a cutie, it almost makes me want one of my own."

"She's definitely adorable," I say with a smile, pulling out my wallet.

This kid has somehow managed to wedge herself into every corner of my heart in record time, and there's nothing I wouldn't do to protect her.

With a swipe of my card, I glance at the jerseys bundled in my hand. "One for my girl," I say, nodding toward Nora, "and one for her mom."

The cashier's grin widens. "I bet she'll love it."

"I hope so." I have no idea what Callie will say when I ask

her to come to the next home game, but I know how it'll feel if she's not there.

Empty.

Off.

I want her in the stands and wearing my number. And I want Nora sitting on her lap with that big smile on her face, waving excitedly.

After the salesclerk bags the jerseys, I scoop Nora into my arms and we make our way to the mall exit. We're halfway there when a loud voice cuts through the noise of the crowd.

"Well, shit."

Recognition slams into me, and my entire body goes still. Without turning, I already know who I'll find.

Zane.

Unfortunately, I'm not wrong.

He's standing a few feet away, looking like he just stepped off the cover of *GQ*. That designer jacket fits him like it was custom made, and his sunglasses are shoved up on his head like he forgot he's indoors. And those skinny jeans? It's entirely possible they're painted on.

The guy has no idea what matters in life and is too damn busy chasing all the wrong things. His smug expression slips the moment his gaze lands on Nora.

He looks from the toddler in my arms to me. "Is that my kid?"

My jaw tightens. "Yup, it is."

He stares, as if struggling to process what I just said. "Why the hell do you have her?"

I adjust my hold as Nora rests her head against my shoulder.

"Callie's parents weren't feeling well this morning," I say, keeping my tone even. "She had work, so I offered to watch her."

Zane's brow creases. "When the hell did you two get so

chummy? Shouldn't I have been the first one she texted if she needed something?"

I skip the first question and go straight to the second. "Would you have watched Nora for the entire day?"

We both know the answer.

He shifts before glancing away. "That's not the point. She should've come to me first. There was no need to involve you."

His gaze drifts back to Nora, studying her a little too long before landing on me again. I can practically see the gears grinding in his head as his face turns pinched.

"There's nothing going on between you two, right?" He lets out a sharp laugh, but it doesn't touch his eyes. "You wouldn't do that to me, bro. Would you?"

Emotion tightens in my chest. I knew this conversation was coming at some point. Maybe it's better to rip the bandage off now and get it over with. My feelings for Callie aren't going to change. If anything, they've only grown stronger.

And now that she's living with me?

I don't want her to ever leave.

"I haven't done anything to you," I say.

Zane's expression shifts as his eyes widen. He doesn't need help reading between the lines. "What the fuck does that mean?"

"Watch your language," I warn, adjusting Nora when she stirs at his sharp tone.

His jaw tightens. "Don't tell me how to talk around my own kid."

"Callie and Nora are staying with me."

He jerks back. "Why the hell would they do that?"

"Her rent shot up five hundred dollars a month and she wasn't able to swing it." I keep my tone even, not wanting to escalate the situation. People are already throwing curious glances our way. The last thing I need is for someone to recognize us and decide to record our conversation. It'll end up on

Railers Rumors before I can blink. Unlike Zane, I don't need or want the attention.

"Maybe you haven't noticed, but she's been working her ass off and is barely scraping by. I have more than enough space. So, I'm helping her out."

Zane's jaw works as he processes the comment. "Sounds to me like you might be doing more than just offering her a place to stay."

It would be impossible to miss the pointed edge in his voice.

Before I can respond, Nora shifts in my arms and her thumb slips into her mouth as her eyes blink with drowsiness.

"Rivvy," she murmurs, curling her hand into the collar of my hoodie. "Go home."

My chest tightens. There isn't a single thing I wouldn't do to protect this little girl. Even if that means the person I need to protect her from is her own father.

Zane watches us, and I see the moment he realizes this isn't a temporary situation. I'm not just some guy helping Callie out. I'm part of their lives now.

"Looks like my ex has gotten real comfortable with you, huh?" he says.

"Yeah, she has." I hold his steady gaze. There's no fucking way I'm backing down. There's too much at stake. "And you don't get to have an opinion about that."

He opens his mouth like he wants to argue before slamming it shut again. Whatever he's thinking, he keeps it to himself.

Without another word, he swings around and takes off.

But the look he throws over his shoulder as he walks away?

It says everything.

I adjust Nora in my arms and press a kiss against her head. She smells like strawberries and cream.

It's comforting as hell.

Maybe Zane thought he could come and go from their lives

whenever he pleased. Maybe he thought Callie would always be waiting in the shadows.

But he doesn't get to be a father only when it suits him.

And Callie?

She's no longer his.

And if I have anything to say about it, she won't be ever again.

27
CALLIE

Sloane wipes her hands on a dish towel before glancing at the clock on the wall. "Want me to stick around and help close up?"

With a shake of my head, I offer a tired smile. "Nope. Go home. I know you've got class tonight."

Her shoulders sag with relief. "Thanks. My brain's already mush, and I haven't even cracked open a textbook yet."

I chuckle as she shrugs into her jacket and grabs her keys. "See you tomorrow."

"Bright and early as always."

She gives a quick wave before slipping out the door. I turn back to the long stretch of counter and begin wiping it down with slow, even swipes. The scent of cinnamon and powdered sugar still hangs in the air.

It's both familiar and comforting.

Less than five minutes later, the door opens again.

Assuming it's Sloane, I don't bother looking up. "Uh-oh, what'd you forget?"

The silence that follows has the hairs on the back of my neck rising. I turn and freeze when I see the person standing there.

Zane.

I can't remember the last time he stopped by the bakery, and definitely not this late in the afternoon. I scan his face, and realize there's a storm brewing in his expression.

Without thinking, I take a hasty step in retreat. "What are you doing here?"

His upper lip curls. "Why the hell are you shacking up with River Thompson?"

The way he says it, like it's something dirty, makes me flinch.

"I'm not," I say automatically, but the words ring hollow the second they leave my mouth. The truth is that I'm living with River now, sleeping in his bed, and letting him touch me.

He makes me feel things I haven't felt in a very long time.

I steady myself and lift my chin. "If you remember, I asked you for help and you couldn't be bothered. So, when River offered, I said yes. It's as simple as that."

Zane steps closer, his jaw tight. "I don't like you messing around with one of my teammates."

Anger sparks in my chest. "That's not what's going on."

He raises a brow in disbelief. "Are you sure about that?"

My mouth opens as I prepare to defend myself and explain that I'm just trying to keep my head above water, but I stop and snap my lips shut. "We're not together anymore. That was your decision. You've moved on and are talking about getting married. As long as your life doesn't negatively impact Nora, it's none of my business. And I won't say a word about it."

Even as his expression tightens, I keep going.

"How I live mine?" I press a hand to my chest. "That's no longer your concern. We both know I would never do anything that compromises our daughter's well-being. I'm the one who's there every single day making her meals, helping with puzzles, brushing her hair, kissing her scrapes, and reading her the same bedtime story four times in a row because she asks me to."

Zane shifts as his face flushes. "What are you trying to say? That you think I'm a bad parent?"

The words sit perched on the tip of my tongue, waiting to be forced out.

Yes. Yes, I do.

You're always late, if you bother showing up at all. Last year, you forgot her birthday. You constantly leave me scrambling and her disappointed.

Not wanting to fight, I swallow everything down.

More than that, I won't let Nora get caught in the middle.

Instead, I take a moment to reel my temper back in. "What I'm trying to say is that I always put our daughter first. And that will never change."

Zane stares at me, and for a second, it looks like he'll argue. Then he lowers his gaze and mutters, "If you need the money so bad, I'll move some things around and see what I can do."

It's not at all what I expected from him.

"Thank you," I say quietly. "I appreciate it."

With a curt nod, he backs toward the door. The moment it closes behind him, I sag against the counter. My legs are shaky, the weight of that confrontation hitting me all at once. Relief crashes over me in dizzying waves, but the tension still clings to the air, stealing the comfort this place usually brings.

I force myself to finish wiping down the surfaces, flipping off lights, and finally, locking the front door. The routine helps to steady my nerves. By the time I grab my coat and purse, the tension has dulled to a manageable thrum.

On the way to River's building, my thoughts circle back to Zane. I'm proud of myself for not shrinking in the face of his anger or trying to soothe things. I stood my ground. And I'm proud of myself for that.

After pulling into the parking garage, I take the private

elevator up to River's place. The quiet hum feels surreal, like I've stepped into someone else's life. The luxury here still throws me off. All the sleek finishes, the curated art, the way everything smells faintly of clean linen and expensive cologne. Every time I step into the elevator or lobby, part of me braces for the staff to question what I'm doing here before reminding me I don't belong.

But I do.

At least for the time being.

I shove those thoughts from my head before stepping into the entryway and heading toward the kitchen, steeling myself for the chaos I'll find. Nora has been River's responsibility all day. By this point in the late afternoon, my parents are usually exhausted and ready to pass off their grandchild like she's a ticking time bomb. I expect to find toys scattered everywhere, the TV blaring, maybe even River half-panicked and questioning every decision that led him to this place in his life.

Instead, I find calm.

Quiet.

It's almost unnervingly so.

I glance toward the living room. There are a few toys lying on the plush area rug. Some are familiar, and a couple look brand new. Which means River went out and bought her more things to play with.

Of course he did.

I shake my head, a reluctant smile tugging at the corner of my mouth.

I'm just about to call out his name when I hear it.

Laughter.

And it's not Nora's.

Or River's.

A woman's chuckle carries down the hallway.

It's both warm and easy.

That's all it takes for something sharp to twist low in my

belly as I slowly move toward the sound, each step heavier than the last.

Maybe the intimacy between us meant nothing to him. Maybe everything he said about wanting me all these years was a lie.

Nothing more than a line to get me into his bed.

It wouldn't be the first time I've fallen for pretty words.

What hurts the most is that after everything I've been through, I believed him.

I'm such an idiot.

River's deep voice floats down the hall, mingling with the woman's. It's low, warm, and familiar, curling through me with the kind of ache that's impossible to shake.

Dread slams into me as I realize it's coming from Nora's room.

No, it's not her room.

Just the space where she's been staying.

I stop a few feet from the doorway, every part of me clenched tight, as if I'm bracing for a blow.

The first thing I'm going to do after confronting River is call my parents and ask if I can crash at their place until I find a new living arrangement. It won't be easy, but I don't have many options.

Instead of loitering in the hallway, I force myself to step into the room. River stands near the windows, talking to a woman I don't recognize. She's tall and polished in a way I could never be. Her dark hair is tucked behind one ear as she leans in to show him something on her phone. The smile gracing her lips is effortless, and her body language is a little too familiar. As if they're well acquainted.

Nora sits at River's feet, flipping through a board book with Gaffy tucked in her lap.

The scene punches me in the chest. It's cozy and casual. As if they're already a little family and I'm the outsider.

Before I can stop myself, I clear my throat.

River's head jerks up, and surprise flashes across his face. "You're home already?"

Umm, excuse me?

He brushes his palms on his jeans and steps toward me. "I wanted the room to be a surprise."

The room?

The woman flashes a bright and airy smile my way. "Your husband is the absolute sweetest. I promise, you're going to love everything we discussed today. Oh! I'm Anna, by the way." She crosses the room and offers a perfectly manicured hand. "It's lovely to meet you."

My brain stumbles over one word.

Husband.

When I open my mouth to correct her, River beats me to it with a wink. "That's what I keep telling my wife."

Anna gathers up her samples and waves on her way out. "I'll be back in a few days to start working on the space. I can't wait for you to see the final result."

I stare at River as her heels echo down the hallway. "You hired someone to decorate your guestroom?"

"No, I hired someone to decorate Nora's room," he corrects. "I figured she deserved a space that felt like her own. Something fun and pretty."

My gaze flicks to the empty doorway again. "Yes, well, she was certainly pretty."

The second the words shoot out of my mouth, I want to shove them back inside where they belong. My wide eyes dart to River.

"You were jealous." The slow smile spreading across his face turns into more of a delighted grin.

"No, I wasn't." My cheeks feel like they're on fire. "It was more of an observation."

"Oh, you were definitely jelly," he murmurs, a wicked glint

igniting in his eyes as he steps closer. "Lucky for you, I think it's sexy as hell."

I open my mouth to deny it before slamming it shut again.

The man is right.

I was jealous.

River swallows up the gap between us with a few sure strides before slipping a finger beneath my chin and guiding my face upward until my eyes can lock on his. "By now, you should know there's nothing for you to worry about. There's only one woman I want... and she just so happens to be standing right in front of me."

My heart flipflops.

His hand falls away. Then, like it's the most natural thing in the world, he retraces his steps and leans down, scooping Nora into his arms before heading for the door.

"Hey!" I call out after him once I'm able to wrap my lips around words. "You need to stop buying her so many toys!"

He glances over his shoulder, a smirk tugging at his mouth as amusement flickers in his eyes. "Oh, she's not the only one I bought toys for."

I blink. "Excuse me?"

Instead of answering, he disappears around the corner with Nora giggling in his arms, leaving me rooted in place, pulse tripping over itself.

"What does that mean?" I call after him.

But there's no reply.

Just the sound of his low laughter mixing with Nora's delighted squeals. And for some reason, it settles deep inside me, locking into place like it was always meant to be there.

28
RIVER

ora has been sacked out for fifteen minutes now. She was so tired that she didn't even put up a fight at bedtime. She just melted against my chest and whispered something about Gaffy before drifting right off.

I couldn't help but stare down at her peaceful little form for a handful of minutes before returning to the bedroom. In the middle of the mattress sits a small black bag.

It's unassuming.

There aren't any ribbons or flashy packaging to disclose what it is or where it came from.

And yet, it's making me sweat. I scrub a hand over the back of my neck and rethink my decision for the dozenth time.

What if I misread the situation?

What if she thinks this crosses a line?

What if it sends her running?

After gradually chipping away at her walls and earning her trust, that would gut me.

This isn't some kind of move, and it's not about sex.

Hell, it's not even about me.

It's about *her*.

Callie gives everything she has to the people around her.

Nora, her parents, friends, customers at the bakery. And she never asks for anything in return.

She just keeps going.

Keeps sacrificing.

Keeps putting herself last.

Maybe I've wanted her for far longer than I should've. Maybe it's selfish of me to want her to see herself the way I do. But she deserves to know she's more than what everyone expects her to be.

This gift is a reminder of that.

A reminder that she matters. That she's allowed to want things. To feel good and take up space. Even when no one's watching.

Especially when no one's watching.

The sound of footsteps approaching from the hallway has my pulse spiking. Callie steps into the room, and her gaze immediately drops to the bag on the bed.

She stops short as her brows draw together. "What's that?"

I swallow and nod toward the gift. "Why don't you open it and find out?"

She hesitates for a second or so before cautiously stepping forward. It's like she expects something to jump out at her. After settling on the edge of the bed, she lifts the bag into her lap. Her gaze darts to me before she opens it, pulling back the tissue paper carefully and then lifting out the sleek black box.

There isn't a label or instructions.

She glances at me with curiosity before removing the lid.

That's all it takes for her to go motionless. "River..."

"Told you I bought some toys," I say gently.

"There's more?" Her voice comes out strangled.

"Yup."

She stares down at the wand, not daring to touch it. "I don't... I don't need this."

I sit beside her, close but not smothering, and slip my

fingers beneath her chin until she has no choice but to meet my gaze.

"Yes, you do." My thumb brushes over her skin. "It has nothing to do with need and everything to do with your pleasure belonging to you. It should never hinge on someone else's willingness to give it. You deserve to feel good whenever you want."

Her lips part but nothing comes out.

"I wouldn't even know how to use it," she finally admits.

"That's okay. It's not about knowing. It's about learning. Exploring. Getting comfortable with what you like and what makes you feel good."

Our gazes stay locked as I drop my hand. This time, she reaches back into the bag without prodding before pulling out the second box.

It's smaller and more discreet.

As soon as she opens it, her eyes widen. With fingers that tremble, she lifts the small oval object from inside.

"It's a vibrator," I offer, like it's no big deal.

Emotion flashes across her face. Embarrassment and then curiosity follow. She nods before setting it beside the other device.

Then she pulls out the next item. Her hand stills. She blinks at it, eyebrows slowly climbing. "This..."

"Is a dildo," I supply helpfully.

Her gaze snaps to mine. "It's pink."

"I was told aesthetics matter."

She lifts it, turning the phallic-shaped toy in her hand, like she's trying to figure out if it came with an instruction manual. "It's, um... big."

"I think it'll fit perfectly."

She lets out a slow exhale. Then, with a slightly shaky laugh, she reaches into the bag and pulls out the final item—a bottle of lube.

Her brows shoot up again. "Wow. You really thought of everything."

"When it comes to your pleasure, I'm nothing if not thorough," I tell her, my eyes locked on the way her lips twitch, like she's fighting back a smile. "Sure, I could've added a couple more items, but I wanted this to feel simple. Easy. Something that wouldn't overwhelm you. Something you could explore, enjoy, and get comfortable with on your own terms and at your own pace."

"Thank you," she says quietly. "I appreciate it more than you know."

"You're worth it, Callie. You deserve to take time out for yourself. To feel desired, wanted, and cherished."

Her gaze lifts to mine, and this time she doesn't look away. She searches my face like she's trying to spot the warning signs or figure out what the catch is.

But there isn't one.

There never has been.

Not with me.

"You're making it nearly impossible to keep my guard up."

"Good." I reach for her hand, threading my fingers through hers before lifting it to my lips and brushing a kiss against them. "You don't need it with me. Not now. Not ever."

She buries her face in the crook of my neck as we sit in silence. Our breaths fall into the same quiet rhythm as her body slowly softens into mine.

I press a kiss to her temple. "When you're ready, I'll show you how everything works. But only if you want me to."

Even though she doesn't answer right away, her fingers curl into my shirt, like she's thinking about finally letting someone in.

And I'll be right here waiting when she does.

29
CALLIE

No man has ever treated me the way River does.

Certainly not Zane.

Not even back when things were good, when I thought love meant compromise and quiet resignation, did he ever truly put me first.

It's hard to explain what that realization does to me. How it hits low and deep, unraveling something I hadn't even realized was wound tight. Like a knot I'd been carrying in my chest for years, too used to the pressure to even notice it was there.

Until River.

What I now understand is that River isn't just kind in the big, sweeping, movie-scene ways.

He's kind in the quiet and thoughtful ones.

The ones no one else sees.

It's the way he watches me out of the corner of his eye, to make sure I'm okay. The way he crouches down to help Nora with her shoes without waiting to be asked, like it's already second nature to care for her. The way he gives me space when I need it, but never enough to make me feel like I'm alone again.

I don't understand him.

How can a man like River, a professional athlete, confident, devastatingly handsome, capable of having any woman he wants, be this gentle?

This generous?

This present?

How is it that he's always thinking of me?

And my daughter?

Of what we need, sometimes before I even know myself?

It's like the weight I've carried around with me for years has finally been lifted.

There's no pressure or expectation in the way he holds me.

Just warmth. A steady strength wrapped around me like a promise I'm not used to being given.

Maybe that's why I don't overthink it.

Why I don't talk myself out of something that feels right.

The word just slips out. "Okay."

River pulls back slightly, just enough to see my face. His eyes search mine with that familiar patience, like he's not just looking for consent but for any trace of doubt I might not even know I'm carrying.

"Okay?" he echoes.

This time, I don't hesitate. A small, nervous smile tugs at my lips as I nod. "I want you to show me."

His brows lift slightly. "Are you sure?"

There's a flutter of nerves beneath my ribs. The thought of him watching me do something so vulnerable sends a flush of heat across my skin, but it's not from fear.

Not with him.

Vulnerability... yes.

But it's so much more than that.

It's trust.

The kind that's deep, quiet, and steady.

"Yeah, I'm sure."

Something shifts in his expression as a tender smile spreads across his face that feels dangerously close to awe. As if I've handed him a piece of my heart, and he knows exactly how fragile it is.

"Why don't you take a shower and relax," he says gently. "I'll be here waiting when you're done."

With a nod, I slip from his embrace, and immediately feel the absence of his warmth.

In the bathroom, I take my time. Each piece of clothing comes off slowly, like I'm shedding old skin and letting go of all the pieces of myself that once believed I had to earn affection or prove my worth.

The tile is cool beneath my feet. Steam curls around me as I step into the shower, and the hot water rains down over my skin, soothing and cleansing all at once.

I wash my hair twice.

Once to clean it.

And then again, just to feel the quiet comfort of the moment stretch a little longer. It isn't hesitation. How could it be when every part of me is buzzing with hope, curiosity, and, yeah... nerves.

And when I finally step out and towel off, I feel a little lighter.

A little steadier.

A little braver.

I reach for his robe. It's thick and plush, wrapping around me completely. What I like most is that it smells just like him. Clean and woodsy, with that warm, spicy undertone that makes my stomach dip and my pulse stutter.

Enveloped in the comfort of him, I take a moment to let everything settle before glancing around the space and pausing near the vanity, checking a drawer, then another, looking for a hair dryer.

When my search turns up empty, I pad barefoot into the bedroom, still towel-drying my hair with one hand. River's sitting on the edge of the bed. His eyes lift the second I appear before slowly raking down the length of me.

His jaw tics slightly. "You look good in my robe."

Heat climbs up my neck again, and I cross my arms, as if I'm not affected by the comment or falling just a little bit more with every conversation.

"Do you have a hair dryer?"

"Yup. It's in the drawer under the sink. Let me grab it for you."

Rising to his feet, he moves past me into the bathroom before opening the one drawer I hadn't thought to check, and pulling out a sleek, high-end hair dryer.

"Sit down." He nods toward the small vanity stool.

I blink, caught off guard. "No, that's okay. I can—"

"Sit, Callie." His voice is quiet yet firm. "Let me do it for you."

There's no push in his tone.

No demand.

Just a steady insistence that's laced with care.

The kind I'm not used to.

The kind that undoes me a little more every time he offers it.

A rush of warmth that has nothing to do with nerves and everything to do with this man, skitters through me as I lower myself onto the chair. River picks up my brush, plugs in the dryer, and runs his fingers gently through my damp strands before starting.

The hum of the dryer fills the room as warm air kisses the back of my neck. His hands move carefully, brushing through the tangles with such patience that it doesn't take long for my muscles to uncoil. The bristles glide across my scalp, followed by his fingers. It's a rhythm that feels strangely intimate.

From beneath my lashes, I watch him in the mirror. His

expression is focused and tender. As if what he's doing is something to be savored.

When the robe slips slightly off one shoulder, he adjusts it without a word, careful to keep me warm. It doesn't take long for my eyes to drift shut as the tension in my spine melts away. The steady strokes through my hair lull me into a state of contentment.

"No one's ever done this for me," I admit, surprised by how raw the words sound out loud.

He pauses for a second, as if allowing the weight of the confession to settle between us. "Isn't it about time someone did?"

Even though his tone is low and steady, there's a quiet intensity behind the question that knocks something loose inside me. I swallow hard, blinking against the sudden prick of tears that threaten. It isn't the gesture. But the care he's taken with both me and my daughter since we've stepped foot in his home.

When he finishes, he unplugs the dryer and sets everything aside before meeting my gaze in the mirror. He doesn't smile or tease. Instead, he looks at me with a serious expression that makes my throat ache.

I turn slightly in the chair to face him. "Thank you."

He reaches out and tucks a piece of hair behind my ear. "Anytime."

That's the one thing I've noticed about River. He doesn't rush or push. He gives me space to choose.

And somehow, that makes picking him feel easier.

I rise to my feet, nerves fluttering like the wings of a hummingbird in my stomach. The bedroom is dim and cozy, the lamp on the nightstand casting golden shadows across the mattress.

River walks ahead of me before settling with his back propped against the headboard and his legs stretched out comfortably in front of him. Only then does he pat the space between them. "Come here."

A shiver of anticipation unfurls within me.

What's happening feels so much more than just physical.

It's the kind of closeness you can't fake.

I climb carefully onto the mattress as my pulse thrums in my throat. My knees sink into the softness as I crawl forward and ease between his legs, letting my spine settle against his chest. His arms wrap around me, low at my waist. They feel both warm and protective. It's exactly what I need. His cheek brushes the top of my head, and I close my eyes.

The robe clings to my damp skin as anticipation coils tight inside me. For now, we stay still. Just wrapped around each other like this is exactly where we were always meant to be.

His thumb brushes lightly along the inside of my wrist. It's a simple touch that feels more like a promise.

When he speaks, his voice is low and rough at the edges. And I feel every word, like they're not just spoken but etched into my skin.

"Do you still want to do this? It's okay if you don't."

I nod, letting my head fall back against his shoulder. "I do."

And I mean it. Every word. Every syllable.

For the first time in what feels like forever, I feel seen. Not for who I'm expected to be, but for who I actually am. I feel taken care of in a way that's quiet and steady, not performative or conditional.

Unconsciously, my gaze drifts toward the toys resting on the nightstand.

River's warm breath brushes my ear. "It's just us. Nothing has to happen. But if you want to explore..." He reaches out and grabs the vibrator before clicking it on. A quiet buzz hums through the air. "Start with this setting. It's the lightest."

Already, my skin feels flushed. I hesitate before my fingers loosen the knot at my waist. The robe falls open slightly, the cool air brushing my bare skin as I shift in his lap and part my thighs.

My hand trembles as I take hold of the oval shaped toy and lower it to the most sensitive part of me. I fumble, the angle all wrong, nerves winding tighter with the passing of each second as it glides across my delicate flesh.

I squeeze my eyes shut as embarrassment swamps me. "I don't know what I'm doing."

River's hand wraps steadily around mine. "Then let me help."

With careful patience, he guides my hand. His fingers rest lightly over mine, never forcing, just offering steady support. He helps me find a rhythm. It's a gentle, teasing drag, along with subtle pressure that turns a flicker into a flame. The vibrator grazes over my clit before dipping lower, and I gasp, my hips jerking as pleasure sparks through me like a live wire.

"Do you like that?" River asks against my ear. His mouth is so close I can feel the brush of his lips on my skin.

"Y-yeah," I confess. "I do."

More than I thought possible.

Even though part of me craves the security of his control, he doesn't take over. He stays with me. His presence becomes a safety net, letting me explore this part of myself at my own pace.

My hips shift instinctively, seeking out more pressure, more friction. More of *this*. My breathing quickens, every inhale catching in my throat. The robe slips even farther from my shoulders, the fabric pooling around me, baring more of my body to the cool air and to him. But I don't reach for it or hide from the intimacy unfolding between us.

I spread my thighs wider, desperate for more of the sensation, the delicious rise of tension cresting just beyond my reach. The vibrator hums, circling with just the right amount of pressure. My body tightens, the coil in my core winding tighter and tighter, until I feel like I'm hanging by a thread.

And through it all, River doesn't touch me.

Not directly.

Not in the way that would change everything.

Even so, it already feels like everything has changed.

"You're so close, aren't you?" he asks.

"Yes," I admit. "It feels so good."

"It should always feel good. You should take your pleasure any time you need to. You deserve it, Callie. You deserve to feel good in your skin. To claim it. Own it. If you were mine…" His words darken with promise, curling around me like crushed velvet. "I'd worship every inch of you. I'd make sure you came every night, sometimes twice, until the only thing you ever craved was the sound of my voice and the feel of my hands on your body. You'd never look elsewhere. You wouldn't *need* to."

His words stroke something deep inside me, something long buried, something that aches to be seen and held. With him, there wouldn't be any empty places.

No doubts.

Only him.

Only this.

The vibrator circles my clit before hitting it perfectly. Pleasure builds to a breaking point, and I arch, my eyes fluttering shut as a sob catches in my throat.

His arms continue to surround me, making me feel protected.

Like it's all right to let go.

"I want to watch you fall apart." His lips graze the shell of my ear. "I want to feel your body shatter from the pleasure you're giving yourself."

It's those words that undo me.

Ecstasy explodes through me like a lightning strike, and my back bows. A raw cry rips from my throat as I come hard and fast against him. My body trembles and my thighs shake. The release is so intense it feels like I'm shattering from the inside out.

I'm floating and weightless in the best possible way.

Once spent, I collapse against his chest. My fingers go limp, the vibrator slipping from my grip as my head drops against his shoulder. My skin is damp with sweat as my legs continue to tremble.

I've never felt more alive or sated.

River gathers me up in his arms, as if I'm the most precious thing in the world.

"Thank you." Emotion careens through me.

He presses a lingering kiss to the top of my head. "You have to know that it was my pleasure." The words settle deep into my bones.

I tilt my face toward his, my gaze snagging on the curve of his mouth. My pulse stutters, each beat pounding louder as the space between us evaporates. When he leans in, his warm breath ghosting over my skin, I quiver with anticipation.

Instead of claiming me outright, he brushes against me once, then again with careful strokes that are dizzying. His knuckles skim along my jaw, steadying me, as if he knows I need the anchor. My lips part on a shaky inhalation as every nerve sparks with the need for more.

When his mouth finally settles over mine, the kiss is unhurried and deliberate. The first graze is gentle, but then his lips caress mine with more certainty before coaxing them open. Heat twists low in my belly, winding tighter as my mouth parts wider.

The slow glide of his tongue tangles with mine. It's a soft clash that weakens everything inside me. The taste of him is intoxicating, and I can't get enough. His hand slides along my jaw, tilting my face to deepen the kiss until the world beyond us blurs.

Every press of his mouth tells me that he doesn't view this as something to be rushed. Everything about our first kiss is intentional, and it's every bit as intimate as the way he guided me through my orgasm.

I sink into him completely, giving myself over without hesitation or fear.

It's only this man and this moment.

And the quiet, life-altering realization that after years, I finally feel wanted.

I wake up the next morning to Callie's warm hand gliding over me, and it feels more like a fucking dream. For a second, I keep my eyes closed and my body still, afraid that even a twitch might break the spell.

Her touch is so damn tentative. Her fingers skim just beneath the waistband of my boxer briefs, like she's memorizing the shape of me.

Like she *wants* this.

Wants *me*.

All I can think about is last night and the look in her eyes when she finally let go. The way her body trembled while she learned how to give herself pleasure. The quiet, broken sounds she made when she fell apart. The way she leaned into me afterward, like she finally felt safe.

In that moment, everything changed between us, becoming more permanent.

Like we crossed some invisible threshold and there's no going back.

Even better, she doesn't want to.

She's not taking a giant step in retreat with the need to regroup.

When her hand drifts lower, growing bolder, I nearly lose it. Before I can say a word, she swings a leg over me and straddles my hips, her bare thighs bracketing my waist.

My eyelids fly open, and I find Callie naked. Her blonde hair tumbles around her shoulders and her cheeks are still flushed with sleep. I don't think I've ever seen anything more beautiful than this woman. My gaze roves over her face, wanting to sear this moment into my brain for all eternity.

"If this is a dream," I rasp, "please don't wake me."

Her lips quirk as a laugh escapes from her. "It's not."

Unable to resist touching her, my hands slide upward along her thighs before resting on her hips. Even though every muscle in my body is tense with restraint, I keep my grip light.

"What is it that you want from me, Callie?" I ask, my gaze locking on hers. "I made you a promise, and I'm not the kind of man who breaks his word. You might not understand that right now, but you will."

Her expression changes. The teasing falls away before being replaced by something raw and open. And it's the sexiest thing I've ever seen in my life.

She leans in as her eyes search mine. "I want you," she whispers. "I want to feel you inside me, filling me up."

Fuck.

The words hit me like a freight train. Hard, fast, and impossible to ignore.

"Are you sure?"

She nods, but it's not enough.

Not for this.

I reach up and brush two fingers across her lips. "Words, Callie. I need to hear you say it. I don't want there to be a single second where you doubt this. Or worse, regret it."

"I won't," she says. "I promise. I want *you.*"

That's all I need.

When she leans down, the soft swells of her breasts brush

against my chest, and I angle my head until my mouth finds her nipple before sucking gently, rolling my tongue against the peak until she gasps, arching into me. Then I move to the other, giving it the same attention.

Her fingers tangle in my hair, tugging as her hips shift against mine.

"Your body is so damn beautiful." I trail kisses along the slope of her breast. "And it made Nora. That makes it a fucking miracle."

She stills.

Just for a second, but it's more than enough for me to feel.

I pause and look up at her. "What's wrong?"

Her eyes shimmer, but she doesn't look away. "Zane didn't think so," she admits, the words so quiet, I almost don't catch them. "He wasn't attracted to me when I was pregnant."

Her words grow so small that it very nearly guts me.

Rage rises in my chest, and I have to beat it down before cupping her face with both hands. I want her to not only hear what I'm about to say but feel it. "I thought you were so goddamn sexy when you were pregnant that it was impossible to think straight."

Her eyes are wide and filled with uncertainty when they lift to mine.

"Do you have any idea how many days I had to stay away from you because I couldn't stop picturing the way your body was changing? How many times I caught myself staring at the fullness of your breasts or the curve of your hips? I'd look at your stomach and think about how radiant you looked. I'm not even going to tell you how many times I got myself off thinking about your beautiful body."

The blush that rises to her cheeks only makes her more stunning.

"I'm not even embarrassed," I add with a huff of dry laughter. "Okay, maybe a little. It was an alarming number. Zane's a fucking idiot. He didn't deserve you or your daughter. Not then, not now, not ever."

She opens her mouth, maybe to deflect or argue, but I don't let her.

"No." I brush my thumbs across her cheekbones. "Don't you dare speak his name right now. Not here. Not when you're with me. If you're still thinking about him, then I'm not doing a good enough job keeping you focused on me."

Color creeps down her neck before spreading across her chest in a flush I want to chase with my mouth. My hands trail down her body, kneading the swell of her breasts, tracing the delicate line of her waist and curve of her hips. I lift her just enough for her to understand what I'm asking. She shifts forward until her thighs bracket my head and her pussy is poised inches above my mouth before lowering herself. The second her warmth presses against my tongue, I lose all sense of time or space.

Of anything but this woman.

She tastes like heaven. I groan against her, wrapping my arms around her thighs and pulling her even closer.

The sound of her moan is enough to leave me reeling.

"You have no idea," I say between strokes of my tongue, "how long I've wanted to do this. How many nights I wondered what you'd taste like."

I work her slowly at first, teasing her lips, flicking her clit before circling deeper, letting the pressure build. Her fingers dig into the headboard above me, anchoring herself as her hips start to move and she unravels one shiver at a time.

It only makes me realize how damn hungry I am for her.

For all of it.

For everything she's willing to give.

I bury my face between her supple thighs. Her honeyed scent, her warmth, the sound of her falling apart above me, it all consumes me. Gripping her hips, I angle her just right and let my tongue worship her delicate flesh.

This isn't about getting her off.

It's about showing her what it feels like to be adored.

To be wanted.

To be cherished in the way she should have always been.

"You taste so fucking good," I murmur against her slick heat. "I could happily stay here all day."

My name comes out on a throaty moan, and it sounds very much like surrender.

I slide one hand around to the small of her back, holding her steady. My mouth is unrelenting. Gentle, then firm. I want her to fall apart and know without question she's safe in my arms.

I'll never do anything to hurt her.

"River... that feels so good."

I press my mouth against her, letting her chase the crest of the wave as it builds. My world narrows until there's nothing but Callie. Her taste, the sounds she makes, and the way she moves above me. If I weren't so intent on devouring this woman, I'd admit she's right... it's that damn good.

But right now?

I don't want to stop.

My cock is rock-hard, aching with the need to sink deep inside her, to feel that tight, wet heat grip me like I've imagined more times than I can count.

But in this moment?

Our first time?

It's all about her.

It's about showing her how a man loves a woman.

Her hips roll against my mouth, her damp skin slick with arousal and heat as she presses herself to my tongue. I lick her harder and then deeper, worshipping every inch. I want her panting as she comes apart. I want to ruin her for any other man with nothing more than my mouth.

She trembles, thighs squeezing around my head, her cries breaking on my name like waves. Her body jolts with the force of her orgasm, hips twitching as her pussy pulses around my tongue. The addictive taste of her floods me, and I realize that it wouldn't take much for me to come from this alone.

If I'm not careful, that's exactly what will happen.

But I don't stop kissing her through the aftershocks. I draw them out until her entire body sags and her fingers curl into my hair, holding me in place.

I press one final kiss to her clit, so tender she lets out a shaky exhale, and then I rise. Carefully, I shift her back and roll her over, my body covering hers as I settle between her thighs. The evidence of her pleasure coats my cock as I slide it gently along her slit, teasing the entrance I've wanted to bury myself in for years. My control hangs by a fucking thread.

"We didn't talk about contraception," I rasp.

Her eyes are soft and liquid as they meet mine. "No, we didn't."

"Are you on something?" The head of my cock strokes along her entrance as it gathers up her arousal.

"The pill."

"I want you to know that I'm clean, Callie. I was serious when I said that I haven't been with anyone since—" I pause. "Since long before Nora was born."

Her hand finds mine, giving it a gentle squeeze. "Me too."

That small, simple touch nearly undoes me.

With my forehead pressed against hers, I slide my cock along her soaked pussy, fighting the instinct to drive inside her and lose myself. "I want to take you bare," I admit. "I want to feel you wrapped around me. Tight and warm and mine. I want to thrust in you so deep that even when I'm gone, you'll still feel me there."

Her pupils dilate and her thighs spread even wider.

"I want you to know exactly what it's like when a man worships you. I want to ruin you for anyone else, the same way you ruined me a long time ago."

Her lips part, but not a sound comes out. I see the response written across her face and feel it in the way her body opens to mine. The way she leans into my words instead of flinching from them.

And still, I need to give her one last truth before taking her.

"Once I'm inside you," I murmur, dragging the head of my cock slowly up her slit, "you belong to me. That pussy belongs to me. I've waited so long, and I'll be damned if I ever give it up. I promise that I'll keep her so happy, so full, so fucked and satisfied, she'll forget anyone else ever existed. And she'll know exactly who owns her."

When she lets out a whimper, my entire body clenches.

"But it's not just that." With one hand, I tilt her chin upward, forcing her to see me. "You already own me, Callie. Every part. Every breath. My cock just wants what it's always wanted. *You.*"

Her eyes glisten, and she gulps like she's trying to swallow everything I just confessed.

In that moment, I can't help but wonder if I said too much.

Peeled back too many layers.

If I've completely shattered the line between wanting her and needing her, because that's what this is.

Need.

I'm not here to play games.

And I don't want to pretend or hold anything back.

My mask is slipping, and I don't give a fuck.

Not with her.

Not anymore.

One taste, and the part of me I've always kept tightly restrained, snapped loose like a leash torn clean.

The beast inside me has broken free.

And he's hungry.

Territorial.

Most of all, he belongs to her.

My eyes lock on hers, and for a second, everything else fades away.

It's just us.

And the ache filling my heart.

Along with the truth I've held inside for years.

"I need you to understand exactly what you're getting yourself into," I say. "I won't let you go. Not easily, anyway. Not like he did."

Her gaze never wavers. "Good."

Something inside me loosens at her easy acquiescence. It's like a knot that's been tied too tight finally gives.

I brush a strand of hair away from her cheek. "And if you end up with a baby in your belly, I'll put a ring on your finger so damn fast it'll make your head spin. I'll be dragging your sexy ass to the altar. No questions asked."

A smile tugs at her mouth. "And if I say no?"

I groan, teasing her entrance with the tip of my cock, watching her arch into me, as if she needs me as much as I need her. It only takes a stroke or two before a moan slips free from her.

"Are you really gonna say no to the man who worships the very ground you walk on?" I rasp, dragging myself through her softness.

With a gasp, she shakes her head. "No, I wouldn't. But—"

"There are no buts," I growl. "Now, are you ready to be fucked the way a man should've been fucking you all along?"

Her head tips back as a needy sound spills from her. "God, yes."

That's all I need to hear.

Every single part of me screams to claim her pussy. To

finally slide into the heat I've been dreaming about for years. To make her mine in every way that counts.

I shift forward, cock poised at her drenched entrance, her body open and eager beneath me—

"Hello?" A woman's voice echoes from down the hall. It's muffled but unmistakable. "River? Where are you?"

Callie stills beneath me as her eyes fly open.

With a groan, I drop my forehead to hers in defeat. "You've got to be fucking kidding me."

"Who is that?"

"My sister," I mutter. "Willow."

We stare at each other for a long beat, her face flushed, chest rising and falling rapidly. I'm still so hard it hurts, and she's panting.

"River?" The voice comes again, louder this time and much closer.

I curse.

And then, as if by silent agreement, we're scrambling. Half-laughing and half-panicking as I roll off her and Callie grabs the blanket, yanking it up to cover her bare body.

With a groan, I push off the bed, still rock hard, still tasting her sweetness on my tongue, and shake my head with a rueful grin. "So damn close."

Callie looks over at me, panting and dazed, her hair a wild halo around her head.

She's seriously the most beautiful woman I've ever seen.

But it's way more than that.

It's just her.

Her lips twitch. "Yeah... close."

As I take one last look at her in my bed, tangled up in my sheets, her lips still parted from all the things we almost did, I know one thing with absolute certainty.

If I wasn't already in love with her, *this* would've been the moment I fell.

And the truth?

I'm not sure I'll ever get back up again.

31
CALLIE

My heart pounds as I stare at my reflection in the mirror and try, for what feels like the hundredth time, to make sense of my life.

I'm about to meet the sister of the man I'm living with.

The one I'm on the verge of sleeping with.

Who I'm not even dating.

Technically.

A few weeks ago, I was drowning, barely able to keep my head above water. The bakery was bleeding me dry, Nora was growing so fast it felt like I couldn't keep up, and I was surviving on caffeine, adrenaline, and the kind of stubbornness that borders on reckless.

And now I'm here.

With River.

Living in his penthouse.

Even though it still doesn't feel entirely real, it feels better.

I'm better.

And Nora is most definitely better.

She's happy and strangely settled.

So maybe that means I'm allowed to want this.

Him.

Us.

Still, I'd be lying if I said I didn't want to hide out in this bathroom for a few minutes longer. Okay, maybe for the rest of the day. My palms are damp and my stomach is in knots.

What if Willow takes one look at me and sees every one of my flaws?

What if she thinks I'm nothing more than a burden to River?

Or a mistake?

Just some struggling single mom who crashed into her brother's life, looking to become a WAG.

I straighten my spine.

She might not realize it, but that's not who I am.

And it's not who River thinks I am either.

After a quick pep talk, I push open the bathroom door, cross the bedroom, and step into the hallway.

I peek into Nora's room, surprised to find it empty.

Well, hell.

Looks like I'm on my own.

My pulse spikes as I walk down the hall, toward the voices, and round the corner. I find Nora sitting in the middle of the kitchen, knees bent, hair wild, giggling. Two other kids surround her, building towers with magnetic blocks.

What can't be denied is that my little girl radiates happiness.

Pure, unfiltered joy.

There's a pretty woman crouched beside them, sliding a juice pouch toward my daughter with a warm smile. Her long blonde ponytail swings behind her as she laughs at something one of the kids says.

Nora beams at her like a little ray of sunshine.

The reason hits me all at once. It's a piercing ache behind my ribs because she doesn't get the chance to laugh and play with other kids on a regular basis. I've been so busy juggling work and bills and stress that moments like this have been few and far between.

But standing here and watching her laugh like that?

It cracks something wide open in me.

It's proof I'm not failing.

I'm still caught in that moment as River slips an arm around my waist.

He leans in. "You made it out of the bathroom. I'm proud of you."

I roll my eyes as a reluctant smile tugs at my lips. "I would've climbed out the window if this wasn't the penthouse."

He chuckles, and the sound of it ghosts over my skin before he presses a kiss to my cheek. "Come meet Willow and her family."

The blonde straightens, wiping her hands on her jeans, before crossing the room with easy confidence. She's beautiful in a natural, effortless way. Sunshine hair and clear blue eyes. It's the same quiet steadiness I've come to recognize in River.

"Hi, I'm Willow," she says, stepping forward without hesitation and wrapping me up in a genuine hug. "I've heard so much about you."

I blink, caught off guard by her warmth. "Oh. Hopefully it wasn't all bad."

The easy sound of her laugh settles something in me. "Only the parts about you being stubborn."

"Guilty," I say with a small smile, feeling the slow loosening in my shoulders, as if a weight I hadn't realized I was carrying has finally been set down.

And then I see him.

Maverick McKinnon.

The Maverick McKinnon.

Right here.

In the flesh.

Dressed casually in joggers and a hoodie, all relaxed charm

and megawatt smile as he crouches beside my daughter on the kitchen floor like he doesn't have the entire hockey world at his feet.

And that smile?

It's just for her.

"All right," he says, holding up two markers. "Which color should we use for the unicorn's hair? Pink or purple?"

"Both!" Nora yells, clapping her hands in delight.

My jaw actually drops open.

Willow catches the look on my face and grins. "He's amazing with kids."

I nod slowly, still stunned. "That's... not what I expected."

"Most people think he's all about hockey, but Mav's a total softie with the little ones. He'd never admit it, of course. But he's the first one on the floor and the last to leave." She leans in, tone turning conspiratorial. "Don't tell him I said that. He'd deny it to his grave."

"Lies," Maverick says with a smirk and a loving glance at his wife. "All lies."

We share a laugh, and the sound feels easy, almost like I belong here with these people in this kitchen. Something about that realization slides quietly into place, threading warmth through me.

I drift toward one of the island stools, my movements almost cautious, as if I'm afraid to jinx the moment. River beelines for the fancy coffee machine before tapping a few buttons with practiced ease. A minute later, he sets a mug in front of me and rests his hand lightly on the back of my neck.

The touch is grounding in a way that makes me feel like it belongs there.

Like *we* belong.

I wrap my hands around the mug and glance at him. His attention is focused on Nora, and his mouth is curved in that crooked smile I realize only appears when he's watching her. There's something in that look that leaves me reeling.

This man brushes my daughter's hair without hesitation. He lets her stir pancake batter, even when it ends up everywhere. He remembers her favorite fruit snacks and how she says *pish* instead of *fish*. He bought her toys, not to win her over, but because he knew they'd make her light up.

Somewhere between the coffee, the quiet laughter, and the feel of his hand resting against my skin, it hits me that I'm falling for him.

Not in the reckless way I've fallen before.

There isn't fear, desperation, or the need to cling to something I know will slip through my fingers.

This feels different.

Steady.

Real.

And I don't just hope it will last.

I *believe* it will.

32
RIVER

Midway through the day, Willow pulls me aside and says, "You should take Callie out to dinner tonight. We'll stay here with Nora, grab pizza for the kids, maybe some ice cream, then head back to the hotel."

And just like that, my entire night gets a hell of a lot better.

I glance at Callie with a raised brow. The last thing I want to do is assume or push. I'd never pressure her to leave Nora behind if she's not ready. I know how hard it is for her to loosen the reins, especially when it comes to the little girl her entire world revolves around.

Callie hesitates, her gaze flicking to where Nora is playing on the floor with Autumn and Haven. In the span of a couple of hours, the three of them have become thick as thieves. It's like they've known each other their whole lives.

I can almost see the silent war playing out in Callie's eyes. The mom in her wants to say no. Wants to stay and be the one in charge of bedtime and juice cups and wiping off sticky fingers.

But the woman?

The woman who hasn't had a moment to relax, to feel desired, to feel seen, wants to give in.

She looks at me again, and something in her expression eases.

"Okay," she says, a small smile tugging at the corner of her mouth before glancing at my twin. "But only if you're sure."

"I am," Willow says easily, glancing at the kids and then her husband. "They're having the best time together."

Callie nods slowly, her arms still crossed, as she watches the scene unfold like it's something precious. Something she hasn't let herself imagine she could have. "They really are."

I don't say anything, but I could kiss my sister for knowing exactly what I needed.

This little moment is everything.

I love having Nora here in my home. She's filled it with so much energy and laughter. I love how effortlessly she fits into my life, how naturally she clings to my hand, how she lights up every room she races into.

And Callie's not just sliding into my life.

She's becoming it.

It's to the point where I can't picture a future that doesn't include the two of them.

Although, getting Callie all to myself, even for a few hours, is a gift I didn't know I needed until it was offered.

We head down the hall to get ready. I shave, throw on a dark crewneck sweater and a pair of jeans. Something simple and understated. Even so, I find myself adjusting in the mirror, wanting to look perfect for her.

I'm halfway through pulling on my shoes when the bathroom door creaks open and Callie walks out. The world goes still as I glance up and find her there.

She's wearing a green dress that hugs her curves in a way that's both delicate and undeniably sexy. It hits just above the knee, revealing legs I've had the privilege of feeling tangled with mine beneath the covers.

There's no glitter, no flash, no stilettos.

Just her.

And holy hell, this woman is the total package.

The real mystery is how she doesn't realize it.

"Is it too much?" she asks, smoothing her palms nervously over her hips. Her tone is light, almost playful, but I hear the flicker of uncertainty buried beneath it. Like she doesn't realize she's just stolen the air right out of me.

Too much?

It's not *nearly* enough.

I swallow hard, my brain scrambling to remember how to do basic things like form words. "You look…" I rake a hand through my hair, as if the movement might help me find them. "You look incredible."

She glances down, as if suddenly shy.

And fuck if that doesn't undo me completely.

It's not just how she looks. It's the softness in her eyes. The quiet vulnerability she's letting me see. She isn't putting on a show.

Callie is just being herself.

And I don't want to look away.

Not now.

Not ever.

We don't say much on the elevator ride down to the parking garage. Instead of the silence being awkward, it's charged. Heavy with the awareness that something between us is shifting. I can feel it in the way she stands just a little closer than necessary and the subtle brush of her hand against mine. The floral scent of her shampoo lingers in the air, making it impossible not to notice her.

Not to want her.

When her fingers graze mine again, I give in and wrap my hand around her smaller one. She glances up, and our gazes catch in the reflective surface of the elevator doors.

Emotion flickers in her eyes.

Uncertainty, maybe.

Or perhaps it's curiosity.

Whatever it is, she doesn't look away.

By the time we reach the truck, I'm fighting the urge to back her against the nearest wall and kiss her senseless. Every part of me hums with restraint.

Barely am I able to hold it in.

Instead, I take her to Gold Coast Table. I called ahead and booked a table outside on the terrace beneath the heat lamps. The atmosphere is quiet and intimate. Romantic in a way that won't scare her off but still makes it clear this isn't just dinner.

She smiles in delight as we're led outside.

"This place is beautiful." She smooths the napkin over her lap, as if trying to keep her hands busy.

"*You're* beautiful," I say before I can think better of it.

Cheesy?

Maybe.

But it's the absolute truth. The words slip out so naturally it feels less like a line and more like the tide rolling in.

Her gaze snaps up, startled for half a second, before she rolls her eyes, the faintest smile tugging at her lips. "Does that line usually work for you?"

I shake my head, leaning forward slightly. "Honestly? I can't remember the last time I used a line on a woman. Or even wanted to. It's been years."

That earns me a laugh. It's the kind that's warm and unguarded, the kind that feels like it's wrapping itself around my heart and giving a slow, deliberate squeeze.

She has no idea how much power she holds over me.

If she asked, I'd give her anything.

The fucking world.

Hell, she could have me on my knees without even trying.

We order pasta and share a bottle of wine. She tells me about riding the train with her mom on Saturdays because parking downtown cost too much. How they'd pack peanut butter sandwiches in foil and eat them on a bench outside the Field Museum before going in with the free day passes her mom was able to snag. She talks about standing on tiptoe at the Shedd Aquarium's big tank, wishing she could stay all day, and how her dad would skate with her at Millennium Park every winter. I tell her about what it was like growing up with Willow. How we were basically a two-kid wrecking crew. If one of us got an idea, the other was already halfway to making it happen.

Somewhere between the breadsticks and dessert, we stop feeling like two people circling around the idea of each other and start feeling like something more.

Something solid.

Something that has the potential to last.

Callie leans in, resting her elbows on the table. There's a beat of hesitation before she pushes past it. "Can I ask you something?"

I nod. "Anything."

"Why haven't you ever settled down?"

The question catches me off guard, but not in a bad way. It's the kind of question that means she wants to know more about me.

I glance out at the city lights before looking back at her. "I don't know," I say honestly. "Maybe I never met someone who felt like home."

She blinks. "Is that what I feel like to you?"

"You do. I can't explain it. It was like... the second I saw you in that club, in that pretty little dress that hugged your curves, I was done for. It was game over."

Her eyes widen slightly.

"And then Zane introduced you as his girlfriend," I say. "That was the first time I ever wanted something that belonged to him."

"River..."

I lift a shoulder. "It's true. I've never wanted anyone so badly. I thought it would pass, but it never did."

She lowers her gaze to her plate. "I'm sorry for the way I've treated you. I was angry. Lost. Coming from a place of pain. And you didn't deserve it."

I reach across the table and slide my fingers between hers before giving them a squeeze. "You don't have anything to apologize for. You were protecting yourself and your daughter. That's never something to be sorry about."

When her eyes find mine again, emotion flickers behind them. "Thank you for not giving up on me."

I grin. "Oh, sweetheart. That was never going to happen."

She doesn't respond.

At least not with words.

Her expression relaxes in a way that makes it impossible to look at her and *not* imagine a life together.

I lift my wineglass. "To tonight," I say quietly. "And to the fact that you're finally where you belong. With me."

She stills before clinking her glass to mine. "It's been a long time since something felt this right."

I lean forward. "I promise you, baby, this is just the beginning. All I need is the chance to show you what your life could look like with me in it."

"You're the first man to come along and look at me like I matter."

That unexpected comment hits hard because she absolutely matters.

To Nora.

To me.

To her friends.

And whether she knows it yet or not, this thing between us?

It's not going anywhere.

On the way back to the truck, I press my hand to the small of her back, feeling the warmth of her body through the thin fabric of her dress. And when she leans into the touch like she's been waiting for it all night, something finally clicks into place.

As much as I want to kiss her right now, I don't.

What we're building is worth waiting for.

Callie is worth waiting for.

And I'll bide my time for as long as it takes to show her that I mean every goddamn word.

33

CALLIE

The elevator doors slide shut as Willow and her family take off for the night.

And just like that, it's the two of us.

Willow's hug still clings to me as her words echo louder in my head than they should.

"I love you with my brother. I hope you realize how much he does too."

I tried to laugh it off.

To deny it.

But she only smiled like she knew a secret I didn't.

Now, Nora's asleep. The lights are low. And River's watching me from across the room like he can read my every thought.

I move around the penthouse like I've forgotten how to be still. I straighten the throw pillows, stack a few books on the counter, and pick up one of Nora's crayons from under the table, pretending I need to put it away.

The entire time, I feel his gaze and the quiet press of this moment.

"Are you okay?" he asks.

I start to nod before stopping halfway, my head moving side to side. "I don't know."

He doesn't push or crowd me with a demand for answers. He stays put, watching me like he's willing to wait all night if that's what it takes.

"I don't know what this is," I finally admit, my arms wrapping around myself, as if that might hold me together. "You and me. It's not supposed to feel like I can finally breathe. It's not supposed to be—" My voice falters, words slipping away.

"Real?" he offers, quieter now.

I blink, throat tight. "Yeah."

He pushes off the kitchen island and crosses the room with slow, deliberate steps.

"That's the problem," I admit. "I'm not afraid of you. And maybe I should be."

Instead of flinching from my honesty, his hand finds mine before lifting it to his chest and pressing my palm over the steady thud of his heart. "Do you feel that?" His gaze locks on mine. "That's for you, Callie. Every single beat. All of it."

I look up, searching his eyes for the truth. I've been wrong before. I don't want to be wrong again.

When he leans in, I don't hesitate. I meet him halfway, pulled by something that's both invisible and undeniable.

Our lips brush, lightly at first.

They're tentative, almost testing.

More of a quiet question suspended in the air.

My breath catches just before he answers with a deeper kiss, one that unfurls slowly, like he's giving me time to decide, to lean in or pull back. His hand slides to the nape of my neck as his thumb brushes over my skin in a gentle caress. The silent message it conveys is unmistakable.

You're safe here. Stay with me.

How can I not melt into him?

The kiss deepens, growing fuller, warmer, edged with the kind of aching tenderness that steals all the thoughts from my mind. My hands find the hem of his sweater, curling into the fabric, clinging like I might fall if I let go.

With a groan, he pulls back just enough to search my eyes, almost like he needs to be sure we're on the same page. He must find what he's looking for because without a word, he lifts me into his arms. My legs wrap around his waist and my fingers tangle in the back of his hair as I press my lips to his again. This time with more certainty.

He carries me to the bedroom, his mouth never far from mine, each kiss fanning the slow-burning heat that coils deep inside me. Every stroke of his lips, every exhale between us, feels like a promise I didn't know I needed.

I don't feel unsure or scared or like I'm walking into something I'll regret.

I feel desired and cherished in the best way possible.

Instead of fighting it, I let myself fall.

When he sets me down, there's no rush. No greedy hands or frenzied movements. Just River as he undresses me with deliberate care. One piece at a time, as though every layer he removes isn't just clothing but another barrier I've fought so hard to keep in place.

His fingers skim over the slope of my shoulder before ghosting along the dip of my waist and lingering along the inside of my thigh.

"You're so damn beautiful," he murmurs over and over, like the words aren't just for me, they're for him too.

As if he can't quite believe he gets to say them.

With each repetition, something inside me unravels. Maybe it's the way he says it like it's the undeniable truth, and not something up for debate. It doesn't take long before I begin to believe it too.

His mouth finds places I thought had gone quiet forever, coaxing them back to life with a tenderness that feels both brand-new and achingly familiar. The hollow just below my ear where his warm breath sends a shiver racing down my spine. The curve of my hip. The back of my knee. Each kiss is deliberate, a vow whispered against my skin. He doesn't move like a man who's trying to prove something. He moves like one who already knows. Like I'm not a body to be conquered but something to be cared for. Something worthy of tenderness.

Arousal pulses low and thick in my core, but it's layered with something deeper. Something weighty and fragile and real.

I tug at the hem of his sweater, needing him just as bare as I am.

Just as vulnerable.

"This needs to come off."

He pulls back enough for his gaze to search mine. "You think so?"

I nod. "Yes."

I want this man naked so I can see all of him.

Every gorgeous inch.

More than that, I want to feel his skin against mine. The weight of him. His undeniable strength. The warmth that is so much more than mere body heat. What I've already seen is more than enough to make me ache.

But now?

I want all of him.

Everything he's willing to give.

"All right." He lifts the sweater over his head with a smirk. "If you're so eager to see the goods, then that's exactly what I'm going to give you. What my baby wants, my baby gets."

My lips curve despite the fire in my veins.

His attention stays locked on me as he tosses the wadded-up material to the floor. A few seconds later, his T-shirt follows, revealing the broad expanse of his chest, the subtle flex of muscle, the ink that winds along his skin like a story etched in permanence.

My gaze drifts to the tattoo on his ribs, Willow's name woven into the design. After meeting her today and watching the way she played with Nora and looked at her brother like he hung the moon in the sky, it hits harder than expected.

That kind of love and bond...

What kind of man tattoos his sister's name on his body?

A good one.

A loyal one.

The kind who makes you feel safe without even trying.

There's the clink of metal as he unfastens his belt.

My stomach flutters in anticipation.

Why is that so damn sexy?

He slides the leather from the loops, the motion unhurried, almost teasing. When he drops the belt to the floor, the sound feels heavier than it should.

Final.

There's the quiet rasp of fabric as he pops the button on his jeans and lowers the zipper. My gaze drops, lips parting when I see how hard he is beneath his boxer briefs. His erection strains against the cotton, sparking a rush of heat under my skin.

The denim catches on his muscular thighs before he shoves it down and steps free. With nothing but confidence and quiet intensity, he peels off his socks and finally, the boxers. The last barrier between us falls away, leaving him completely bare.

Unapologetically exposed.

River Thompson is seriously gorgeous.

Hard and thick. Sculpted like a work of art. He's power and grace in perfect harmony. And the way he stands still, letting me take him in, tells me this moment is as vulnerable for him as it is for me.

I don't realize I've spoken the words out loud until he says, "No, baby. You are."

His tone melts something deep inside me.

"You're the gorgeous one," he murmurs, climbing onto the

mattress. The bed dips beneath his weight, and the second he reaches me, our gazes find each other and cling. There's nothing playful about his expression.

It's heated and raw.

"All the nights I spent dreaming about you didn't do you justice," he says, lips brushing over mine.

It's the kind of kiss that makes your heart ache. Then he deepens the caress until it becomes slow and searching. Our tongues meet and tangle. I moan into his mouth as he devours me like a man starving and I'm the only thing that can satisfy his hunger.

When he finally pulls back, I'm trembling with the need to be claimed.

Even though he must sense my desperation, he doesn't rush a single moment. His mouth drifts lower, kissing the underside of my jaw and then the delicate hollow of my throat. I don't think about tipping my head back and baring my neck.

I just do it.

A silent offering.

He lingers there, bathing my pulse with open-mouthed kisses that make my skin prickle and my toes curl. His lips trail down to my collarbone as his hands glide over my body like he wants to take as much time as necessary to learn me.

When he palms my breasts, I arch into his hold, needing more. He cups me, his fingers teasing the sensitive peaks until they're stiff and aching.

And when he finally takes me into his mouth, I feel everything.

Not just the arousal or heat, but the tenderness.

The worship.

I arch against him as he draws one tight bud into his mouth, sucking before pulling it deeper with a languid stroke of his tongue. Heat zips down my spine. My fingers slide into his hair, holding him in place.

A low groan breaks loose from him, and the sound vibrates against my skin before he releases me with a soft pop. His mouth trails to the other peak, and he lavishes it with just as much care. He licks and teases my body until I'm trembling beneath him.

And then he's on the move and sliding lower.

Each kiss he plants is like a silent promise that this time will be different. That *I* am different. That I'm wanted, not just for how I look or what I can offer, but for every fragile part of me too.

By the time River settles between my thighs, I'm already shaking.

He pushes my legs wider, coaxing them open with hands that are equal parts strong and gentle. When his eyes lift to mine, the force of his gaze pins me in place. I feel seen in a way I never have been before.

His thumb strokes through my slick heat, the pad circling with deliberate pressure. A shiver slides through me as my hips twitch.

"Did I mention just how beautiful you are?" His voice is thick with desire.

"Pretty sure you did," I say on a gasp as he continues stroking me, this time more firmly. A sharp jolt of pleasure zings through my body.

His gaze holds mine. "I don't ever want you to doubt just how much I desire you."

How could I?

When his every touch tells me exactly that.

This man makes me feel like I'm the only woman who's ever existed.

When his thumb circles my clit, my legs fall open wider, my body accepting him without hesitation. I don't even try to fight it.

His gaze drops to my drenched center. "Do you like when I play with your pussy?"

I manage a shaky, "Y-yes."

"Good." He leans in, thumb still circling. "I want you so addicted to my touch that you ache for it. For what only I can give you."

A broken sound slips from me. A moan, maybe a plea. But without question, it's surrender.

"Please, River."

He growls, like he's savoring every second of my capitulation. "You have no idea what it does to me when you beg." His strokes become tighter. Slower. "There's nothing better than the sound of my name sliding from your lips."

I release another needy whimper.

"Tell me what it is you want," he says. "My tongue or cock? It's your decision. I'll give you whatever you need. All you have to do is ask."

I don't even hesitate. "Your cock."

His eyes darken with heat. "Good choice."

And in that moment, I feel how he's not just about to make love to my body but every single piece of me I've kept hidden away.

And I'm ready to let him.

He rises onto his knees, settling between my thighs like he belongs there. Like he's always belonged there. His hand wraps around his thick length, stroking slowly from the base to the tip until a single drop of moisture beads at the slit.

The sight of him so hard and full of need sends another wave of arousal through my core. He shifts, hips flexing with slow, deliberate control as he drags his cock through my center. The hard, velvety length glides against me until my body trembles beneath the relentless friction. Every pass steals another piece of my sanity, winding me tighter, making me ache for more.

My head tips back against the pillow, lips parted on a sigh, eyes fluttering shut as I lose myself in the delicious sensation.

"Oh no, baby," he rasps, the warning curling through me like smoke. "I want your eyes open for this. I want you to see exactly who's filling up your pussy and giving you every ounce of pleasure. I need you to see who's worshipping your body. Every fucking day, if you let me."

His words jolt through me. My eyes snap open, and another wave of molten desire crashes over me, flooding every nerve.

The way River looks right now, kneeling over me, muscles tight, thick cock gripped in his hand as he strokes it against me, is an image that will forever be seared into my mind.

"Are you ready?" The muscle in his jaw tics a mad rhythm, as though holding back is costing him everything.

"Yes."

When he finally pushes inside, the movement is measured, as if every inch is deliberate. He doesn't rush or slam into me. He sinks in as if this isn't just about sex but about the moment.

About me.

My body stretches to accommodate him, greedy for the fullness, the heat, the dizzying sensation of being taken and claimed in a way that leaves no room for doubt about who's inside me.

And I'm shaking. Not from nerves or fear, but from the weight of everything I've been holding back. From the cracks splintering through walls I swore would never come down.

Once he's filled me completely, he holds still, letting me feel every inch. His solid weight settles over me as his forehead presses against mine.

"Are you okay? Should I keep going?" he asks.

I nod, my fingers curling into the hard muscle of his back. "Please, don't stop."

When he moves, each deep stroke feels like a promise. Each thrust is a tie that binds us tighter. There's no rush or careless push for release. Every motion is controlled, as if he's pouring meaning into it.

This man doesn't just take, he gives.

It's with the subtle drag of his mouth along my jaw and the way his eyes lock on mine, as if I'm the only thing in the room worth looking at.

Heat builds in waves as my legs loop around his waist, drawing him closer. I want all of him. Every inch, every ounce of weight and pressure. I want to feel him deeper, until there's not a single millimeter of space left between us.

I arch beneath him, chasing the pressure, the orgasm building in my core. But it's not just the pleasure that undoes me. It's this man. The way he murmurs my name like a prayer. The way our fingers tangle together. The way his mouth finds mine, as if he's trying to memorize me with every kiss.

His hand cradles my face. "It's okay to fall apart, Callie. I'll always be there to catch you."

Tears blur my vision as emotion surges through me. With a nod, I draw him closer, my fingers twisting in his hair.

"Don't stop," I gasp. "Please, don't stop."

"Just let go, baby," he says against my neck. "I've got you."

And I do.

I surrender to him.

And to us.

To this moment that feels like everything.

My orgasm tears through me. The intensity is both raw and consuming. My body bows beneath him, my cry caught somewhere between a sob and a gasp.

It's not just a release.

It's more of a breaking.

A becoming.

A reclaiming of something I'd lost over the years.

He follows moments later, groaning against my skin, his

body tensing before he thrusts deeper, shuddering as he lets go inside me.

Afterward, he doesn't pull away or roll to the side. He stays with me, forehead pressed against mine, our bodies connected, like we're breathing from the same set of lungs.

"You feel like home." He kisses my cheek and then my jaw before his lips find the corner of my mouth.

And when he pulls back to look at me, his eyes are steady and clear. They're full of something I didn't know I needed.

"You're mine now," he says into the darkness. "And I'm yours. For as long as you'll have me."

I curl into him, my body warm and loose from the aftershocks of pleasure.

And in that moment, I let myself believe it.

34
RIVER

I wake to find Callie tucked into my side, one hand resting across my chest, her breath warm and even against my skin. Her hair's a wild mess across the pillow, and her lips are parted in sleep. One bare leg is draped over mine.

And damn if the sight of her doesn't knock the air from me.

I could stay like this forever. Wrapped up in the quiet, in her, in the feeling that everything I've ever wanted is finally within reach.

A faint sound from down the hall pulls me back to reality.

Nora.

I ease carefully from beneath Callie's arm, trying not to jostle her. She shifts but doesn't wake. Unable to help myself, I press a kiss to her forehead before reaching for the sweats I dropped on the chair.

The hallway is dim as I beeline for the door to Nora's room and peek inside. She's in the center of what can only be described as a stuffed animal battlefield. Plush creatures are strewn in every direction, fallen like tiny soldiers who never stood a chance.

Her face lights up when she sees me. "Rivvy!"

My heart flips as I cross the room in two strides and scoop her up. She giggles, flinging her arms around my neck.

"Want breakfast, ladybug?"

She hums happily against my shoulder as I carry her to the kitchen and settle her in the highchair. Once she's occupied with a few toys, I pull ingredients from the fridge and cabinets. Eggs, milk, cinnamon, and bread. All the necessary ingredients for French toast. Nora babbles away, mimicking me with her own invisible bowl and spoon.

I want mornings like this forever.

Fifteen minutes later, footsteps pad across the hardwood, and I glance up to find Callie. She's barefoot, sleepy-eyed, and wearing one of my old T-shirts that hits mid-thigh. Her hair is still tangled, and the sight of her slams into me like a freight train.

She pauses in the doorway like she doesn't know where she fits in this picture.

But to me, it's obvious.

She belongs right in the middle of it.

"Morning," I offer, flipping a slice of toast onto a plate.

"Morning." She runs her fingers through her messy hair. "You made French toast?"

"Oh, I think you earned it," I say, unable to stop the slow smile that tugs at my mouth. "Sit down. I've got this."

She hesitates for a beat before lowering herself into a chair. Her smile is small and a little unsure, but there's something genuine blooming behind it.

Nora's too busy devouring her breakfast to notice the shift, but then she grins at me with syrup smeared across her cheeks and shouts, "Mo!"

When we both laugh, Nora pauses, blinking like she's not sure what's funny and then giggles anyway. The sound of it fills the kitchen, wrapping around me and squeezing until I don't know how I'll ever go back to my life before this.

Before her.

Before them.

This right here feels like everything I've ever wanted.

And if this isn't what family looks like, I'm not sure it exists.

All I know is I'll do whatever it takes to keep it.

When the plates are empty and stacked in the sink, the warm hum of the morning gives way to the press of the day ahead. Callie glances at the clock and exhales. "I should head to the bakery. I've been MIA way too long."

I nod, even though a part of me wants her to stay. "You go. I've got cleanup."

She gives me a smile before scooping Nora into her arms with practiced ease and walking toward the hallway. Just before she disappears, I remember the gift I picked up at the mall.

"Wait," I call out.

She pauses before turning, curiosity filling her eyes as she meets my gaze.

"I have something for you."

Her brows arch in surprise. "For me?"

"And Nora."

I reach under the counter for the plastic shopping bag. My palms are slick with nerves as uncertainty twists in my gut.

Callie shifts Nora to her hip, balancing her effortlessly as she crouches to set her down. With one hand steadying her daughter, she reaches for the bag, peeking inside like she's not sure what she's about to find before pulling out a tiny Railers jersey that's Nora-sized, complete with my name stretched across the back in bold block letters.

She stills, fingertips brushing over the stitched fabric. Her eyes widen before she looks up to meet mine. "River…"

"There's more." My pulse hammers in my ears, knowing exactly what this means, what I'm saying without doing it out loud.

Carefully, as if it's something fragile, she sets the little jersey aside. Her hand dips into the bag again and pulls out the second one in her size. Her movements falter, and it takes a moment before she lifts the fabric to her chest. When her gaze finds mine, the unspoken questions swimming in her eyes are impossible to miss.

"You got us matching jerseys? With your name and number?"

I shrug, feigning nonchalance. "I was hoping you'd wear them tonight at the game."

The moment thrums with anticipation and a hint of anxiety.

This isn't just about a jersey.

It's about what it represents.

It's about us.

About what we're building, even if neither of us has dared to label it yet.

"I wasn't planning on going tonight," she admits quietly.

"It would really mean a lot to me to have you in the stands, supporting me. Both of you. I'm playing my brother-in-law, and Willow and the kids will be there rooting for Mav. I need my own cheering section."

She steps in close and presses a kiss to my cheek. It's quick, light, and gone before I'm able to react.

"Oh," she says slowly, lips twitching like she's fighting back a grin. "That's right. You're playing Maverick's team tonight. Well, now you've given me something to think about."

I'm sorry... what?

I arch a brow. "So let me get this straight. You weren't sure about watching me, but the second Mav hits the ice, you're suddenly clearing your schedule?"

She smirks. "What can I say? He's nice to look at."

I eat up the distance between us and brush my knuckles along her jaw. Only then do I tip her chin until our gazes lock. "Careful, Callie. You keep talking like that, and I'll spend the whole damn night making sure you remember exactly who you belong to and whose name you'll be screaming long after the game's over."

She wavers but doesn't back away.

Not even a little.

And damn if that doesn't make me want her even more.

My hand falls away as she picks up Nora and turns toward the hallway, as if the conversation has already been settled. As I watch her leave, every muscle winds tight and my pulse races.

That's the moment I realize I'm already hers.

Body.

Heart.

Every damn piece of me.

I just hope when she's ready, she'll choose to be mine as well.

35
CALLIE

From the second I step into the bakery, I'm off-balance and out of sorts.

The bell over the door chimes the same way it always does, and the glass display case gleams without a smudge in sight. Behind the counter, Sloane is elbow-deep in a mixing bowl, folding chunks of chocolate into dough.

This place has always been my safe space.

A sanctuary.

And yet, today, nothing soothes my rough edges. It's as if the comfort I've always known has slipped into something I don't entirely recognize. It's disconcerting that I'm unable to lose myself in the usual routine.

Maybe it's because I woke up next to River, and before I could find my bearings, the man was making breakfast for me and Nora like he's been doing it for years. He kissed my daughter's cheek, slid a plate of French toast in front of her, and smiled like this was just a normal, everyday occurrence.

Or maybe it's because, right before I went to get dressed, he handed me a jersey with his name on the back and asked me to wear it to his game tonight. As if we've been dating for months and our relationship is clearly defined.

Sloane glances up just as I shrug out of my coat and tie on my apron. Her eyes narrow. "You're making that face again."

"What face?"

"The one that tells me something's eating at you," she says, arching a brow.

When I force out a laugh, it comes out sounding just as flimsy as it feels. "I'm just tired."

"Uh-huh," she says slowly, watching me like she's able to read every thought as it pops into my head. "Does whatever you're chewing on have anything to do with the fact that you're practically glowing? Although, to be fair, you also look like you might throw up, which is an interesting combination."

I grab a towel and start wiping down the counter just to give myself something to do. "I don't know. It's just River, I guess. He's turning out to be more than I expected. Actually, he's wonderful. Not just to me, but with Nora."

Sloane's lips curve into a knowing smile. "I had a hunch he was behind the look."

Air rushes from me in a huff. "I think I'm just confused. And I can't sort out my feelings when I'm with him. He makes me feel like everything will be all right, and I'm not used to it. I've had to rely on myself for so long. It doesn't feel real. Honestly, everything with him feels way too easy. Maybe that's what scares me."

Sloane wipes her hands on a dish towel before walking around the counter and leaning a hip against it. Her steady gaze remains fastened to mine. "After everything you've been through with Zane, no one can blame you for being cautious about letting your guard down."

Nervous energy hums through my body, and with a sigh, I toss the towel aside. "It's like I'm waiting for the other shoe to drop. For the moment I have to pack up, grab Nora, and walk away before it all goes to hell."

Sloane's expression lightens as she folds her arms against her. "I think you might be forgetting that River isn't Zane."

"Logically, I realize that," I admit, my voice catching just enough to betray me. "But there's still something inside me that won't let go of the fear. He's patient, thoughtful... And he looks at me like I matter. Like I'm not just this mess of bad choices and baggage. More than anything, I want to believe it's real. I want to believe him. *In* him. But it's all happening so fast."

Sloane tilts her head. "You're right. It is fast. But have you considered that maybe it's not automatically a bad thing?"

I sink onto the stool behind the counter as my palms press against my thighs. "I keep thinking about what this could mean for Nora and me. What if I'm wrong again? What if I let him in and screw everything up?"

"That's not going to happen," she says gently. "You're scared. That doesn't make you broken, Cal. It makes you human."

I blink hard, trying to keep my emotions in check. "I've followed my heart before, and it turned out to be a disaster. I don't know if I can survive making the same mistake twice."

Sloane closes the distance between us before crouching in front of me and resting her elbows on her knees so we're eye to eye. "You're not making the same mistake as before. You're not choosing a man who makes you feel small or chasing someone who doesn't show up. From everything I've seen, River shows up. Not only for you, but for Nora as well. From where I'm standing, that counts for something."

My throat constricts. "You're right. It counts for a lot."

"Then maybe it's time to stop running, and let yourself enjoy the moment. Even if it's terrifying."

I stare at her for a long, silent beat. "What if I fall again?"

Sloane takes my hand and squeezes it. "Then I hope like hell he's already waiting at the bottom to catch you."

The sound of my phone ringing slices through the air, startling both of us. My belly dips when I recognize the number flashing across the screen. Every instinct tells me to let it go to voicemail, but I force my thumb to swipe.

"Hello?"

"Good morning!" The woman on the other end is way too chipper for what I assume is a collection call. "I just wanted to let you know the property deed is in the process of being transferred into your name. It'll take a couple of weeks for the paperwork to be finalized, but that's more of a formality at this point."

I frown. "I'm sorry... I don't understand."

"The loan for Lakeshore Sweets was paid in full yesterday. You own the property free and clear. Congratulations. I'm so happy you were able to find a solution."

My gaze jerks to Sloane. She's watching me with a crease between her brows.

"Is everything okay?" she mouths.

I nod, but my head is spinning. "Are you saying someone paid off the loan for the bakery?"

"Yes." There's a pause. "You sound surprised."

A nervous laugh escapes. "Yeah, I guess I am. Can you tell me who made the payment?"

The sound of keystrokes fills the line. "No, I'm sorry. I don't have access to that information in the system. Only that the loan was paid in full."

My pulse pounds in my ears. "Okay. Thank you."

"Congratulations again. We really love when women business owners succeed."

Even after the call ends, I can only stare at the phone in my hand.

"Well?" Sloane prompts, stepping closer. "Don't leave me hanging. What happened?"

"That was the bank. My loan for the bakery has been paid off." I swallow. "Completely."

Her jaw drops. "You're kidding! Who did that?"

I shake my head as one name drifts to the surface. "Maybe it was Zane? He stopped by the other day and offered to help." Even as I push the words out, they feel wrong somehow. "I just can't believe he came through for me in such a big way."

Skepticism flashes in Sloane's eyes. "Zane? You really think so? I hate to say it, but that man doesn't have an altruistic bone in his body."

"Under normal circumstances, I'd agree with you," I admit. "But there isn't any other explanation."

Even as I say it, my thoughts start to spin.

Why would Zane pay off the bakery loan after years of letting me scrape by alone?

It feels like I've uncovered a version of my ex I don't recognize.

Maybe one who's finally trying to do the right thing.

36
RIVER

The buzz of the crowd hums through the arena, a steady thrum of energy that vibrates beneath my skin. I push off from the boards, carving a slow loop around the ice, letting the movement settle in my limbs. Warm-ups are usually mindless. It's all muscle memory, breath control while operating on autopilot.

But that's not the case tonight.

Tonight feels different.

I'm not just skating against another team.

I'm skating against family.

"Hey!" a familiar voice calls out from behind me, smug and loud enough to carry over the music. "Try not to embarrass yourself out here, got it, Thompson?"

I glance over my shoulder and smirk. "Please. With your lineup? Shouldn't you guys be playing in the AHL?"

Maverick skates up beside me, his grin sharp beneath the visor. "Says the guy we crushed last time."

I scoff. "If you remember correctly, I was out with an injury. Wasn't even on the ice."

"Likely story," he mutters, bumping my shoulder like we're

just two guys at a pickup game, not about to go head-to-head in front of a sold-out crowd.

The contact is easy and familiar. After all the years we spent grinding against each other on opposing teams, it's funny how life turned out.

"Lilah invited Willow to sit in the suite." His gaze shifts to the glass above center ice. "The whole McKinnon crew's up there."

"Yup, she texted earlier to let me know," I say, already scanning the luxury box. My gaze locks on Willow almost instantly. She's standing near the glass with my niece on her hip and my nephew waving like a maniac. As soon as she catches my eye, a grin lifts her lips.

That's all it takes for the tightness coiled within me to ease.

There's nothing better than having family in the stands cheering you on.

All right, maybe that's not altogether true.

My gaze drifts to the box after another pass around the zone.

Callie is still MIA.

Part of me wonders if she plans to attend.

And if she does show her face, will she be wearing my jersey?

Will she let me claim her in front of everyone?

"Not here yet, huh?" Maverick asks, keeping pace with me.

Ten years ago, we were bitter rivals, both on and off the ice. I stole his high school girlfriend, and he ended up having a secret relationship with my sister in college.

I was afraid he was using her to get back at me.

And I couldn't have been more wrong.

It took some time for us to see eye to eye, but now the guy is more than just my brother-in-law. He's one of the few people I trust with my sister, niece, and nephew. Maverick McKinnon has turned out to be a good man.

He's an even better husband and a phenomenal father.

Not to mention, a damn good friend.

"Nope," I say, my gaze searching the suite for what feels like the hundredth time.

"You think she's going to show?"

"I sure as hell hope so," I mutter, more to myself than him.

I've played in hundreds of games and scored more goals than I can count. But I've never wanted anyone in the stands the way I want to see her smiling face in the crowd.

Knox skates up beside us and bumps shoulders with Maverick.

A cocky grin simmers around the edges of his lips. "Hey, old man. Nice to see you finally decided to join a winning team for a change."

Mav snorts. "You're hilarious, McNichols. You couldn't pay me enough to be teammates with you."

"Yeah, I can imagine. It would really suck not being the best out there, wouldn't it?"

Maverick just shakes his head, refusing to take the bait. "You remind me so damn much of your brother. That's not a compliment. How's Colby doing these days?"

Knox's grin transforms into something more genuine. "Expanding the bloodline. Avery's still got him wrapped around her little finger, and Britt's due with baby number three in the spring."

"We're playing Milwaukee next month," Mav says, shifting his stick between his gloved hands.

Knox chuckles. "Do me a favor and lay him out flat with a nice clean hit and tell him it's from me."

Mav smirks. "I'll deliver the message personally."

He glances toward his teammates on the far side of the rink. "I better get moving before they accuse me of fraternizing with the enemy."

"Seriously, man. No one could blame you."

With another shake of his head, Maverick skates off, leaving Knox and me alone on our side of the ice.

Even though I tell myself to focus on warm-ups and get my head on straight, I still find my gaze settling on the suite.

Knox follows my line of sight. "Looking for someone special, huh?"

I give him a bit of side-eye. "Maybe."

He lets out a low whistle. "You must have been working on your manifestation skills because there she is."

My eyes snap back to the glass at the upper bowl, and lock on Callie.

Nora is in her arms as she steps into view, her expression is a mix of nerves and determination. When her gaze lifts, it collides with mine. A small, quiet smile curves her lips.

Time slows as she shrugs off her coat, and everything in me falters.

Not only is she wearing my jersey, so is Nora.

When she turns to hug Willow, I catch sight of my name stretched across her back in crisp white lettering. The pride that fills me is almost enough to bring me to my knees.

I glide to a stop directly below them, and stare up like an idiot as Nora climbs into the seat beside Willow, trying to get Haven's and Autumn's attention.

Pressure swells inside me until it feels like it might just burst.

Knox taps my shin with his stick. "Come on, lover boy. We've got a game to win. There's no damn way we can let McKinnon think he's better than us. I don't care if your sister is sleeping with the enemy or not."

With a low laugh, I push off again and start moving. If I thought I was distracted before, it's nothing compared to knowing that Callie and Nora are up there watching me. It feels like everything I've ever wanted is finally coming to fruition.

As much as I love seeing my woman wearing my jersey, I'm

looking forward to stripping it off her body and making love to her once we get home.

I'm jerked from those thoughts when I get shoved from behind. After finding my balance, I swing around, prepared to knock Knox on his damn ass. The guy seriously doesn't know when to quit.

Instead, I find Zane. His normally happy-go-lucky expression is nowhere in sight.

I straighten to my full height and glare at him. "What the hell is your problem?"

I know exactly what it is, though, and I should have been prepared for it. Especially after our last conversation.

Instead of meeting my gaze, his cuts past me and up toward the suite. "You really think that's a good idea?"

"What I think," I reply carefully, "is that if you gave a damn about Callie, you'd want the best for her. You'd be happy she found someone who treats both her and your daughter right."

His jaw tics, the muscles clenching. "Callie's not yours."

"And she hasn't been yours for years," I fire back.

Zane skates closer until he's crowding my space. "There are plenty of women you can screw around with. Pick one who doesn't have my kid."

Before I can wrap my lips around a response, he takes off.

It's doubtful this is the end of it. I'd hoped he would cool off and think about what's best for his ex, but apparently that's not the case.

After ten more minutes, the players file off the ice as the starting lineup is announced. The puck is dropped and the game gets underway. As soon as it does, the noise fades and the rest of the world narrows to hockey.

It's filled with quick shifts, clean passes, and hard checks.

It's tight from the start.

Every line grinds it out, and every play becomes a battle. No one can say Maverick isn't on fire tonight, and I'm matching his energy with every shift. Since we're both defensemen, we don't go head-to-head, but when our paths cross at the boards or at the blue line, neither of us hold back. There's pride in how we play. A mutual respect threaded into every shove, every sharp pass, every clean check.

But then the energy shifts. It would be impossible not to notice the extra hits that come my way. Or the elbows that get thrown after the whistle and the subtle jabs behind the play.

At first, it's nothing major. It's just enough to piss me off.

But that's to be expected in a tight game.

What's not anticipated?

That it's coming from my own teammate.

Zane.

Initially, I second-guess my suspicions, figuring it's accidental and I'm reading into things.

But then he catches me with an elbow as we pass on the bench, and shoves me harder than necessary when there's a skirmish near the crease. He mutters something just out of earshot of the refs.

I grit my teeth and keep my head down. The guy is trying to get under my skin, and I refuse to give him the satisfaction of knowing he hit a nerve.

No matter how much I ignore him, he refuses to back off. During a board battle, we get tangled again. Only this time, there's nothing subtle about it. His shoulder drives into my ribs. It's sharp and deliberate. The air gets knocked from me, and I stumble, twisting around with a glare. But he's already skating off. There's nothing playful or remorseful about the look he throws over his shoulder.

It's cold and calculated.

The guy is trying to rattle me.

Shake my focus.

For a moment, it almost works.

Until I glance up and find Callie. She's watching from the

suite, hand resting on Nora's back. Her wide eyes are locked on mine and flooded with concern. Somehow, they manage to do the impossible and ground me.

I take a moment to center myself.

This game might be personal, but so is everything I'm playing for.

At every opportunity, Zane keeps pushing. He throws slashes that ride higher than they should. Knocks me off the puck any chance he gets. Elbows me in tight scrums when the refs aren't looking.

I take every cheap shot and dirty play.

As hard as it is, I don't retaliate.

Not yet.

During the media timeout, Oliver glides up beside me. "Hey, Thompson. Check out the Jumbotron."

I look up, and there they are. Callie and Nora, front and center, caught by the camera.

The announcer's voice booms through the arena. "Looks like number twenty-three has his own fan club in the house tonight! Check out those matching jerseys. Talk about too cute to handle!"

The crowd erupts, the noise vibrating through me. Nora grins so big it lights up the whole damn screen, and her arms flap like she's ready to take flight. Beside her, Lilah, Rina, and my sister are laughing.

But it's Callie who captures my attention. Our gazes lock, and my heart clenches so hard it feels like it might burst. She gives the smallest wave, her smile hesitant, discomfort evident beneath the spotlight.

Even so, all I can think is that she and Nora are mine.

They're my girls.

I'm still riding high from that moment when the third period starts.

I dish the puck off to Knox, already shifting my weight to loop around when Zane barrels into me.

I don't even see the hit coming. His shoulder crashes into mine, and I slam into the boards with a bone-rattling thud. My head snaps forward, and pain explodes across my ribs and down my arm.

The crowd gasps and the whistle shrieks. The trainer is on the ice before I've even caught my breath.

"Are you good?" he asks, squatting beside me, hands moving carefully over my body.

I grit my teeth and nod, even though it's a lie. "I'm fine."

It takes effort to push to my feet as my lungs burn and my vision swims. I glance up and find Callie standing, one hand pressed to the glass, eyes locked on mine.

There's no way in hell I'm crawling off the ice.

Not in front of Zane.

The guy who's supposed to be my teammate.

The one I considered a friend.

More importantly, I'm not crawling off in front of Callie.

I wave off the trainer and force myself upright, pushing through the fire blazing down my side. My skating is slow and steady as I pretend like the impact didn't drive the air clean out of me.

When I reach the bench, Coach is already waiting. His face is red and his jaw is clenched tight enough to crack his molars.

"You two want to make a goddamn spectacle of yourselves?" he barks. "If you can't keep it together, I'll bench both your asses for the rest of the season."

Zane shrugs like he doesn't give a shit.

But I do.

I care about this team and our shot at taking home a Stanley this season.

I also care what happens if this locker room turns on itself.

Even more than that, I care about Callie and Nora, and doing what's best for them.

I refuse to throw any of that away because Zane can't get his larger-than-life ego in check.

The rest of the game passes by in a blur of adrenaline and impact. My shoulder throbs. My ribs feel like they've been cracked in half. Every time I think Zane's cooled off, he clips me again. Elbows, slashes, body checks that toe the line. Always just subtle enough to look like nothing if you weren't paying attention.

With gritted teeth, I play through it.

Every time I glance up at the suite and see Nora cheering, I remember exactly who I'm doing this for.

And when the final buzzer sounds and we edge out a win by a single goal, there's no celebratory fist pump. Instead, I skate to the bench with sweat pouring down my back. Only then do I look up and find them watching me.

They're still here.

I don't give a shit if Zane keeps coming for me, trying to tear down what I'm building with his ex. I'll take every fucking hit and keep on going.

Just as long as Callie and Nora are mine at the end of it all.

37
CALLIE

The moment I step into the suite, a familiar pang hits me. The sense I don't belong.

Or at least, that I never used to.

When I came to watch Zane's games, I sat in the lower bowl, crammed somewhere near the glass. It was loud and rowdy. The air thick with beer and sweat. I never really watched the game. Mostly, I watched him and the way he came alive under the spotlight. It was impossible not to notice the way other people stared at him. And I smiled like I was supposed to, like I was lucky to be there.

To be his girl.

But the truth is that I was never really part of his world. I was just someone he brought along for the ride. It took both time and distance to realize that.

This feels different. There's a warmth here I didn't expect. A comfort that steals over me before I can shake it off. Lilah is the first to spot us.

She turns and waves, already crossing the room with open arms. "You made it!"

As soon as she's close enough, she pulls me into a hug that's tight and sincere.

Then she pulls back with a grin, and her gaze settles on Nora. "And you brought a cheerleader."

Nora beams and immediately wiggles out of my arms when she spots the cluster of kids playing near the lounge area. Willow turns at the sound, her face lighting up as she rises from the plush couch.

"Nora!" she calls, crouching just in time for my daughter to barrel into her.

Watching them together makes something sharp and unexpected twist deep inside me. Not only in how easily Nora fits into this space, like she was meant to be here all along, but in the way I'm starting to feel like I do too

Willow rises to her feet and hugs me next, her embrace warm and full of quiet reassurance. "It's so good to see you again."

"You too." My throat tightens. "Thanks again for watching Nora the other night."

"It was our pleasure." Her gaze flicks to the kids, where Nora is now in the thick of it, proudly showing off Gaffy. "Autumn and Haven absolutely adore her."

I can't help but smile as my heart clenches at the sight. "Trust me, the feeling is mutual."

From the corner of the suite, Rina lifts one hand in greeting, the other is curled around a drink. Her sharp gaze slides over me before landing squarely on the jersey beneath my jacket.

Her brows lift in amusement. "Well, damn," she says, tilting her head. "You really went all-in, huh?"

A self-conscious laugh slips out as I glance down and smooth my hand over the blue material with River's name and number stamped across the back.

"He gave it to me this morning," I admit. "Right after he made French toast."

Rina stares for a beat. "Girl, if a man gives you his jersey and makes you French toast in the same twenty-four-hour period, that's your sign to marry him."

My laughter is real this time as it bubbles up unexpectedly. Beneath the humor, there's something unsteady in my chest. Part of me wants to believe in this fairy tale I've been dropped in the middle of.

Even if it still scares me to death.

Warm-ups have already started on the ice below, and I instinctively scan the rink for River. He's easy to spot. A blur of blue and white as he cuts across the ice like it's second nature.

Like he was born to play this game.

And then he looks up and our eyes lock from across the distance.

He doesn't smile or wave.

Just holds my gaze, like there's no one else in this arena but the two of us.

The moment stretches until I watch his gaze drop, landing on the jersey I'm wearing.

The one he gave me.

Something in his face changes. That hard, focused expression eases just enough for a flicker of emotion to break through.

I have to swallow against the sudden tightness in my throat.

This quiet moment of connection is more intimate than anything I ever experienced with Zane. My ex used to flash those camera-ready grins and reach for my hand when he knew someone was watching.

But with River, everything feels different.

Real.

Honest.

The atmosphere in the suite shifts as Hugh enters. He murmurs something to Evelyn, who stands with her back partially turned to us. She doesn't respond right away, but when she finally glances over her shoulder, her eyes are sharp and full of irritation. The tension between them is subtle, but it cuts deep. Like a wound neither of them ever let fully heal.

There's history there.

And clearly, it's not over.

The announcer's voice booms over the speakers. "Ladies and gentlemen, welcome to tonight's game!"

Nora gasps and claps her hands, bouncing on her toes like she's about to take flight. And when River's name is called, her voice carries above the noise.

"Rivvy!"

She's so proud and innocent in her joy. The grin stretching across her face might be the cutest thing I've ever seen.

As soon as the puck drops, the energy on the ice changes.

Zane is out there, his movements erratic. He's playing like he's out for blood. I'm afraid of who's blood he's trying to spill. My gaze sharpens just in time to catch the way he slashes his stick a little too close to River's skates.

"Is he seriously starting this shit now?" Rina mutters from beside me, her gaze glued to the action below.

Willow leans forward as her eyes narrow. "What's that guy's problem?"

My stomach knots. It's like a traffic accident I can't rip my attention away from. I'm hyperaware of every second Zane and River share the ice. The way River manages the pressure but never retaliates. He's holding it in and, somehow, keeping his cool.

But I can see it in the set of his jaw and tension in his shoulders.

The restraint is costing him.

"That's Nora's father," I say quietly.

Willow stills, and her brows rise as realization flickers across her face. "Oh."

Her expression turns to one of understanding.

Or maybe it's sympathy.

We can all see what River is up against and how he's choosing to respond instead.

I can't believe what Zane is doing, and I hate even more that River has to put up with it.

They're supposed to be teammates.

Zane shouldn't be behaving like this.

If I wasn't already terrified of how deep I've fallen for River, I am now. There's a different kind of torture in watching someone you love become the target of a man you once trusted.

A man you once thought you'd build a life with.

Nora tugs at my leg. "Uppy, Mama."

I blink out of the trance that has fallen over me, and lift her into my arms, holding her tight before resting my cheek against her curls as the game halts for a commercial break.

"Look, Nora! You're on the Jumbotron!" Rina exclaims from beside me.

My head jerks up, and sure enough, the massive screen above center ice is lit up with an image of me and Nora in our matching jerseys, framed in the muted glow of the suite. River's number is impossible to miss on our sleeves in bold white.

The announcer's voice booms through the arena. "Looks like number twenty-three has his own fan club in the house tonight! Check out those matching jerseys. Talk about too cute to handle!"

The crowd cheers and laughs. Nora squeals in delight, her small hands waving to the sea of strangers.

Lilah, Willow, and Rina grin, clearly loving every second of this. Even Evelyn chuckles from behind the rim of her wineglass.

I remain frozen, somehow managing a small, awkward wave before my gaze drops to the ice and I find River staring up at the screen with a smile.

No, not just a smile.

He's beaming, as if he's proud we're here and wants the whole arena to see us.

The screen fades to something else, and the noise around us dips back to normal.

On legs that shake, I sink onto my seat, arms still wrapped around Nora.

Rina leans over, her hand covering mine. "Don't look so panicked," she says. "That man is smitten. Anyone with eyes can see it."

I force a shaky exhale, but the tension inside me refuses to ease.

Whatever River and I are doing is now out there for public consumption.

My gaze drifts to my ex, and the expression on his face says it all. If he was irritated before, it's nothing compared to the storm brewing there now. Instead of shrinking away from it, fire simmers in my veins.

He moved on in the blink of an eye. And the man certainly hasn't shied away from parading his new life in front of me. How dare he act like a spoiled child because I'm finally doing the same.

I lift my chin, meeting his glare head-on.

Let him be angry.

I'm done allowing him to control the narrative.

38
RIVER

I barely register the door to the locker room slamming shut behind me with a metallic clang that echoes through the large space. My blood is still running hot, adrenaline pulsing through every vein like wildfire.

My jaw throbs from where Zane slammed me into the boards. My ribs burn with every inhale. But none of that pain touches the warmth flooding me at the image of Callie and Nora wearing my jersey. It's one I'll carry for far longer than any bruise Zane leaves on my body.

He's standing in front of his locker, peeling off his gear at a maddeningly slow pace, like he's trying to wait me out.

As if he knows I'm coming.

Well, guess what?

He's right about that.

The restraint I forced myself to keep during the game is long gone.

"Do you want to tell me what the hell that was out there?" I snap, striding on my skates toward him, not bothering to mask my fury.

Zane barely blinks as he tosses his gloves into his locker. "Not sure what you're talking about, Thompson."

Bullshit.

We both know he spent the entire game fucking with me.

"Do you really think you're proving something by cheap-shotting me in front of your daughter?"

That jab lands exactly how I mean it to, and his smirk falters.

"That's right," he says, jaw tightening as he thumps his chest. "*My* daughter."

The entire locker room stills as the chatter around us fades. The guys are all watching now, sensing something volatile building, but none of them step in to stop it from spilling over.

My hands curl into fists at my sides. "I never said Nora wasn't yours. Maybe if you acted like she mattered, we wouldn't be having this conversation."

Zane's eyes flash. "What the hell is that supposed to mean? Do you think you're better than me?"

I don't blink. "That's not even a question. I know I'm better."

He swallows up the space between us. Adrenaline surges through me, pounding in my ears like a war drum.

"Come on, man," he says, his voice low and cutting. "Do you really believe she wants you? She came to you because she had nowhere else to go. You were just the first warm body she found."

My vision tunnels, the edges going dark, my jaw ticking as I fight the urge to rearrange his smug face.

"She was desperate," he continues, each word slow and deliberate, twisting in me like a blade. "And you were convenient. Nothing more."

He's hitting exactly where it'll hurt me most, in that dark corner of my mind I try to ignore. The part that wonders if he's right. I need Callie to choose me because she wants me and what we're building is real. Not as a last resort because I happened to be standing there.

Zane's lip curls. "You're not her savior. You're just a pit stop.

A quick fix until she wakes up and realizes you'll never be enough for her. Or my daughter."

I don't feel my arm move, but the crack of my fist connecting with his jaw echoes through the room like a gunshot.

Zane stumbles back, slamming into the lockers.

And still, I'm not sure it was enough.

Movement erupts around us. Zane's back on his feet in seconds, fury written in every line of his face. Before he can lunge, Steele's in his way, shoving him hard against the lockers.

"Shut your fucking mouth. That's the mother of your child you're talking about. Show some goddamn respect."

Jax and Knox lock their arms around my body from behind, dragging me back before I can make another mistake. Oliver's right there with them, muttering curses, ready to step in if it blows up again.

Laiken's got Zane pinned, one arm looped around his shoulders, holding him in place with a calm that somehow feels more dangerous than rage. "Don't even think about it, dumbass," he grumbles.

"What the hell is going on in here?" Coach booms from across the locker room.

No one responds.

A heavy silence descends over the room. It's the kind that hums with barely restrained violence.

When seconds tick by, Coach swears under his breath before storming out without waiting for an explanation.

Laiken doesn't release Zane right away. "You done?" he asks, his tone low but deadly.

Zane jerks his head in a clipped nod before shrugging out of Laiken's hold. Blood drips from his split lip as he straightens, wiping it away with the back of his hand. His furious glare never deviates from mine.

"If you were ever my friend," he says, voice quiet as it drips venom, "you'll back the fuck off."

I slowly shake my head. "That's not going to happen. Unless Callie looks me in the eye and says she doesn't want this, I'm all-in."

The words hit harder than I intend, and they're more honest than I'm ready to admit.

The locker room goes still.

Even Laiken looks rattled by the declaration.

Zane's jaw flexes as his mouth twists into a sneer. "Have it your fucking way."

He turns away, peeling off the rest of his gear before stalking toward the showers. At the edge of the tiled space, he pauses and glances back. "Just realize that she's with you because you're safe and easy. You're the kind of guy she can use to steady herself until she's ready for the real thing. And trust me, you're not it."

He steps into the steam, the sting of his words hanging in the room.

"What a prick," Knox mutters, breaking the tension.

Oliver exhales, dragging a hand through his hair. "Honestly, I'm surprised he even noticed you and Callie. He's so fucking wrapped up in himself, I doubt he sees anything that's not in the mirror."

Steele steps closer and asks, "Are you okay?"

Nope. Not even close.

Instead of admitting that, I nod and drop down onto the bench, the last of the adrenaline draining from my system. My breath continues to come hard and fast. Every muscle in my body feels strung tight, like I'm one wrong word away from spiraling out of control.

Still, there's no part of me that regrets it.

I'd do it all over again.

I'd take the punch.

The hit.

The fallout.

The whole damn mess.

Zane didn't fight for Callie and Nora when it mattered.

I sure as hell won't make the same mistake.

39

CALLIE

The final buzzer blares, and everything in me seizes. The roar of the crowd swells below me, a tidal wave of noise I can't seem to break through. I'm on my feet, but it feels like the ground just shifted beneath me, leaving me unsteady as I try to brace for what comes next.

Everyone in the suite is celebrating, humming with energy over the Railers' hard-fought win. Nora is curled against Evelyn's shoulder, sound asleep, her fingers clutching the edge of the older woman's cashmere sweater.

I should be floating.

Instead, I feel mired down, like I'm being swallowed up by quicksand.

The players skated off the ice minutes ago, and I haven't stopped replaying the final moments. The glare Zane threw me as he disappeared down the tunnel, the tightness in his shoulders, the hard set of his jaw.

That wasn't a man pissed about the game.

It was personal.

When my phone buzzes, I pull it from my pocket. The message lights up the screen and sends a cold ripple down my spine.

Zane: *We need to talk. Alone. Meet me by the back entrance.*

I stare at it for a beat, trying to decide what to do.

Evelyn glances up from where she's gently rocking Nora. "Is everything okay?"

I force a nod. "Would you mind watching Nora for a little while?"

Her eyes soften with something like understanding as she smooths a hand over my daughter's hair. "Of course, sweetheart. She's out cold." She hesitates. "Although, are you sure that's a good idea?"

"I think so. If she wakes up or there's a problem, just text me," I say, slipping from the suite before anyone else can stop me or ask questions I'm nowhere near ready to answer. My thoughts race, knotted with worry and something darker, as I take the elevator down and follow the private corridor toward the arena's back entrance.

Zane's already there waiting for me. He's hunched near the shadows, hood pulled low over his forehead, hands shoved deep in the pockets of his jacket.

As soon as I approach, he turns, and I freeze.

His lip is split and his cheekbone is already purpling beneath the swelling.

"What happened?" I ask.

His expression twists with bitterness. "The guy you decided to shack up with is what happened."

Even though his words are ugly, I lift my chin. "I saw what was going on during the game, Zane. Don't you think he had a reason to be pissed?"

It almost surprises me when he doesn't snap back. Instead, his gaze sweeps over my face, like he's searching for an answer to a question he can't bring himself to ask. Or maybe he's just looking for the version of me he once knew.

"What the fuck are you doing with River Thompson?" he

finally demands, each word clipped. "Trying to hurt me? Get my attention? Make me jealous? Is that what this is about?"

A sharp, incredulous laugh slips out before I can stop it. "Believe it or not, my private life has nothing to do with you."

He inhales hard, like he's gearing up for another attack, but then he just exhales slowly. His glare flickers, the hard lines of his jaw easing just enough for the exhaustion to show through. His gaze drops briefly to the floor before coming back to me, slower this time, less sharp.

"I'm sorry, Callie," he says. "I made a mistake. I let the fame go to my head. The girls, the parties, the money, the TV show. I thought I could have it all. And in the process, I lost what mattered most."

I freeze, stunned by the sudden change in attitude.

This isn't the Zane I know. Not the one who fed off attention like oxygen and measured his worth in headlines and camera flashes. The very same man who walked away without looking back.

This Zane's shoulders sag under some invisible weight. His eyes, once electric with ego, are dimmer now, shadowed with regret. And for maybe the first time, he looks a little bit honest.

"I've changed, Cal. I want another shot," he says, stepping closer until I can feel the heat of his body. His fingers thread through mine, and for just a second, it feels like the beginning again. "I want our family back."

My mouth falls open before I manage to shake my head. "I'm sorry... Did you say you want another chance?"

"Yeah." His tone is low but steady. "I've been thinking about us a lot lately. What we had and how we used to be. We were good together once, Callie. We could be good again."

None of this makes sense. "What about Gigi? I thought you loved her. You're planning a wedding."

"I'll end it." The words come quickly, almost desperate, as if she's nothing more than an afterthought. "If that's what it takes to get you back, I'll end it tonight. Right now. Just say the word."

Air leaves me in a rush. This isn't how I expected our conversation to go.

Not after everything that's happened.

"You don't get to say all the right things and think it'll erase the past." It takes a moment to realize I'm shaking. "It destroyed me when you walked away."

"I know. And I'm sorry. I'm not asking you to forget." He steps closer, gaze burning into mine. "I'm asking you to give me another chance. For Nora. For our family. Our daughter deserves that, doesn't she?"

A hard knot forms in my throat. "That's not fair."

He reaches out, his thumb brushing along my cheek with a practiced familiarity that makes my skin prickle. "The truth is that I never stopped loving you, Callie. I know I've got a long way to go, but think about it. Please. I'll even go to counseling. We can work on it together. Just give me another chance. Give our family another chance."

His words echo in my head, colliding with a flood of emotions impossible to untangle. I open my mouth to push back, but another thought pops into my mind.

My tongue sweeps over my lips. "Were you the one who paid off the bakery loan?"

Zane doesn't answer right away. His hand drops from my face as his jaw tightens.

"It was you, right?"

He exhales slowly. "Yeah."

My stomach twists. "Why?"

"Because I understand how much that place means to you," he says. "And I know how hard you've fought to keep it. I didn't want you drowning in stress while raising Nora. It wasn't about control or guilt, it was about doing the right thing, even after screwing up everything else."

For a moment, I'm unable to find the words. I'm caught somewhere between shock and something dangerously close to gratitude. "Why didn't you tell me?"

"I was waiting for the right time," he says with a shrug.

Everything feels so tangled. The moment, the past, the wreckage we left behind.

The man in front of me isn't the Zane I remember.

But that doesn't mean I trust him.

Not yet.

Maybe not ever.

And now, it feels like I have more questions than answers.

40
RIVER

The elevator doors glide open, and Callie steps out with Nora asleep in her arms. Her tiny Railers jersey is bunched beneath her chin, one small cheek nestled against her mom's shoulder. Her inhalations are slow and steady, lashes fanned out across flushed skin. She was out cold within five minutes of leaving the parking structure.

I follow a few steps behind, not saying a word.

Not yet, anyway.

Callie's been silent since we left the arena. It's not the I'm-exhausted kind of quiet, or the my-kid-just-fell-asleep-on-me kind. This silence feels heavier. Like she's mentally grappling with something that she's not ready to talk about.

A pit has taken up residence in my gut.

She doesn't glance back as she moves down the hall, murmuring to Nora while carrying her into the room that's becoming hers more and more every day. I hang back and watch as she goes through the familiar nighttime routine. Her hands are steady as she removes the jersey and swaps it for pajamas.

I get the feeling she's holding herself together just long

enough to get her daughter settled. And I hate that. Hate that she won't tell me what's going on in her head.

She hums quietly as she tucks the blanket under Nora's chin and smooths her hair with aching tenderness.

I don't think Callie realizes how truly strong she is.

And I don't think I can stand here much longer without saying or doing something.

For years, this penthouse felt too big, too sterile, and much too silent. All that changed when they moved in. The quiet has been replaced by the sound of Nora's footsteps and Callie's laughter echoing off the walls.

It's not just a place anymore.

It's become a home.

Our home.

When she finally closes the bedroom door behind her, I force myself to say, "Hey." I keep it soft. Careful. As if I'm tiptoeing through a minefield. "Is everything okay?"

Her gaze doesn't meet mine as she asks a question of her own instead. "What happened in the locker room?"

Thrown off, I tense. "Zane and I had a few words."

Her gaze locks on mine. "Did you hit him?"

The truth sticks to the roof of my mouth for a beat. "Yeah, I did."

She nods once, like she was expecting the answer. "Why?"

There's no way I'll repeat the shit Zane said. I won't let that poison touch her.

"I was irritated with how he acted during the game," I say instead. It's not a total lie, but it's nowhere near the truth.

Disappointment flashes across her face, and I hate myself for not knowing what she needs from me in this moment.

"Zane reached out after the game, and we met. He wants another chance," she admits quietly. "He wants Nora to have her family. He knows he screwed everything up and wants to make it right. All I have to do is say the word and he'll break everything off with Gigi."

Her voice cracks a little at the end, and that's all it takes for me to eat up the distance between us. Two strides and I'm in front of her, cupping her face in my hands, desperate to remind her of everything we're building together.

"Is that really what you want?" I ask, trying to keep the panic from flooding my system. "You want Zane back after everything he put you through?"

She shakes her head. "I don't know. I want to give Nora the best life I can."

"You don't need Zane to create a loving home for her. You've done that all on your own."

Her eyes lift to mine. They're glassy and just a bit lost. Like she's standing in front of a door she's terrified to open, afraid to find out what's waiting for her on the other side.

"I don't know what to do," she admits.

My throat tightens. "I get it."

"No," she says with a shake of her head. "You don't. You've never had someone rip you apart and then come back saying all the right things. It messes with your head, River. It makes you question what's real, what's regret, and if you're being manipulated."

More than anything, I hate that Zane still has this kind of hold over her.

With her face cradled in my hands, I rest my forehead against hers.

"Then don't choose for him," I choke out. "Don't even choose for Nora. Choose what you need and what makes you happy."

"I don't know what that is anymore."

"If you give me a chance, I'll help you figure it out," I tell her. "All you have to do is trust me."

She leans into me slowly, like someone testing the edge of something fragile but real.

It's not a yes.

But it's not a no either.

We stay like that for a long, quiet beat. Just soaking each other in and steadying ourselves in the stillness.

And for now, that's enough.

It has to be.

41
CALLIE

The room is dark and quiet, save for the gentle rhythm of River's breathing beside me. He's fast asleep, one arm flung over his face, his chest rising and falling in a slow, steady pattern that should be comforting.

And normally, it is.

Tonight, though, the stillness does nothing to soothe me.

It only makes everything louder.

My thoughts won't stop spinning.

The game.

The locker room.

Zane.

The loan.

The way River looked at me like I was his whole world, even after I told him everything.

I roll onto my side and watch him in the faint silver wash of moonlight that leaks in through the curtains. His lashes are feathered against his cheek, his jaw dark with stubble, and one hand curls loosely against his bare stomach.

Physically speaking, the man is beautiful.

But he's so much more than that.

He's kind.

Generous.

Reliable.

And he's still here after everything I confessed. He didn't walk away or tell me to pack up and get out.

Zane might've said all the right things earlier tonight, but River's been showing them from the moment he opened his door and let me and Nora in.

Every breakfast he made.

Every book he read at bedtime.

Every small moment he didn't have to offer but gave anyway.

He's loved Nora without hesitation, like it's woven into his DNA.

And she's fallen for him, completely and without question.

If I'm being honest, so have I.

The ache inside me expands so quickly, it nearly swallows me whole.

The truth is terrifying.

My heart hammers as I push upright in bed, the only sound the slow, steady rhythm of River's breathing beside me.

With trembling fingers, I reach for the hem of my tank and drag it over my head. The thin cotton slides across my skin and then pools beside the bed. My underwear follows, slipping down my legs in a whisper of fabric before I let it fall to the floor.

I shift the covers before straddling him, my knees bracing on either side of his hips. The sheets rustle around us, the quiet movement amplified by the hush of the room. River stirs beneath me, a low murmur falling from his lips. His brow furrows and then relaxes, his body stretching instinctively toward mine.

His eyes flutter open. "Callie?"

I lean down and kiss him, savoring every second as his arms

circle my waist and draw me closer. A groan vibrates through him as our mouths move together.

His hands skim over my bare skin, awakening every nerve in their path.

"What's wrong?" he asks, voice hoarse as his lips brush mine.

I press my forehead to his. "Nothing. I just need you."

His grip on my hips tightens, and the feel of him does the impossible and grounds me in this moment. "You have me."

His words are gentle and fierce all at once. A life preserver in the dark I can cling to.

I exhale as my fingers curl around the waistband of his boxer briefs. Slowly, I ease them down over the firm lines of his hips, past the powerful cut of his thighs, until he kicks them off.

I shift, letting my body glide against the thick ridge of his cock. The friction is instant, and it sends a thousand shivers racing across my skin.

My spine arches as every nerve ending sparks to life, drawn to the heat of him.

I don't just want this man.

I *need* him. Every inch, every part of him pressing into me until there's nothing left between us.

Nothing in my life has ever felt this right.

Or this real.

Like something I never truly believed I could have but stumbled into when I needed it most.

"Callie," he groans. "That feels so damn good. *You* feel so damn good."

His fingers flex against my hips, digging in just enough to keep the control from slipping through his hands.

Every breath he holds is a silent promise that he'll never rush me. That this will happen on my terms.

And that only makes me want him more.

I move slowly, teasing him, rocking my hips until I'm soaked and aching, until every part of me throbs with the need to be filled.

To be his.

His jaw clenches, the muscles in his arms trembling with the effort not to rush ahead, but still, his gaze never leaves mine.

He waits patiently.

He's steady and unshakable.

Instead of demanding, he offers every part of himself.

And when I can't take another second of space between us, I shift and guide him to my entrance. The thick head of his cock presses against me.

It's hard, hot, and absolutely perfect.

I lower myself onto him, inch by inch, until he's buried deep inside me and we're fully connected.

I release a moan and settle against him, bracing my hands on his chest. He cradles my hips, anchoring me as we move together. And in this quiet hour, wrapped in shadows and everything that's still unspoken between us, there's no confusion.

No fear.

No past.

Just this.

Just *us*.

42
RIVER

The sheets are cool to the touch when I reach for her. My hand drags over the place where she should be, searching for her warmth and curves.

At this point, it's instinct.

Much like breathing.

But she's not there.

I sit up quickly, my chest heaving. My heart slams against my ribs as last night rushes back in vivid flashes.

The way Callie climbed on top of me before we started moving as one.

Almost like I was her choice, and it meant something.

And maybe it did.

I glance around at the emptiness that surrounds me.

Then again, maybe it didn't.

My bare feet hit the floor as I shove a hand through hair that's still mussed from her fingers tugging at it last night. My body aches in all the best ways, even though my insides feel as if they've been carved out.

After throwing on a pair of flannel pants, I rush across the hall to Nora's room. A month ago, it was a barely used guest room, now it belongs to a two-year-old with golden curls and a smile that melts everything inside me.

My lungs constrict as I quickly scan the space.

Nora's gone.

Just like I suspected she would be. But everything else is still here. The baby monitor on the dresser. Nora's fuzzy blanket folded at the foot of the bed. The Railers teddy bear I brought home last week is propped against the pillows. And there's a pair of tiny sneakers by the closet door.

All of her things are still here.

Relief and confusion roil within me until it's impossible to ignore.

She didn't take anything.

Which means that she didn't leave me.

It's always possible that she just stepped out with the need for air.

Space and time to think.

Although, try telling that to the part of me that's already panicking that I've lost her.

I head to the kitchen, hoping to find a note. Something that will stop the mental spiral.

But there's nothing.

Why didn't she wake me before taking off this morning?

No matter how hard I try to reason it out or how many scenarios I run through, my gut keeps dragging me back to the same conclusion.

She ran back to Zane.

The thought lodges like a splinter that's impossible to dig out.

I pour a glass of water, more out of habit than thirst. It sits untouched on the counter, my hand wrapped too tight around the glass to lift it. My fingers are shaking. My whole body feels like it's vibrating just beneath the surface.

Every step I take echoes too loudly in the silence she left

behind. The space feels wrong. Off. Too quiet, too still. Almost like the air itself has gone stale without her in it.

Every room I pass feels empty. Like she somehow managed to take the warmth with her.

Did I push too hard?

Did I make her feel cornered?

What if I turned this into a choice when all she needed was time to figure out what she wanted?

What if last night was her way of saying goodbye?

My fingers curl around the edge of the counter, gripping it so tight my knuckles turn bone white.

I've never wanted something this badly.

Not the game.

Not a contract.

Not the numbers on the back of my jersey or the team logo stitched across the front.

I want Callie.

And Nora.

I want the quiet mornings, the messy evenings, the laughter from the next room. I want the routine of them in my space like they were always meant to be there.

For the first time since she walked into my life, I wonder if I let myself believe in something I was never meant to keep.

The sharp ding of the elevator breaks the stillness, and my heart kicks hard in my chest. I spin toward the door as hope surges within me.

Callie.

She came back.

She didn't leave me.

She—

The doors slide open and Willow steps out first, her expression shifting the second she sees me. Maverick follows behind her with the kids in tow.

The hope rising within shatters, the air rushing out of me like a punch to the gut.

Willow's gaze scans my face. "What happened?"

I swallow hard, the knot in my throat thick and unforgiving. "She's gone."

Maverick frowns. "You know, this whole twin telepathy thing you two have going on is creepy as fuck."

The kids race into the penthouse, shouting Nora's name as they search for her.

Not bothering to respond to her husband, Willow steps close and wraps her arm around my waist before resting her head on my shoulder. "It'll be okay, River. I know it will."

I nod, even though I don't believe it. "Thanks."

More than ever, I need my sister to be right.

43

CALLIE

After dropping Nora off at my parents' house, I head straight to Lakeshore Sweets.

This place is the one corner of my life I built entirely on my own. The ovens. The recipes. The early mornings and long days. There's a rhythm to baking that usually quiets the noise in my head.

Flour. Sugar. Butter.

Stir. Scoop. Bake.

It's simple, soothing, and predictable.

But not today.

No matter how many muffins I mix or croissants I roll out, my thoughts won't stay put. They keep drifting back to last night like a song stuck on repeat.

To River's face as he circled the ice.

To Zane watching me from across the arena.

To the moment River's mouth met mine in the dark.

As much as I try to shake them off and focus on the dough beneath my hands, the memories won't stay silent.

They're loud and tangled.

And they're taking up way too much space in a mind that usually finds peace in precision.

Two hours later, the front door swings open with a gust of cold air that sends a shiver down my spine. Sloane breezes in, bundled up in an olive-green utility jacket over her sweatshirt, with cheeks that are flushed from the wind.

She stops short the moment she sees me behind the counter, and her eyes narrow. "Uh-oh. Is it really so bad that you're stress baking?"

I glance up from the tray of cinnamon rolls I'm icing, and force a tight smile. "This isn't stress baking."

She drops her purse on the counter with a thud. "Please. I've been around long enough to know what you look like when you're mentally spiraling."

"I do run a bakery," I remind her, gesturing to the register. "Some of this is kind of required. We already have orders to fill."

She arches a brow. "Callie. It's Wednesday. All the pre-orders are filled. Unless someone booked a party I don't know about, no one needs twelve trays of cinnamon rolls before ten a.m."

She glances around, eyeing the croissants cooling on the racks and the double batch of muffins on the prep table.

"From the looks of it, you've been here a while."

"Since five," I admit.

"That tells me everything I need to know." She's already shrugging out of her coat and pushing through the swinging kitchen door. "I'm texting the girls."

"Sloane," I groan. "That's not—"

She waves me off, pulling out her phone like someone summoning backup to a crime scene. Her fingers fly across the screen.

Sloane: *SOS at the bakery.*

Lilah: *OMG. What's going on? I'm not even out of bed yet.*

Rina: *I was headed to the arena, but I'll swing by the bakery instead. Make sure there's coffee. And a cinnamon hustler. Extra dirty.*

Sloane: *Girl... we all know how you like it dirty.*

Rina: 😏

Lilah: *It is way too early for this.*

I roll my eyes, but I can't stop a small smile from breaking through. The kind that sneaks in, even when everything inside me feels twisted and uncertain.

No matter how bad things feel, these women show up every single time.

And somehow, knowing they're on their way makes everything feel a little more manageable.

"I haven't even told you anything," I say.

"You didn't have to," Sloane replies, pulling mugs from the cabinet. "We've indulged in enough late-night wine and post-breakup debriefs for me to recognize all the classic signs."

She hands me a mug of fresh coffee before giving me a wink. "Drink that. We'll talk when the whole crew gets here."

Forty minutes later, the bakery is quiet again, the morning rush leaving behind an empty pastry case with a few stray crumbs. I join the girls at the table near the window, where Lilah and Rina are already seated with a platter of pastries between them.

Lilah peels apart a croissant, her eyes locked on me. "Okay. Spill."

I slide into the empty seat and wrap my hands around my mug. The warmth seeps into my fingers, but it doesn't quite make it to my chest.

All three watch me without judgment. Just patient, steady concern. It's more appreciated than any of them realize.

I let out a slow exhale. "It's Zane."

With a groan, Rina rolls her eyes. "Of course it is."

Sloane leans back in her chair as she crosses her arms loosely in front of her. "What happened?"

"The guy was a real dick on the ice to River," Rina mutters. "I was *this* close to marching down there and beating him with his own stick."

"I would've actually paid money to see that," Lilah says with a snort.

Rina raises a brow. "Now you tell me."

Lifting her mug, Lilah's gaze slides to mine. "Sorry. Got distracted by the mental image. Please continue."

The corner of my mouth twitches. Even now, they manage to make me smile. But it fades as quickly as it came.

I set my mug down and say what I've been holding in all morning. "After the game last night, Zane told me that he wants to get back together. He wants us to be a family again for Nora's sake. That he's changed."

The silence that follows is instant and heavy.

None of them speak at first, and I don't blame them.

"He also paid off the bakery loan," I add. "All of it. Lakeshore Sweets belongs to me now. Free and clear."

Rina is the first to recover as she sits up straighter. "That's... unexpected." Her expression twists into a frown. "And what about Gigi? Wasn't she supposed to be the love of his reality TV life?" There's a pause. "Hold up." She unlocks her phone and starts typing. "I think Railers Rumors posted pics of them at a club after the game."

I blink. "Are you sure it was taken last night? Maybe they're old photos."

She hands me the phone, and the second my eyes land on the first image, my stomach drops. His lip is split and he's wearing the same clothes he had on after the game.

And there's at least half a dozen of them. In every single one, Zane and Gigi are tangled up in each other, grinding against one another, laughing, kissing like nothing in the world exists but the camera and the attention it brings.

More confusion crashes over me as I stare at the photos.

Why would he go out of his way to lie to me?

I don't understand any of this.

Lilah reaches across the table to squeeze my hand. "I'm sorry, Callie. I know he said all the right things, but I just don't think he's being genuine."

"No," I murmur. "It certainly doesn't seem like it."

With a tilt of her head, Sloane asks quietly, "Are you one hundred percent sure he's the one who paid off the loan?"

My head snaps up. "He told me he did when I asked about it."

Rina and Sloane exchange a quiet, knowing look. It's enough to send a ripple of unease through me.

"Callie," Rina says gently, "I'd verify that information before you take his word for it."

I take a sip of coffee to buy myself a moment, but instead of offering comfort, it scorches all the way down.

"Maybe what I need to do is talk to Zane," I say, setting the mug down.

"I think that's a good idea," Lilah agrees.

"You've been asking him to step up for years," Sloane adds. "And now, only after you've started something with another man, he suddenly decides to act?"

"Honestly," Rina cuts in, "I'm not convinced he did anything except muddy the waters because he doesn't like seeing you move on. It has nothing to do with Nora and everything to do with control."

Lilah tears off another piece of croissant. "What does River think about all this?"

My throat tightens. "River's been everything Zane never was. He's steady and kind. Nora adores him. And I..." My words trail off. "I think I'm falling in love with him."

Lilah rubs circles on my back. "Then let yourself fall."

"It's not that simple," I admit.

"Sure it is," Rina says, her tone blunt but not unkind. "Zane talks a good game. River lives it. One's a performance. The other's real."

"You don't need someone who *says* he's changed," Sloane adds. "You need someone who *shows* you every single day without asking for credit."

I stare into my coffee as their words settle within me, heavier than I expected. "It's hard to believe Zane would lie about paying off my loan. That he'd take credit for something another man did."

Even as the words leave my mouth, doubt creeps in. If there's one thing Zane's always been good at, it's bending reality to fit his narrative.

"That's exactly what you need to find out," Lilah says gently. "You deserve the truth so you can make a decision based on facts, not assumptions."

The door opens, and my head snaps up, a spark of hope flaring before I can stop it. But it's just the delivery guy, balancing a crate of milk and cream in his arms.

The breath I've been holding slips out in a shaky exhale, and I press a hand to my chest, as if it will calm the pounding underneath.

It doesn't.

I go through the motions of signing the receipt, offering a polite smile, and thanking him, but my thoughts are all over the place. They're still caught on the phone call from the bank. On the weight of the loan hanging over my head for years. And the quiet, steady man who has shown up for me in ways I never asked for but desperately needed.

Deep down, in a place that realized the truth long before logic caught up, I already know who paid off the debt.

It wasn't Zane.

It was River.

It's *always* been River.

The man who let me and my daughter move into his home

without hesitation. Who gave me his bed, his trust, and his protection without needing anything in return.

The man who didn't need to say the right things because his actions have always spoken louder than his words.

He's been there.

Every single time.

Without questions or conditions.

And suddenly, the weight of the lies Zane fed me feels suffocating.

"Sloane," I say quietly, setting my coffee down on the table. "Would you mind holding down the bakery for a bit? I need to take care of something."

Her eyes narrow, already sensing the direction this is going. "Where are you headed?"

"Zane's place," I say as I rise to my feet and untie my apron. "I think it's time we had an honest conversation."

Sloane nods. "Of course."

"I'll stay and help too," Lilah says, rising and gathering empty mugs. "Go get your answers."

"Same," Rina chimes in, already pulling her long dark hair into a high ponytail. "I'm in full-on avoidance mode today anyway."

"Oh?" Lilah smirks. "Let me guess... Oliver finally figured out what being auctioned off actually means?"

A slow grin tugs at the corner of Rina's mouth. "Bingo. The look on his face was priceless. I haven't laughed that hard in weeks."

A reluctant smile lifts my lips as I shake my head. "You're so bad."

"Guilty as charged," Rina says with zero remorse. "He should try to remember that more often."

"Thank you," I say, glancing at each of them in turn. Their support isn't flashy, but it's solid and steady.

Much like River.

As I make my way to the door, Rina calls out, "Let us know if you need backup. I'm only half joking."

"I'll keep that in mind," I toss over my shoulder as relief threads through me.

For the first time all day, I feel a little more grounded and a little less like I'm unraveling at the seams.

44
CALLIE

Once I'm in the car, I pull up the address for Zane's new high-rise he moved into not long after filming started for his reality show with Gigi.

I've never been there before.

When he visits with Nora, it's always at my place. Occasionally, he'll take her to the park or out for ice cream, but those visits are short-lived. He panics if she cries, gets flustered when she refuses to eat, and has absolutely no idea what to do when she's overtired or clingy.

It doesn't escape me that River is the exact opposite. He stepped into our lives with quiet confidence, responding to Nora's needs as if he's been doing it for years.

As if he enjoys it.

As if he always saw us as a package deal and never questioned if it was too much.

A lump forms in my throat as I pull out of the lot behind the bakery and merge into the slow crawl of mid-morning traffic.

It's hard not to compare the two men.

Zane may be Nora's biological father, but River's been showing up for her in all the ways that matter.

Right now, what I need more than anything is clarity.

And the truth.

Twenty minutes later, I pull up in front of a sleek glass-and-steel high-rise a few blocks off Lakeshore Drive. I maneuver into a metered space and then sit for a moment, staring up at the modern facade. Gold-lettered signage glints in the sunlight, and two valets stand at attention in tailored coats, ready to open doors with gloved hands.

Even from here, it's obvious this place is far beyond anything I could afford on my own. I grab my purse and step out of the SUV, nerves stretching taut with every step toward the entrance.

A doorman in a dark suit gives me a quick nod as I pass, his attention fixed on the cluster of photographers loitering just outside the revolving doors.

"Miss! Are you here for Gigi?"

"Is the wedding still on?"

"Can you confirm the pregnancy rumors?"

Their questions are fired off in rapid succession without time for a response.

I duck my head and push through the glass doors, the noise trailing behind me like static I can't quite shake.

Inside, the lobby is stunning. Marble floors gleam beneath my shoes, polished to the point where they reflect every light and shadow. Navy velvet chairs are arranged in perfect symmetry around low, brass-trimmed tables stacked with glossy magazines I doubt anyone actually reads. Above it all, a massive chandelier drips from the ceiling like glass rain, refracting light in a thousand directions.

It's the kind of space that feels curated. As I move across the lobby, I pass two staff members standing behind the concierge desk.

One mutters, "These reality TV people are a nightmare. Why did the board approve their application?"

"Don't get me started," the other replies. "There's a camera crew coming again this afternoon. Third time this week."

Their voices trail off as I keep walking.

I half-expect to be stopped, questioned, or redirected. But one of the photographers from outside manages to slip in behind another guest, and security rushes to deal with him.

The moment buys me enough time to step into the elevator and press the button for the fifteenth floor. My fingers tremble as they leave the panel, and the doors close with a barely audible *whoosh*. The car begins its smooth, soundless ascent.

In the mirrored walls, my reflection stares back at me with shoulders that are squared, eyes that are sharp, and a mouth set in a firm line. Determination wars with dread on my face, and I'm not entirely sure which one is winning.

Once the elevator glides to a stop, the doors open to a hallway wrapped in quiet luxury. Plush carpeting muffles my footsteps as dark-paneled walls glow under muted, recessed lights. Everything about this place radiates exclusivity and power.

It's a far cry from the modest apartment Zane used to rent.

This isn't merely a different address, it's a different world.

My pulse stutters the moment his unit number comes into view, and I slow to a halt in front of the door. My knuckles hover in the air before I force myself to rap them against the wood.

Silence.

I wait ten long seconds and then knock again. It's louder this time, the sound sharper than I intend.

Still nothing.

Unease twists low in my stomach, warning that maybe this was a mistake. But I didn't drag myself all the way here just to turn around. Not when I need answers and there's so much at stake.

I shift my weight, teetering on the edge of retreat, when the lock clicks and the door swings open.

Gigi fills the doorway, framed by chic, modern lines and a warm glow that spills from inside. A rose-colored silk robe hangs precariously off one shoulder, exposing golden skin and a fair amount of cleavage.

She looks me over with a flat, disinterested gaze. "So, where's the food?"

I blink, momentarily thrown off by the question. "Sorry. What?"

"The takeout," she snaps. "Aren't you from Gold Coast Table?"

"No." I straighten, trying to reclaim some sense of control over the situation. "I'm not here with food. I'm Callie. Nora's mother. We met at the Railers event last month."

She squints, her perfectly glossed lips twisting slightly, as if she's trying to place my face. There's absolutely no flicker of recognition in her expression.

"Oh. Right," she finally mutters.

I can't help but wonder if she remembers Zane even has a child.

The robe slips again, this time leaving little doubt if she's wearing anything underneath.

I quickly avert my gaze. "Is Zane here? Can I talk to him?"

Without answering, she turns her head and yells, "Zane! Your baby mama's here!"

The words land like a slap. Before I can respond, she's already walking away, her bare feet silent on the polished floors, leaving me standing awkwardly at the threshold.

I hesitate for only a moment before stepping inside.

The apartment is massive and pristine. Floor-to-ceiling windows overlook the lake in the distance as sunlight glints off the water. The kitchen gleams, untouched and showroom ready. Everything is minimalist and expensive looking, from the modern light fixtures to the oversized sectional sofa that looks like it's never been sat on.

This place isn't just nice. It's high-end. Custom and luxurious.

It's nothing like the one Zane used to live in, or the modest two-bedroom townhouse Nora and I called home. The contrast is stark.

While I've been clipping coupons and skipping meals to stretch our budget, he's been living like a king.

A sharp pang twists in my stomach.

Even though I shouldn't be shocked, I am.

Where was all this money when I needed help buying formula or paying the rent?

I take a moment to remind myself why I'm here.

The loan.

And the truth.

Zane appears in the hallway, tugging at the waistband of a pair of skintight jeans, the top button undone. His chest is bare, revealing the bruises and scrapes from last night's game.

He drags a hand through his tousled hair, eyes widening slightly when he sees me standing in the entryway.

"Hey, Callie," he says. "What are you doing here?"

"I needed to talk to you." My weight shifts uneasily from one foot to the other.

His brow arches. "About what?"

My thoughts tangle in my head, too many crashing into each other to make sense of just one. I stare at him, stunned by how different this moment feels from the one we had last night.

I thought he'd know exactly why I was here.

That he'd be expecting an answer.

Instead, I'm standing in front of a half-naked man, fresh from someone else's bed, after a woman in a silk robe called me his *baby mama* and then disappeared without a second glance.

Even though the truth is obvious, I still have to ask. "Last night… did you mean any of it?"

When he blinks and says nothing, my voice turns sharp. "What you said about wanting to be a family again. Was any of it real?"

His silence is deafening.

"I'm such an idiot," I murmur, more to myself than to him.

"Callie—"

I raise a hand to silence whatever pathetic excuse he's about to offer. "Just answer one more question and then I'll get out of your way."

He hesitates. "Okay. What?"

"Did you pay off the bank loan for the bakery?"

His lips part like he's about to lie, but a flicker of guilt, too quick to catch fully and too familiar to miss, flashes across his face. He glances over his shoulder, like maybe he's afraid of being overheard before stepping closer.

"No."

The word lands like a slap. "Then why would you tell me that you did?"

He shrugs, shifting on his feet. "I thought…"

When his voice trails off, something inside me snaps. "What? What did you think, Zane?"

"That it was probably River," he mutters. "And I don't like the thought of you two together. He shouldn't be going after something that's mine."

I reel back a step, floored by the sheer arrogance. "I'm not yours. I've never been yours. You don't get to claim me like property."

"You don't get it. I—"

"No, you're the one who doesn't get it," I cut in, temper rising. "You don't care about me or what's best for our daughter. You care about control and spinning your life for some damn show. How dare you try and destroy someone else stepping up when you couldn't be bothered."

His tongue darts out to lick his lips as he bounces between defensive and pathetic. "He's breaking bro code."

I let out a short, humorless laugh. "That might be the most ridiculous thing I've ever heard. River has been kind, loving, and steady to both me and Nora. And you tried to blow that up because you couldn't stand the idea of someone else doing what you should've done all along."

"That's not true—"

"It is," I snap. "You don't get to rewrite history. And you don't get to lie to me and take credit for something he did."

My body shakes, but I don't let myself cry.

Not here in front of him.

"You know what? I actually feel sorry for you." My tone gentles. Not with sympathy, but with pity. "You're missing out on your daughter's life. The real moments. All the ones that matter. Someday you'll realize that. I just hope it won't be too late to undo the damage you've inflicted."

Instead of giving him a chance to respond, I turn on my heel and head for the elevator. Even when he calls out my name, I don't look back.

Because the man who actually loves me already gave me the truth without ever having to say a word.

45
RIVER

I t feels like I've been pacing the penthouse for hours. Back and forth. Again and again. Like a man on the edge of splintering apart, because that's exactly where I am.

Outside the floor-to-ceiling windows, the city blazes in sharp daylight. Sunlight bounces off glass towers, but I barely register the scenery. The brilliance blurs together, smearing across the glass like a watercolor left out in the rain. I've stopped seeing the view. Stopped feeling anything but the restless churn inside me.

My phone is clenched in one hand, screen still lit with the glow of the location-sharing app. I hate that I've been staring at it all day like some obsessed asshole. I hate how badly I've needed the reassurance that she's safe. More than that, I hate that I've reduced myself to watching a blinking dot to know if she's coming back to me.

This morning, she was at the bakery.

For a few hours, my heartrate slowed and my brain quieted. I told myself she was where she needed to be. Back in the rhythm of her own life. Surrounded by the women who always have her back.

But then the dot moved.

To Zane's address.

And just like that, my world tilted on its axis. My hand was already on my keys, my body halfway to the door before my brain caught up. The urge to storm over there and rip her away from him nearly swallowed me whole.

Zane fucking Holloway doesn't deserve her.

Or Nora.

He never did and he never will.

As much as every instinct in me screams to fight for her, this isn't a battle I can win with brute force.

Not with Callie.

She's not some problem I can fix or a prize to be claimed. She's a woman who's had to be strong for too damn long. Who's been let down, disappointed, and dismissed more times than I probably even know.

And if there's one thing I've learned since she and Nora came into my life, it's that the only way this works is if she chooses me on her own.

Not because I begged or showed up with a list of reasons why she should.

But because she *feels* it and she wants this as much as I do.

So I wait.

Even if it kills me.

Which it just might.

I've replayed last night over again on an endless, painful loop. The way she climbed on top of me like she needed me just as badly as I've always needed her. The way her eyes stayed locked on mine, filled with everything we haven't said out loud.

And then she was gone.

No note or explanation.

Just a hollow space where her warmth had been.

The memory of her in my bed still clings to me like smoke. The feel of her skin, the way she moaned my name, the trust in every sigh and arch of her body.

It all felt so damn real.

Although maybe not real enough.

I drag a hand through my hair and turn back toward the window, trying to breathe through the ache inside me, when I hear the arrival of the elevator. The sound slices through the silence like a gunshot, freezing me in place.

A second later, the doors glide open and Callie steps out. Her hair is pulled into a loose ponytail, and her cheeks are pink from the cold.

She looks tired.

Beautiful.

So achingly familiar, it knocks the air from me.

I want to wrap my arms around her and never let go.

Instead, I remain rooted in place. If this is the moment she's come to say goodbye, I'll need every shred of control I have left just to stand here and take it.

She meets my eyes from across the distance. There's hesitation in hers. But also something steadier. A quiet kind of resolve I haven't seen before.

"Where's Nora?" I ask.

"With my parents. I needed to talk to you. Alone."

My pulse stutters.

Well, fuck.

That can't be good.

The need to be closer wins out, and I take a cautious step in her direction. "Are you okay?"

She nods just once. "I am now."

Those three words nearly bring me to my knees.

But still, I don't know where this is going. I don't know if she's here to stay or to say goodbye. And that uncertainty guts me.

"Why didn't you tell me?"

Adrenaline rushes through my veins. I don't need her to explain the question. I already know what she means.

I take another step. "I never wanted you to feel like you owed me anything. If you chose me, it needed to be because your heart wouldn't let you do anything else and the world feels quieter when we're together. Because being with me feels as natural as breathing."

Unable to help myself, I close the remaining distance between us. "I wanted it to be because you love me as much as I love you," I say quietly.

And now I'm standing right in front of her.

When I look into her eyes, I see it.

Everything I've been hoping for.

Everything I've been afraid to believe in.

"I do love you," she confesses.

I blink, almost afraid I imagined it. "You do?"

Her lips curve. "Yes. I love you, River."

She says it like it's the simplest truth in the world.

And maybe it is.

Maybe it always has been.

Emotion grips my throat. "Say it again, baby."

She steps closer, pressing her palms to my chest. "I love you."

I close my eyes as her words wash over me, splitting me open in ways I never knew were possible.

I drop my forehead to hers. "Thank fuck, Callie."

Her fingers curl into my shirt. "I was so scared," she admits. "Not of you. Never of you. But of letting someone all the way in and then losing them. Of trusting the wrong person again."

"That's never going to happen with me."

"I realize that now." She draws in a breath and leans back just enough to look up at me with eyes that shine. "You were always there. Every single time. When I needed help, when I needed quiet, when I didn't even know what I needed—you showed up. You were already there."

"Always," I rasp. "And I'd do it again. A thousand times over."

She smiles through the tears. "Even when I didn't deserve it."

"Don't." I cup her jaw, brushing my thumb along her skin. "Don't ever say that again. You deserve every fucking thing this world has to offer."

Her throat works on a swallow. "Zane said all the right things, but he's never shown up. Not for Nora or for me. You have. Every moment and in every way that matters."

"I will never stop showing up for you," I promise. "I don't care how hard it gets. I'm in this. All the way."

When she launches herself at me, I catch her without hesitation. She buries her face against my neck, her body trembling in my arms, as if the weight of everything she's let go has finally caught up to her. My hands smooth over her back, wanting to offer comfort.

"I wanted to tell you this morning," she admits. "But I needed time to think. And I needed to be sure."

I pull back just enough to look at her, brushing my fingers along her cheek. "And are you?"

Her nod is firm. "I'm done questioning what we have. And I'm done letting fear speak louder than love."

I press a kiss against her forehead. "Good. Just know I'm not going anywhere." I can't help but stare at the woman who's changed everything for me. My entire world. "Not ever."

46
CALLIE

River laces our fingers together as we step into the private elevator, and I lean into his side, pressing my cheek against his shoulder. My heart is still pounding from everything we said earlier and the truths we finally spoke aloud, but it's no longer from fear or uncertainty.

It's anticipation.

Every step, every floor we ascend, feels like moving closer to something new. Something that's been building between us for years.

When the doors slide open on the rooftop level, my breath catches at the sight that greets me from the other side. Fairy lights twinkle around the space, strung between the trees that circle a rectangular pool. The glow they cast is soft and golden, painting everything in an amber light that feels unreal. Lush greenery surrounds the space. Tall planters and potted palms giving the illusion of a secret garden perched high above the city skyline. A few stone sculptures peek out from the foliage. It's as if the entire rooftop was designed to be more of a dream.

As soon as I take a step, River bends and lifts me into his arms without effort. His hold is strong and steady, as if I'm something precious he'll never let go of.

"Oh my God," I gasp, taking it all in.

"This is all for you," he murmurs, his lips brushing the crown of my head. "For us. No noise, no pressure. Just you and me."

Something inside me falters and races all at once as he carries me toward the water. Loungers are strategically placed around it with space heaters to ward off the chill of the night. He brushes a kiss against my lips before gently setting me down.

His hands find the hem of my sweater, his fingers hovering there for just a beat. Even though he doesn't ask, I give him a nod.

That's all the permission he needs before slowly lifting the fabric. His fingertips skim over my skin as the sweater slips from my body. His touch leaves a trail of heat behind, and it awakens something deep inside me.

Leaning in, he kisses my shoulder, my collarbone, and the gentle curve of my breast through my bra. Every inch he bares, he worships with his lips.

"You are so damn beautiful," he mutters against my skin, like it's a truth he needs me to believe.

I tremble under the weight of his words, his hands, the way his eyes stay focused on me. He makes me feel as if I'm the center of his entire world. As if it's always been that way and only now am I catching up.

He kneels in front of me, sliding my leggings down inch by slow inch before pressing his lips to my hipbone. And then lower, to the inside of my thigh. I shiver as his warm breath grazes my sensitive skin.

"I'm nervous," I confess. "What if someone else wants to use the pool?"

River looks up at me with a smile. "No one's going to come up here, baby." He runs his palms down the backs of my calves and up again with reassuring strokes. "This oasis? It belongs to me. Private access only. No one can come up here without me knowing. It's just for us."

His hands settle on my hips, his thumbs stroking gently. "There are heat lamps around the edges, and the pool is a balmy eighty-five degrees year-round. I had all the lights put in last summer. I've never brought anyone else up here." His gaze holds mine. "I made it with you in mind.

Tension seeps from my muscles as gratitude fills me.

With his eyes locked on mine, he hooks his fingers in the band of my panties. "Okay?"

I nod, suspended in a space between disbelief and desire. "Okay."

He kisses me again.

This time lower.

A whimper slips out as he lifts me effortlessly into his arms and carries me to one of the plush loungers near the pool. As soon as he lays me down, the warm air wraps around me, but it's his mouth that sends a shiver dancing across my skin.

He kisses along the center of my body, pausing at the curve of my belly. His lips linger there, and when he speaks, it's a low vow that brands me from the inside out.

"Someday soon," he murmurs, "you'll grow round with my baby. I want to watch your body change in the most miraculous way and know it was us. I want to give Nora a sibling, and to build a life together. I've never wanted that with anyone else, Callie. Only you."

It's everything I've always wanted to hear. Before I can tell him that I want it too, he moves lower, settling between my thighs.

"River..." My hands slide into his hair, anchoring him to me, as his mouth finds my center.

He touches me as if he's never wanted anything more, and tastes me like a man starving. He loves me with his tongue. Each flick and stroke is a silent declaration. His hands hold me as if this moment matters more than anything else in the world.

And what I realize is that it does.

He's memorizing me, and I'm giving him every piece of myself without fear or uncertainty.

My hips rise of their own accord, chasing that pressure, that rhythm, as he groans against me. Every sound he makes is fueled by hungry devotion. It doesn't take long until I'm falling apart in a flood of sensation. The cry that escapes me echoes into the night sky. It rings off the steel and stars before getting carried away by the autumn breeze.

Barely am I able to catch my breath as River rises and strips off his clothing piece by piece until he's standing in front of me gloriously naked. The fairy lights glow against the hard lines of his chest, the ink on his skin, and the need burning in his eyes.

He's absolutely gorgeous.

Strong.

And most importantly, he's mine.

This man is *mine.*

I sit up slowly and drink in his masculine beauty before sliding to my knees. Not once do I break eye contact as I wrap my hand around him and guide his thick erection to my mouth.

The sound that rips from him is filled with pent-up desire and longing.

"Jesus, Callie," he groans, fingers threading through my hair. The way he holds me doesn't feel forceful, it's almost as if he needs to ground himself in this moment.

I take my time, worshiping him with the same level of attention he did to me. Every flick of my tongue, every pass of my lips tells him what I haven't stopped feeling since the moment his mouth touched mine.

All the emotions I was too afraid to admit even to myself.

I love you.

I love you.

I love you.

His muscles tense beneath my hands, his breath turning ragged as I push him closer to the edge. His other hand trembles against my jaw, and when he finally comes, it's with my name a hoarse cry on his lips.

River stares at me like I'm everything.

And when I rise, his mouth settles on mine in a deep kiss that consumes me. One that feels like a thank-you and a promise all rolled into one before he scoops me into his arms and carries me to the pool. The second my skin hits the water, a shiver racks my body. It's not from the temperature but from the weight of his gaze. The heat in his eyes makes me feel exposed even though I'm submerged.

He settles me on his lap in the center of the pool, his hands bracketing my hips as he slowly sinks inside me. Needing to be even closer, I wrap my arms around his shoulders and hold on tight. I just want to singe everything about this moment into my memory. The weight of his body, the depth of his love, the way we move together like we were always meant to be this.

Months ago, I couldn't have imagined a future with River.

Now I can't imagine one without him.

His mouth finds my neck, my jaw, the place just beneath my ear that makes me tremble. "I love you," he confesses. "I've loved you for so long."

"I love you too."

His arms tighten around me as we keep moving. Surrounded by the water, fairy lights, and stars, this sliver of time feels almost magical.

We make love like two people who've finally found what they never thought they'd have. Every touch is sure, every kiss is steady, because he's always known I was his, and I'm finally ready to admit he's mine. And when he pulls me close afterward, it doesn't feel like an ending. It feels like the beginning of everything.

47
RIVER

The flood of people hasn't slowed since the first bottle of champagne popped hours ago. Every time I take a sip of beer, someone else shows up, arms loaded with housewarming gifts.

"I gotta say, domestication looks good on you, Thompson." Laiken grins, clapping a hand on my shoulder. "The place looks awfully cozy for a guy who used to be more of a minimalist."

With a smirk, my gaze slowly sweeps across the room.

It's not just my penthouse anymore.

It's ours.

The three of us.

A neroli and white jasmine candle glows on the counter. Nora's sparkly sneakers sit askew on the mat, one tipped sideways like she darted out of them mid-step. And Callie's favorite cookbook is open beside a mixing bowl.

The air smells like sugar and citrus and something that feels distinctly like home.

"I like it better this way," I tell him, meaning every word.

The place is packed wall-to-wall with people I've fought beside, bled beside, and trusted with everything short of my heart, because that's always belonged to the woman who's chatting on the other side of the room.

Steele's in the kitchen, locked in a heated debate with Knox over whose bourbon reigns supreme. They're each gripping a bottle like it's a trophy, neither willing to back down.

On the sectional, Maverick and Willow are curled up together, glasses of red wine in hand, wearing the kind of expressions that make it obvious they're in a world of their own making. His arm rests comfortably around her shoulders, his smile easy and content, like he knows exactly how lucky he is.

I couldn't have picked a better man for my sister. She deserves someone who sees her quiet strength and appreciates her softness. They're the perfect complement to one another.

Jax is trailing after Sloane like a persistent golden retriever who doesn't understand the concept of personal space.

"You need to stop staring at me," Sloane warns, striding past him. "Or I'm going to pour this drink over your head."

My teammate grins, completely unfazed by her prickly demeanor. "If you're trying to find a deterrent," he says, letting his gaze drag slowly down and back up her body with deliberate insolence, "you'll need to do better than that."

Laiken chuckles under his breath, and I do the same. Neither of us bother to hide our amusement. Whatever's brewing between those two is going to be interesting to watch.

My gaze catches on Callie again. Her hair is pinned up, a few silky tendrils framing her face. She's wearing a black wrap dress that hugs her curves and makes her skin glow.

The second our gazes lock, everything in me seizes. Not with nerves but with certainty.

She's always been the endgame.

Even when she belonged to another man.

One who used to be my friend.

She cuts a path straight to me, her fingers brushing my arm

like she needs that small connection as much as I do. "I think everyone we invited has shown up."

I glance around the room at the friends and family crowding the space. People who mean the world to both of us. "Pretty sure they're all just relieved you finally took pity on me and gave me a shot."

"I can one hundred percent attest to that," Laiken says with a grin.

Callie's lips curve. "Maybe I should've stopped keeping you at arm's length sooner. It feels like I missed out on so many wonderful moments."

I brush a kiss across the tip of her nose. "As much as I would've loved that, I think we found our way to each other at exactly the right time."

From the corner of my eye, I catch Rina leveling a death glare at Oliver.

"I swear to God, if you make one more comment, I'm going to—"

Oliver flashes a lazy grin over the rim of his tumbler. "What, baby? What are you gonna do? Tell me. I'm curious."

Her eyes narrow as her tone turns sharp enough to draw blood. "Why don't you try me and find out."

His brows lift, but the smirk never fades. "You make it damn hard not to push the envelope when you threaten me like that."

She lets out a low growl before spinning on her heel and stalking off, muttering something under her breath that's definitely not fit for polite company.

I shake my head as Oliver's gaze follows her, his expression equal parts amused and fascinated. "If you're trying to get on her good side, that isn't the way to do it."

Oliver's gaze drifts to mine. "Who said I wanted to be on her good side? Maybe I like the view from where I'm at."

Laiken snorts. "Should we take bets on whether he gets traded before next season?"

With a shrug, Oliver strolls off in the same direction Rina disappeared in.

Even if he's acting like he's not following her, I know better. We all do.

"Those two are like oil and water." Callie tilts her head as she watches them. "They just don't mix."

"Oh, I wouldn't be so sure about that," I say with a chuckle, sliding my arm around her waist and pulling her into me. She fits there like she was made for the spot. "You good, baby?"

She nods, her gaze slowly sweeping the room. Her eyes soften as they take in the friends, the laughter, and the life we've started building together, piece by piece. "I am. I didn't realize what home felt like until now. And that has everything to do with you."

I brush my lips against her temple. "No, baby. That has everything to do with *you*."

My pulse thrums a frantic rhythm. I've been planning this moment for weeks, but now that it's here, I'm nervous as hell.

Before I can lose my nerve, I press one last kiss against her forehead and then step away, lifting my glass high. "Hey, everyone. Can I have your attention?"

Someone turns the music down, and the hum of conversation dies away until the room is quiet. All eyes shift toward me, but the only ones I'm locked on belong to the woman standing a few feet away, her brows furrowed as confusion flickers across her expression.

Callie leans toward me. "What are you doing?"

"Making sure everyone knows exactly how I feel," I say with a small smile.

Facing the room, I force my voice to stay steady. "When I moved into this place a couple years ago, it was just a penthouse. Four walls that were cold and sterile, echoing with quiet. It didn't feel like a home until the day Callie and Nora walked through the door."

Willow presses a hand to her chest as Nora races over to us. Evelyn's lips curve into a tender smile as Hugh positions himself just behind her, drink in hand, eyes intent.

I take in the friends who've become family and, in the center of that, the two people who changed everything for me.

"Tonight isn't just a housewarming party," I continue. "It's a celebration of the life we're building together."

Callie's eyes widen when I sink to one knee in front of her daughter and slip a hand into my jacket before drawing out a small velvet box. Flipping it open, I reveal a delicate heart-shaped locket with a picture of the three of us inside.

"Nora," I say, my voice catching just enough to give me away, "I don't know what I did to deserve you, but I want to be your family for the rest of my life. If you'll have me... this is for you, ladybug."

She claps her hands, squealing, and launches herself into my arms. "I love you, Rivvy!"

"I love you too," I choke out against her curls, holding her tight before gently setting her back down again and rising to my feet.

My gaze shifts to the woman I've spent years waiting for, and my hands tremble as I pull out the second box. Inside is a diamond ring that is simple, stunning, and timeless. Just like Callie. On the inside of the band, five small words are engraved, carrying every truth I've ever wanted her to know.

Where you are, I'm home.

"The very first time I saw you, I knew you were going to change my life. And I was right. You've given me love and purpose. And you've made me a father in every way that matters."

Tears spill down her cheeks as she presses her hands to her mouth.

"I want to spend the rest of my life proving I deserve you," I continue, taking a step closer as nerves twist in my gut. "So, Callie..." I draw in a breath. "Will you marry me?"

For just a beat, she doesn't speak. She just stares, her whole heart shining in her eyes before she nods. "Yes," she says on a shaky exhale. "Yes, of course I will."

The room explodes in applause and cheers. Champagne corks pop, laughter rings out, but all I see is her. All I feel is the way she fits against me, her arms tangled around my neck, and the press of her lips to mine.

I ease back just enough to meet her gaze. "I love you."

Her lips tremble into a smile. "I love you too. You gave me everything I didn't know how to ask for."

A warmth unfurls inside me as I brush my nose against hers. There is nothing I wouldn't give this woman. "And you gave me something I never thought I'd have. A family. A future. A reason to fight for every single day."

Her kiss is tender and full of promise. Against my mouth, she murmurs, "Then let's do everything we can to make it count."

In that instant, the laughter and music fade into silence. All that exists is her. Us. And the unshakable truth that forever isn't waiting somewhere down the road.

It starts right here, in her arms.

48
CALLIE

Lakeshore Sweets is bathed in morning light, the kind that filters through the front windows in golden streaks and makes the glass display case gleam. The scent of fresh coffee and warm sugar hangs in the air as I slide the last cupcake into its box, fingers tugging the ribbon into a neat bow with more care than usual.

For once, everything feels easy.

From our usual corner table, Lilah, Rina, and Sloane are caught up in a fit of laughter over something I only half catch. Lilah's in a floaty, bohemian top, and her blonde hair shines in the sunlight. As she lifts her hand to rest absentmindedly on her belly, I stop short.

"Look at you," I say. "You're starting to pop."

Lilah beams, and her whole face glows. "I kind of feel like I swallowed a cantaloupe."

Laughter ripples around us, and for a beat, I let myself simply enjoy being here, surrounded by my friends.

The door opens, and I glance up to see River walk in, wearing Railers gear and looking entirely too good this early in the morning with messy hair and a hint of stubble on his jaw.

The man is ridiculously handsome.

And trailing behind him is Oliver.

River doesn't hesitate. He strides straight toward me before cupping my face in his warm hands and kissing me as if he's been thinking about it all morning. The world narrows to the minty freshness of his breath and the solid press of his body against mine.

I smile against his mouth as the bakery explodes in commentary behind us.

Rina whistles. "Well, damn. Is it me or did it just get a little hotter in here?"

"I always knew there was a happily ever after in their future," Lilah says with a dreamy sigh.

Oliver lounges against the counter, his gaze locked on Rina. "I've been looking for you."

Rina arches a brow. "Unfortunately, it looks like you found me."

A slow grin curves Oliver's mouth. "There's no place you can hide that I won't find you."

"That sounds like a threat," she shoots back.

"Consider it a promise, sweetheart," he counters smoothly.

Color blooms in Rina's cheeks, and for once, she doesn't fire back with something sharp enough to draw blood.

I glance at Lilah, who's biting her lip to keep from laughing. "Who knew we'd get breakfast and a show?"

"As long as it doesn't turn into a crime scene, we're all good," Sloane says with a chuckle.

Rina looks seconds away from wrapping her hands around Oliver's neck and wringing it.

Or... maybe not.

Sometimes I get the feeling there's more between them than either of them is willing to admit.

River leans in, brushing a smudge of flour from my cheek with his thumb. "I missed you this morning. I don't like waking up without you next to me."

I melt a little before teasing, "I had cupcakes to frost and a bakery to open."

"I'll let it slide this once." His eyes darken, fingers skating along my jaw. "But tonight, you're all mine."

My breath hitches as I manage a nod. "Deal."

He gives my hand a quick squeeze before stepping back. "We should probably get moving before Coach fines us for being late."

Oliver's gaze stays fixed on Rina, who takes a deliberate sip from her mug without meeting his eyes. "Catch you later, Reynolds."

"I sincerely hope not," she mutters under her breath.

I watch him go, my hand drifting to my stomach without conscious thought. I'm not sure why the gesture feels so right.

Maybe it's nothing.

Or maybe it's everything.

What I do know is that the future doesn't scare me.

It feels wide open, full of promise, and I can't wait to step into it with River by my side.

EPILOGUE
CALLIE

If someone had told me two years ago that my life would look like this, I wouldn't have believed them. Not in my wildest, most desperate dreams.

Lakeshore Sweets is closed today, but the air inside is sweeter than any recipe I've ever whipped together. My bakery, the place I poured my soul into, has been transformed into something magical. White ribbons drape from the ceiling beams, fairy lights twinkle along the walls, and bouquets of wildflowers spill from mason jars on every table. Thick white candles flicker across the counters, their light spilling in a honeyed glow.

It's not extravagant or over the top.

It's simple, honest, and real.

A lot like us.

Rina, Lilah, Sloane, and Willow surround me, helping me into my dress. It's not the kind of gown you'd find in a glossy magazine. The soft, flowing fabric feels like it was made just for me. My hands tremble as I smooth it over my hips.

"You look absolutely stunning," Lilah whispers, eyes shining.

Sloane, always prepared, hands me a tissue before I realize I need it. "Don't start crying yet. You'll ruin your makeup."

A shaky laugh breaks loose, and emotion swells inside me for these women. My chosen family.

The door creaks open and Nora bursts in. She's a blur of tulle and sparkly white sneakers, clutching her little flower basket as if it's the most important job in the world. Petals spill behind her as she races into the room.

"Ready, Mama?" she asks, eyes bright.

I crouch down, pressing a kiss to her forehead. "I am. But the real question is if you're ready."

She nods with exaggerated seriousness, and my throat tightens.

It's time.

The second I step into the main room and see River waiting, the rest of the world disappears. His blue eyes lock on mine, as if I'm the only person who exists. The music swells, and every movement toward him feels like stepping into the rest of my life.

When I reach him, he leans in. "I didn't think I could ever be this happy until you came along. And even then, I wasn't sure I'd ever get to call you mine."

Tears sting my eyes, but I don't let them fall. I want to remember every second of this moment.

Our vows are quiet and intimate. There aren't any speeches or grand gestures. It's just us with our hands linked, hearts bare, surrounded by the people who matter most.

"I promise to choose you. Every day, in all the ways that matter," I tell him, meaning every word.

"I promise to protect the love we've found. To protect you. And Nora. Always," he whispers back, brushing his thumb across my knuckles.

Later, there's laughter, teasing, and raised glasses. I look around at this messy, wonderful family we've built, and know I couldn't ask for anything more.

When River pulls me into the middle of the space for our first dance, his hand firm at my waist and his lips brushing my temple, I feel light and loved.

Even more than that, I'm no longer afraid of falling.

Because I know deep in my heart he'll always be there to catch me.

BONUS EPILOGUE
RIVER

Two years.

That's how long it's been since I stood at the end of a makeshift aisle in the bakery, heart lodged in my throat, watching Callie walk toward me with tears in her eyes and a bouquet of wildflowers in her hands. Two years since I promised her forever.

And every day since, I've fallen a little more in love with her.

"Daddy!" Nora launches herself onto the bed like a pint-sized missile, curls bouncing wildly. "Time to wake up! It's game day!"

The mattress dips and rocks under her as she bounces with the kind of enthusiasm only a five-year-old can summon at this hour.

Beside me, Callie groans, eyes still closed, one hand clutching the comforter and the other curved protectively over her very round belly.

"Five more minutes," she mumbles.

Nora doesn't even hear her. "You said I could wear your jersey! Look!" She tugs it proudly over her head, the oversized

Thompson jersey swallowing her small frame. "I look just like you!"

With a laugh, I catch her mid-bounce and pull her into my lap. "You look even better, ladybug. Are you ready to cheer us on?"

She nods enthusiastically. "Yup! We get to sit in the fancy suite with Aunt Lilah, Aunt Rina, and Aunt Sloane!"

"I know," I say, brushing her hair back and kissing her forehead. "They've got the best snacks in there, don't they?"

She grins.

Callie attempts to sit up and fails with a sigh. "I might need a forklift."

Grinning, I lean over to help her, sliding an arm around her before carefully lifting. "You've got two tiny hockey players in there, babe. You're already doing all the heavy lifting."

She smiles sleepily, and even with messy hair, swollen ankles, exhaustion written on every line of her face, she's the most stunning woman I've ever laid eyes on. "You say that now," she mutters. "Talk to me when I'm waddling my way to the bathroom during the intermission because my bladder is seconds away from exploding."

I crouch down to slide her slippers onto her feet before pressing a kiss to her temple. "Then I'll stop the game and carry you to the bathroom myself. Just say the word, you know I'll do it."

The babies kick under my palm like they're chiming in, and Callie winces. "They're going to be bruisers like you."

"Maybe," I say with a grin. "But they'll be strong like you."

Twins.

Our lives are about to change in the best way possible, and I can't wait. Neither can their big sister. Nora keeps asking when her siblings will finally get here.

Downstairs, the dogs bark at something outside the

window, and Nora is already tugging me toward the hallway by the hand.

"Can I have French toast?" she asks, bouncing in place. "And the strawberries shaped like hearts? You know, the way Mommy does it?"

"I'll see what I can do, ladybug," I say, ruffling her curls.

"I can do it," Callie says, tying her robe around her waist as she trails after us.

"No way. Why don't you take a nice, warm shower, and we'll make breakfast? When you're done, I'll have scrambled eggs ready with extra cheese, just the way you like them."

"Are you sure?"

"Absolutely," I say, gently steering her back up the stairs when she tries to follow us. "You know how much I like taking care of my girls."

She smiles at that, and I know she hears the truth beneath the words. There was a time I didn't know if she'd ever let me in. If she'd ever believe I wasn't going anywhere, if she could trust me enough to build something real.

It took time to earn that trust, but we made it.

Now she's my wife. The mother of my daughter, and very soon, our sons. The woman I get to wake up next to for the rest of my life.

I'm the luckiest bastard in the world.

And I know it.

After breakfast is cleaned up and Nora's dressed, the morning unfolds the way it usually does in our house. Imperfect and full of little moments that already feel like memories in the making.

Nora chatters nonstop about how she's going to play on a real hockey team next year.

"I'm gonna skate fast like you," she tells me. "And then, when I score, I'm gonna do a cool celebration!"

"Show me how you're going to celebrate," I say.

She drops to one knee and pretends to play the guitar. "Just like that."

I laugh and give her a fist bump when she pops back up. "I can't wait to see it."

By the time we pull into the arena that evening, Nora is practically vibrating with excitement. She clutches Callie's hand while the other is wrapped tight around the stuffed Railers bear I gave her when they first moved into the penthouse. Back then, it was just a gift. Something small I'd hoped would make her feel safe and loved. Now, it's so much more. A symbol of where we started, of everything we've built together, and of all the moments still waiting for us.

We made a lot of amazing memories in that penthouse. And I still own it. Sometimes, when Nora spends the weekend with Zane, Callie and I slip back and create new ones. Zane's more involved in Nora's life now, and while it's far from perfect, we've all learned how to co-exist for the little girl who ties us all together.

Unable to help myself, I glance at my wife. She's laughing at something Nora just said, her hand absently rubbing circles over her stomach the way she always does when she thinks no one's looking. Her glow isn't just from pregnancy. It's from the life we've created together.

The sheer weight of how lucky I am nearly undoes me.

When I finally hit the ice, I'm locked in, but it's not the same as it used to be. This game isn't about stats or glory anymore.

It's about the moments that matter.

This is the life we've built.

The family we've made.

I've played a lot of games and scored a lot of goals. I've had big wins and career highs. But nothing has ever meant as much as this.

This is the win that matters.

I take one last glance at them in the suite. Nora is waving

like her arm might fly right off, and Callie's hand is resting instinctively over the gentle swell of her belly. I feel that same pull I've known since the moment they stepped into my life.

They're my heart. My reason. My future.

I'm reminded of the promise I made to them both.

To protect them and give them every piece of me.

Always.

It's the easiest vow I've ever spoken and the truest one I've ever known. As I skate back onto the ice, I know it's not just a promise for today. It's a vow I'll keep for every tomorrow we're given.

EPILOGUE
EVELYN

Night of the engagement party...

The rooftop terrace is quiet.

Blissfully so.

Below, the penthouse hums with laughter and clinking glasses as music pulses low and the celebration rolls on.

But up here?

It's just me, the Chicago skyline, and the hush of an autumn breeze brushing against my skin. The night is unusually warm, a small gift this late in the season. One of the last, if I had to guess.

I move to the ledge that surrounds the rooftop, my heels clicking against the stone, and draw in a slow breath scented with the greenery that lines the terrace. Potted trees, climbing ivy, and bursts of seasonal blooms. The city sprawls before me, a sea of shimmering lights that stretch endlessly into the distance.

It's only in this stillness that the tension knotted within me begins to loosen.

When the elevator chimes behind me, my breath stalls. I don't need to turn to know who it is. My spine goes rigid as my shoulders tighten instinctively. Hugh Landry steps out of the elevator and into my stolen peace.

No matter where I go, he finds me.

Lately, it feels more deliberate.

He doesn't speak, just moves toward me with slow, measured steps until his presence looms at my back. Tall, broad, and unapologetically masculine. Living with him has been a test of willpower I never signed up for. Sharing a home with Hugh should be simple.

It's turned out to be anything but.

Not when I've seen him barefoot, hair mussed from sleep, skin still damp from the shower with a towel slung low around his hips. I close my eyes, banishing the image before it can dig in deeper and do more damage.

There's a shift of fabric as he stops behind me.

His low voice is dangerously close to my ear. "I thought I'd find you up here."

I keep my lips pressed together, refusing to give him the satisfaction of a reply.

He edges close enough for his body heat to seep into my skin. Near enough that my breathing turns uneven despite my best efforts.

"Funny thing," he says, voice laced with humor. "For a woman who claims she can't stand me, you keep ending up in all the places I want to be."

His nose grazes the curve of my cheek before tracing the line of my jaw.

I fight the shiver threatening to betray me, and lose.

"You said," I whisper, "you wouldn't touch me unless I begged you to."

His chuckle is rich and warm as it slides down my spine like silk. "You're right. I did."

"That will never happen," I add quickly, though it sounds more like a warning to myself than to him.

"That's all right." His voice is even closer now, pitched low. "I've waited years for this. If I have to wait a little longer, I will. You're worth it."

He steps closer, resting one large hand on the ledge, just an inch from mine.

My fingers curl in reflex, but I refuse to move.

Tension buzzes in the air as my gaze drops to the sliver of space between our hands.

"You still wear the same jasmine perfume," he murmurs.

"Yes," I reply tightly, surprised and a little unsettled that he would remember.

He leans in, his breath feathering across my neck. "It always takes me back to the summers at the lake and the first time you kissed me."

"You were the one who kissed me first," I fire back without thinking.

His laugh is low and rough. "You're probably right about that. Even then, I couldn't get you out of my head. That hasn't changed in all these years."

I freeze. "Hugh…"

"I remember every second we spent together, Evie," he says. "I know mistakes were made, but it's not too late for us to get our happily ever after."

My pulse riots dangerously beneath my skin.

"I look at those kids in there," he continues, "and I'm envious. They're not afraid to put themselves out there or take a chance on love."

"Love?" I swallow. "I think you might be delusional."

"Not at all," he says simply. "What I am, though, is patient."

I steel myself before turning to face him. "If you're hoping I've forgotten what happened after that summer—"

"There's no forgetting," he cuts in quietly, his gaze sharp and unyielding. "If I could go back and redo it all, I would in an instant. There were people who didn't want us together, and I let them win. I let them take away the one pure thing in my life. That's a regret I'll carry with me forever."

"No," I agree quietly. "There's no rewriting history. As much as either of us might wish it were possible."

A hint of sadness pricks me unexpectedly, but I shove the emotion aside before it can take root.

"I know," he says. "Trust me, I do."

Just when I consider stepping away and leaving this dangerous closeness behind, he says, "If I could touch you, I'd start right here."

His finger hovers above my bare shoulder, close enough for the heat of him to ghost across my skin. Even though he doesn't make contact, my body reacts all the same.

"I'd trace every inch of you," he continues, "until you forgot about everything except this very moment."

I freeze, pulse stuttering, as his gaze falls to my parted lips. For one reckless, terrifying second, I want to close the distance between us. I want to feel his mouth on mine, coaxing me into forgetting the past. Every reason and every scar that once tore us apart.

Instead, I retreat, taking a shaky step back until the railing presses into my spine. "Don't."

"I didn't break the rules," he says after a beat. "As much as I wanted to."

Every nerve ending sparks to life as I lift my chin. "Forcing me to move in with you was a disastrous idea."

"Maybe," he admits, eyes locked on mine. "But it was my call to make. And you're running out of reasons to keep pretending you don't still have feelings for me."

I hate that he's right.

Worse, I hate that my skin tingles where his breath touched it, and that I can still smell his cedar and warmed amber cologne. And that even now, I want more.

He steps back at last, giving me the space I desperately need but don't actually want.

And then, just before he turns away, he says, "You need to understand something, Evie. I'm not going anywhere."

I watch him walk away as my pulse continues to race and heat blooms under my skin. Every piece of me is at war with the only part that matters.

The one that still wants him.

BONUS EPILOGUE

HUGH

The city stretches out beyond the glass wall, glittering like a thousand restless points of light. From this high up, it all looks calm.

Controlled.

Contained.

Exactly how I like it.

Normally, that would be enough to quiet the noise in my head.

Tonight, that's not the case.

And the reason is sleeping two rooms down the hall in my bed, wrapped in a whisper of silk that tests every shred of my control. Her perfume lingers on my sheets, haunting me the way it has for nearly three decades.

That was the deal.

She'd move in for the season and share my home along with my bed.

Nothing more.

Nothing less.

And I promised not to touch her unless she asked.

Begged.

Even though it's killing me, I've kept that promise.

Every damn night.

"Hugh? Have you even heard a word I've said?"

The humor in Dominic's voice drags me back from the skyline and my wayward thoughts. I blink and focus on the man sitting across from me in the leather armchair opposite my desk. His coat is slung over the back, posture relaxed in that way that says he's much too comfortable in my space. What can't be denied is that he's earned the right.

"Yes," I lie, swirling the untouched bourbon in my glass. "You were giving me a recap of what happened with Lionel."

His mouth pulls into a smirk. "We covered that ten minutes ago." Before I can respond, he adds, "You're thinking about her."

It's not a question.

My jaw tightens, but I don't bother with a denial. He'll see right through it. That's what happens when you surround yourself with people who know all your secrets.

He tips his head toward the door as his eyes glint. "Let me guess, she's waiting in your bed right now."

I lift the bourbon to my lips, take a slow sip, and let the heat burn down my throat. "I wouldn't say waiting."

"No," he says with amusement. "I wouldn't think so. Evelyn Kingston was never the wait-around type."

"No," I agree, a faint tug at the corners of my mouth, "she isn't."

"And how exactly do you see this little scheme you've orchestrated working out?"

I level him with a hard look. "You didn't come here to talk about her. So, let's move on."

His easy smile fades as his gaze sharpens. "You're right. There are far more pressing issues to contend with. The kind that involve people who like to stick their noses where they don't belong. We need to figure out what we're—"

"Not here," I cut in.

Dominic rolls his eyes. "Are you afraid she might overhear?"

"She doesn't need to know."

He studies me for a beat, like he's weighing whether to push before exhaling slowly. "And how's that supposed to work?"

"I'm not sure yet."

"You didn't honestly think it would be easy, did you?"

"Not for a second." Although I'll admit, I expected her to crumble a hell of a lot sooner.

"It's one of the reasons why you've never been able to forget her."

"You're overstepping," I say flatly.

"As usual." His mouth curves. "But you haven't killed me yet."

"The keyword in that sentence is *yet*. There's still time, my friend."

With a chuckle, he rises to his feet. "I should probably go before I push my luck. Just remember, we need to move fast—"

Before he can finish, the door to the study creaks open and Evelyn pads barefoot inside the space. Her dark hair spills around her shoulders, making her look younger, and the green silk nightgown clings to every delicious curve.

We both still.

"Dominic?" she says, surprise flickering in her eyes.

His gaze sweeps over her, resting on her far longer than necessary.

My fingers tighten around my glass. "If you enjoy having eyes in your head," I growl, "you'll avert them."

Dominic chuckles but looks away. "Still territorial, I see."

"Still alive," I remind him.

He grins at her. "It's good to see you, Evelyn. It's been far too long."

"It certainly has. I didn't realize you two were still friends."

"Forty-five years and counting," Dominic replies. "We were born friends, and we'll die friends."

Her attention snaps to me, sharp with unspoken questions.

"Well, I should get going." He brushes past her, pausing in

the doorway just long enough to add, "There's more to the past than what you know, Evelyn."

Before she can ask what that means, the door clicks shut behind him.

If he hadn't left of his own volition, I would've tossed him out on his damn ass for that last comment.

She stares at the closed door for a long moment before crossing the room and perching on the edge of my desk. It's impossible to ignore the way the silk rides high on her thighs. She's still the most beautiful woman I've ever seen.

"I didn't realize you and Dom were still friends," she muses.

"There's a lot you don't know," I answer.

"Then do us both a favor and enlighten me."

"I wish I could."

When her mouth curves, it's not with humor but challenge. "I'm pretty sure you can do whatever you want."

"You give me far too much credit," I say with a dry laugh.

Her eyes narrow, but instead of pressing for more information, she slides off the desk in a whisper of silk, and closes the distance between us. Her hands rest on my shoulders as she settles onto my lap, straddling me so we're face-to-face.

I arch a brow. "Are you giving me permission to finally touch you?"

Her chuckle is low and warm, curling down my spine. "Not a chance."

My hands clamp onto the arms of the chair instead of her hips. The second I touch her, I'm finished.

If she knew the kind of men I've kept from her door, she'd understand why I pushed her away. It was always about protecting her.

Her warmth settles over me, the thin silk barely a barrier.

Then she shifts.

Her movements are both slow and deliberate. The friction

punches the air from my lungs. Without a shadow of a doubt, I know she can feel exactly what she's doing to me.

Her smile turns wicked. "Interesting."

"Evelyn." There's a warning in my low tone. The woman must realize she's playing with fire.

Her fingertips trail over my chest and along my shoulders before sliding into my hair. "You've always kept so many secrets. And even now, twenty some—"

"Five," I cut in. "Twenty-five years, Evie."

"Twenty-five years later, and you're still keeping them from me." She rocks against the thick erection that strains against my pants, her gaze never leaving mine.

Every muscle in my body coils tight.

"Tell me what's going on," she whispers, her mouth so close I feel the heat of her breath against my lips.

"No."

Her attention drops to the evidence of my arousal, and when it lifts again, both triumph and desire burn in her green eyes. She's savoring the way I'm dancing on the edge.

"What's more important, Hugh?" she murmurs. "Protecting me or letting me know exactly what you're so afraid of?"

"Both," I rasp.

She leans in, close enough for her lips to graze mine. Almost a kiss, but not quite. "Then I'll find out for myself," she says coolly. "And when I do, you won't be the one who decides what happens next."

With that, she slides off my lap, the silk of her nightgown ghosting over my thighs as she walks out with her head held high.

My hand shakes as I wrap my fingers around the tumbler and toss back the rest of my bourbon. The amber-colored liquor burns down my throat, but the fire she left raging inside me is much worse.

I have to hand it to Evelyn... The woman certainly knows how to bring a man to his knees.

And her threats?

She means them.

Which is a problem.

I lost her once.

There's no damn way I'll allow it to happen for a second time.

Thank you so much for reading Hold Me Tight! I hope you enjoyed Callie and River's story as much as I loved writing it!

Ready for the next book in the Chicago Railers Hockey series? Check out Rina and Oliver's story in Show Me Forever!

SHOW **Me Forever** is an enemies to lovers, forced proximity work romance featuring an unexpected pregnancy, a protective hero who falls first—and harder—and the kind of obsessive devotion that changes everything.

DID you know Willow and Maverick have their own story? It's one of my absolute favorites!

WHAT COULD BE WORSE *than having a one-night stand with my twin's biggest rival on the ice?*

Umm...nothing.

Nothing is worse than that.

It's the reason why my brother can never find out that I hooked up with Maverick McKinnon, ridiculously hot defenseman for the Western Wildcats. It doesn't matter if the memories from our night together are enough to make my toes curl and my panties—

Well, you get the idea.

He's the first guy to come along and not treat me like I'll shatter into a million pieces when he lays his hands on me. Even if there's a teeny tiny part within that would like to see him again, the fallout would be brutal.

I have enough to deal with. Like trying to break out of the box my family has placed me in since my diagnosis.

The only problem?

I've lost something valuable.

Something I need back.

And I'm pretty sure whose bed I'll find it in.

"**I LOVE this book** (and really, the whole series). Maverick and Willow are total fire together. Watching them figure out how to navigate their relationship is an awesome journey. Great book - highly recommend giving this one a read! -Cindy, Goodreads

"So many fun tropes.... brother's rival, mistaken/hidden identity, instalove (although both of them deny it) best of all... no third act break up! **If you want or need a fun sports romance then this is the book for you!**" -Tamara, Goodreads

Turn the page for an excerpt...

MINE TO TAKE

WILLOW

"Exactly how did I let you talk me into this?" my bestie asks as we navigate the crowded corridor.

"Because you love me." I flash an overly sweet smile in her direction.

With a scowl, she flattens her lips before grumbling, "Well, you got me there."

Holland and I became fast friends back in elementary school. She's my sister from another mister. The yin to my yang. Whenever I've needed her, she's been there. I'd like to think that I've done the same, but at this point, she's definitely put in more time.

She's a true friend in every sense of the word.

And there's nothing I wouldn't do in return for her.

Holland gives off major don't-fuck-with-me vibes. But beneath her hard, crunchy exterior lies a soft, nougat filling. Although, if you said that to her, she'd probably take a chunk out of your backside with her teeth.

But she can't fool me. We've been friends long enough that every so often, she'll drop the mask and allow her vulnerability to take center stage. I love that she's comfortable enough to give me those rare and precious glimpses of the real Holland.

"Added bonus, you enjoy watching River play."

A devilish smile lifts the corners of her lips. "Actually, what I enjoy is watching your brother knock grown men on their asses. There's something immensely satisfying about it. Especially when he does it to one player in particular." She glances at me. "Which is the real reason I agreed to this outing."

I knock my thinner shoulder into hers. When she meets my eyes, I waggle my brows. "It wouldn't be the worst start to a relationship."

She snorts. "I'm sorry, have you totally lost your mind? I have zero interest in hockey players and even less in your brother."

"Are you sure about that?"

Her tone turns steely. "One hundred percent."

My brain tumbles back to our childhood. "You might not realize this, but I've always secretly hoped you two would fall in love and get married. Then we'd truly be sisters."

"What are you talking about? That's never been a secret. You used to leave sticky notes on my books with our names surrounded by little hearts."

For years, I tried nudging them in each other's direction with no luck. Neither seem interested in the other. River treats Holland like the sister he never wanted or asked for.

"Plus, your brother is a total bonehead."

I loop my arm through hers and draw her curvy body closer before adding in a cajoling voice, "Just think, if you play your cards right, he could be *your* bonehead."

"Hard pass. I'm focused on finishing up college and getting the hell out of here. In that order." There's a pause before she mutters, "And Marcus left a lasting impression. One that has been singed into my soul."

It's not often that my friend dredges up her ex.

"That was years ago," I say carefully.

I hate that he hurt her so much. Holland has always been a master at keeping her emotions tightly contained. I can hardly blame her with the way she grew up. I'm just glad our house was something of a refuge for her.

She jerks her shoulders and brushes off the comment. "Once burned, twice shy and all that bullshit."

"I'm just saying that you should be open to the idea of love if it presents itself. That's all."

"Maybe after college, once I'm a boss-ass bitch," she concedes.

That reluctantly given admittance feels like a major victory.

When my phone vibrates in my pocket, I slip my hand inside and fish it out before glancing at the screen.

"Let me guess—it's Becks."

Even though I try not to let it affect me, everything inside me deflates. "Yup."

"She wants to make sure you've taken all the necessary precautions this evening."

"Right again."

"You realize that woman would put you in a bubble if it were socially acceptable?"

"Don't give her any ideas," I grumble.

A smile trembles on her lips. "Oh, I'm pretty sure she's already investigated it. Must not have been feasible."

I hate to admit just how spot-on Holland is in her assessment of the situation.

"How hilarious would it be if you showed up in a biohazard suit?"

I glare. "She'd be thrilled."

"Yeah, probably. The woman is a total nutjob." She glances at me. "Sorry, but it's true."

"I'm aware," I say with a reluctant sigh.

We follow the swiftly moving crowd until finding our seat

section. Even though I'm a student at Western, the only time I attend their games is when my brother's team is playing the Wildcats. My twin has been involved in the sport since kindergarten, so I grew up watching it. More times than not, Holland was dragged along to keep me company.

As soon as we enter the arena, I glance around, searching for my parents. Mom pops to her feet and waves erratically. The people surrounding her swivel in her direction and stare. Somehow, they managed to secure amazing seats right up against the plexiglass.

"Oh good, there's Becks," Holland mutters. "I've missed her. What's it been? Seventy-two hours since she stopped by our place to do a deep clean?"

I shake my head at the nickname. "You know she hates when you call her that, right?'

She flashes a grin. "Why do you think I do it?"

Even though I shake my head, I can't help but be amused by my bestie. She does and says things that I would never dream of.

It would be difficult not to admire her spunk.

I return the wave, hoping Mom will settle down.

"Think she got here early and sanitized our entire section?"

"Probably."

It would be amusing if it weren't true.

My mother has always been nervous by nature. My diagnosis in high school only amplified those tendencies.

Once we make our way to the seats, Dad rises to his feet and pulls me in for a warm embrace. He's way more chill than Mom. After a handful of seconds, she elbows him out of the way to do the same. Her grip borders on bone crushing. When the embrace stretches a few seconds too long, I pat her back. Only then does she draw away enough to study my face, as if looking for telltale signs of fatigue or illness.

"How are you feeling, sweetie? I hope you've been taking

those new immunity boosters I bought. When I didn't hear from you yesterday, I was concerned."

I bite back the sigh that sits perched on the tip of my tongue, and paste a smile in place. "I feel great. I told you when you stopped by the other day that I'd be busy with classes and the tutoring center."

Her brows pinch at the mention of my job on campus. "You're just asking to pick up an illness working there. All those germs... I really hope you're taking the necessary precautions. Washing your hands, using sanitizer, wearing a mask, and social distancing when possible. And when you return home from school, make sure you're changing right away and throwing your dirty clothes into the laundry."

"Mom..."

"I'm serious!" Her voice rises as fear flickers in her eyes.

"We talked to Dr. Edwards about it at my last appointment, remember? He agreed that it was fine. I'm not putting myself at risk."

She presses her lips together before muttering, "I still don't like it."

"She's fine, Becks. Willow hasn't even caught so much as a cold this semester."

Mom turns glaring eyes on my roommate, and her voice flattens. "Oh, I didn't notice you there, Holland."

My roommate grins. "It's nice to see you too."

After all these years, my mother has finally learned to tolerate Holland because I love her so fiercely and refuse to listen to one bad word she has to say about her or her family. What Mom can't deny is that she's been a steadfast friend through everything.

As far as Mom's concerned, it's Holland's only saving grace.

"I'm being careful. Promise," I say, cutting into their conversation before it can spiral out of control and ruin the evening.

It's happened before.

We're here to support River, not talk about me.

It won't be long before she launches into a spiel about me going into elementary education and how many germs children carry. She'll probably end up stroking out when I begin my student teaching placement next year.

Or she'll show up every day armed with a can of disinfectant, sanitizing wipes, and masks.

I wouldn't put it past the woman.

Just as I'm about to drop down onto the seat, she says, "Wait! Let me wipe down the chair again."

"Mom," I groan. "That's not necessary."

She meets my beseeching gaze with a determined look of her own. "It'll only take a second."

Embarrassment claws at my cheeks as she pulls out a travel-size pouch of wipes and scrubs the plastic and metal. A few people seated in the row above us stare as she grabs a small bottle of spray and then disinfects it.

The alcohol scent, masked by something that can only be described as artificially floral, stings my nostrils.

Once she tucks away her cleaning supplies, she waves toward the seat. "Now it's ready."

"Thanks."

"No problem, sweetie. Do you want to wear a mask?" She glances around with a frown. "There are so many people packed in here."

"If the germs don't kill her," Holland mutters beneath her breath, "your smothering will."

By the way Mom narrows her eyes, she heard the comment loud and clear.

Before either one can take another swipe, the lights in the arena are dimmed as the music volume is raised, cutting off the possibility of further conversation.

When the players from the East Town Rattlers are

announced, we whistle and cheer as River's name reverberates throughout the arena. Then it's time for the home team players to be introduced. I glance around as the fans cheer and applaud until the noise becomes deafening. The Jumbotron gives their fans a close-up shot as each player takes to the ice with a wave.

Since transferring to the university in the fall, I haven't paid much attention to the athletes on campus. Although, it would be impossible not to be aware of them. Hockey and football are by far the most popular sports at Western. Each team generates a ton of revenue for the school, and they have more groupies than they know what to do with.

It's been the same for my brother in both high school and college.

It only takes one glance to notice a few girls in the visiting team's section holding up signs with my brother's name and number scrawled across the white posterboard.

That's reason number one as to why I would never get involved with an athlete.

River is the other.

My twin would have a conniption if I looked twice at one of his teammates. He's always been quick to run off any of the guys who show even a hint of interest.

His behavior is almost as overbearing as my mother's.

Last year, I reached my breaking point and brought up the idea of switching universities. Holland encouraged it and offered to be my roommate. Even though both my mother and brother objected to the move, I transferred last summer and started at Western in the fall.

So far, it's been one of the best decisions I've ever made.

I only wish I'd done it sooner.

There's freedom in the people I meet not knowing who I am or my backstory.

I'm knocked from the tangle of my thoughts when the puck

gets dropped at center ice and the players explode into action. I unzip my jacket, revealing my brother's jersey.

His dream is to play professional hockey.

When River was a junior in high school, he reached out to Brody McKinnon, who owns a sports management agency, in hopes of representation. The former NHL player turned him down, saying that they weren't taking on any new clients.

My brother was crushed.

Especially since his son is Maverick McKinnon. They played on opposite teams in high school, and it's the same in college. Over the years, it's turned into something of a rivalry.

A none-too-friendly one.

I blink back to the action on the ice when one of River's teammates makes a quick pass to him. As soon as the puck lands on the end of his stick, my brother takes off, maneuvering around players as they attempt to swarm.

Energy buzzes through the arena as Western's fans shout for River to be shut down. A look of intensity settles on my brother's face as he darts across the ice. I leap to my feet and cheer when he skates closer to the goal. He's one of the top scorers on his team. Just as he veers toward us to avoid a defenseman, another player slams him into the boards. My eyes widen as my hands fly to my mouth. The sound of the collision reverberates throughout the vast space as I stare at the defenseman who just took out my brother.

Our gazes lock for a heartbeat.

And then another.

Time stands still as icy air gets clogged in my throat. The cheering crowd fades as I stare into eyes that can only be described as the color of rich mocha.

When his gaze drops to my jersey, the loss of eye contact is instantaneous. His lips twist into a scowl. That's all it takes for my heart to explode into action, racing beneath my breast as my brother scrambles to his feet and plows a gloved hand into Maverick McKinnon's wide chest.

My knees weaken now that the intensity of his stare is no longer drilling into me.

Players from both teams descend, trying to pull Maverick and River away from one another. I don't have to hear the words that fall from my brother's lips to know that he's pissed off. Frustration wafts off him in thick, suffocating waves.

Mom shakes her head and scowls. "I've said it before and I'll say it again—that McKinnon boy is an animal."

"Damn," Holland mutters. "I was hoping more of a fight would break out. Maybe a little bloodshed to break up the monotony."

Mom shoots her another glare as my gaze slices to my twin's rival. His teammates have their arms wrapped around him as the ref blows his whistle, ending the possibility of a brawl breaking out.

When Maverick's hard-edged stare slices to me for a second time, my fingers rise to play with the silver W pendant that hangs loosely around my neck. River wears a matching one with his initial. He bought them for us after my diagnosis, and there's never been a day that I haven't worn the delicate piece of jewelry. It's become a good-luck charm.

As the game gets back underway, anticipation crackles in the air like an impending storm. Instead of keeping my attention focused on my brother the way I should, I find myself staring at the handsome defenseman.

MORE BOOKS BY JENNIFER SUCEVIC

<u>Chicago Railers Hockey</u>

Make Me Yours

Hold Me Tight

Show Me Forever

Promise Me This

Keep Me Close

<u>The Campus Series</u> (football)

Campus Player (Demi & Rowan)

Campus Heartthrob (Sydney & Brayden)

Campus Flirt (Sasha & Easton)

Campus Hottie (Elle & Carson)

Campus God (Brooke & Crosby)

Campus Legend (Lola & Asher)

<u>Western Wildcats Hockey</u>

Hate You Always (Juliette & Ryder)

Love You Never (Carina & Ford)

Always My Girl (Viola & Madden)

Dare You to Love Me (Stella & Riggs)

Never Mine to Hold (Fallyn & Wolf)

Never Say Never (Britt & Colby)

Mine to Take (Willow & Maverick)

Break my Heart (Ava & Hayes)

Never Your Girl (Holland & Bridger)

<u>Parent Books for the Western Wildcats</u>

Hate to Love You (Hockey) (Natalie & Brody)

Just Friends (Hockey) (Emerson & Reed)

The Breakup Plan (Hockey) (Whitney & Gray)

<u>The Barnett Bulldogs</u> (football)

King of Campus (Ivy & Roan)

Friend Zoned (Violet & Sam)

One Night Stand (Gia & Liam)

If You Were Mine (Claire & JT)

<u>The Claremont Cougars</u> (football)

Heartless Summer (Skye & Hunter)

Heartless (Skye & Hunter)

Shameless (Poppy & Mason)

<u>Hawthorne Prep Series</u> (bully/football)

King of Hawthorne Prep (Summer & Kingsley)

Queen of Hawthorne Prep (Summer & Kingsley)

Prince of Hawthorne Prep (Delilah & Austin)

Princess of Hawthorne Prep (Delilah & Austin)

<u>The Next Door Duet</u> (football)

The Girl Next Door (Mia & Beck)

The Boy Next Door (Alyssa & Colton)

<u>What's Mine Duet</u> (Suspense)

Protecting What's Mine (Grace & Matteo)

Claiming What's Mine (Sofia & Roman)

<u>Stay Duet</u> (hockey)

Stay (Cassidy & Cole)

Don't Leave (Cassidy & Cole)

Standalone Football

Love to Hate You (Daisy & Carter)

Collections

Claremont Cougars

The Barnett Bulldogs

The Football Hotties Collection

The Hockey Hotties Collection

The Next Door Duet

ABOUT THE AUTHOR

Jennifer Sucevic is a USA Today bestselling author who has captivated readers worldwide with her sizzling new adult romances. With over thirty novels to her name, her stories of love, heartbreak, and swoon-worthy heroes have been translated into six languages, including German, Italian, and Portuguese, making her a truly global voice in the genre. Armed with a bachelor's degree in history and a master's in educational psychology from the University of Wisconsin-Milwaukee, Jen initially worked as a high school counselor before embracing her passion for writing full-time. Her background in psychology lends a depth to her characters that resonates with fans everywhere.

When she's not crafting irresistible love stories, Jen enjoys biking along scenic trails and soaking up the sun at the beach. She currently resides in Michigan with her family, where she continues to dream up heroes and heroines you'll want to fall in love with again and again.

If you would like to receive regular updates regarding new releases, please subscribe to her newsletter here-
Jennifer Sucevic Newsletter

Or contact Jen through email, at her website, or on Facebook.
sucevicjennifer@gmail.com

Want to join her reader group? Do it here -)
J Sucevic's Book Boyfriends | Facebook

Social media links-
https://www.tiktok.com/@jennifersucevicauthor
www.jennifersucevic.com
https://www.instagram.com/jennifersucevicauthor
https://www.facebook.com/jennifer.sucevic
Amazon.com: Jennifer Sucevic: Books, Biography, Blog,
Audiobooks, Kindle
Jennifer Sucevic Books - BookBub

www.ingramcontent.com/pod-product-compliance
Lightning Source LLC
Chambersburg PA
CBHW021406310726
48971CB00005B/1228